I0739396

LIVING IN THE LOWER CHAKRAS

LILY'S TURN CAME. SHE GRABBED A BOOK OFF THE PILE AND handed it to him, fumbling it. He caught it and their hands touched. Her fingers felt as if they'd been asleep their entire lives and now they lit up like candles. Sparks shot through her entire body.

"What's your name?" he asked, smiling.

"Lily, Lily Toureau. But it's not for me. It's for my friend Bree. She's sick and couldn't come."

He looked into her eyes and Lily felt as if she were melting into a giant primordial blob.

"So you braved the elements to help her out. That was very kind of you," he said.

Lily felt sure it was a reference to her wet T-shirt. Her cheeks felt hot, but she said, "Thanks."

Just in case he was sincere.

After Sean finished signing the book, he handed it back. Her hand touched his and their eyes met. He looked amused. She felt dizzy as he looked at her and her head tingled. The sensation traveled down her spine, then became overwhelming until her entire body resonated with it. She felt herself wilting to the floor.

When she came to, Sean knelt over her, along with one of the bookstore women and Heather.

"Lily, are you all right?" Heather asked.

She nodded, sure her face must be on fire with embarrassment.

ALSO BY LINDA JORDAN:

Notes on the Moon People

Bibi's Bargain Boutique

Continental Divide

Horticultural Homicide

Faerie Unraveled: The Bones of the Earth Series, Book 1

Faerie Contact: The Bones of the Earth Series, Book 2

Faerie Descent: The Bones of the Earth Series, Book 3

Faerie Flight: The Bones of the Earth Series, Book 4

Faerie Confluence: The Bones of the Earth Series, Book 5

Come on over to Linda's website and join the fun!

LindaJordan.net

Don't miss a release!

Sign up for Linda's Serendipitous Newsletter while you're there.

LIVING IN THE LOWER CHAKRAS

LINDA JORDAN

METAMORPHOSIS PRESS

Copyright © 2013 by Linda Jordan

All rights reserved

Published by Metamorphosis Press

www.MetamorphosisPress.com

ISBN-13: 978-0-997797107

This is a work of fiction. Names, characters, places or incidents are either the product of the author's imagination or are used fictitiously. Any resemblance to actual events, or persons, either living or dead, is entirely coincidental.

For Michael & Zoe

LILY

The cold November rain pounded onto the windshield making it almost impossible to see. The brooding clouds didn't help. It was rush hour and almost dark already. The wipers on her battered Subaru wagon needed replacing. Even at top speed, they couldn't cope. Lily shifted in her seat, tapping her long, manicured nails on the steering wheel, waiting for the light to turn.

Her friend, Heather, said, "Go, go, go!" the instant the light turned green.

Lily wove back and forth between lanes, driving from the rain spattered crowds of Capital Hill to the completely drenched students in the U. District.

Heather pulled out her cell to check the time and shrieked, "We'll make it. We will!"

Lily smiled at Heather's exuberance. She pulled into the small parking lot, only to find it full. They had to park in the overflow lot a block away, snagging the last open spot and nearly mowing down a newspaper box, trying to get into the space.

She sighed, grabbed her bag, decided to leave her coat, locked the car and raced up the street after Heather. Where did Heather get her energy? Lily was thirty-eight, but she didn't remember having that much oomph at twenty.

They ran the block and a half to the University Bookstore. Her white T-shirt and black capri leggings were soaked. Her long, blond hair was tangled in the bag she carried. It hurt, but she'd have to get it all untangled later.

Just as Lily made it to the crowded doorway, she ran into a girl coming out. A girl smothered in purple and gold, the UW colors. A girl carrying a chocolate ice cream cone. Which went all over the front of Lily's t-shirt.

"Watch it, bitch," snarled the girl, catching the ice cream in her hands.

"Sorry," said Lily. God, she was such a klutz. She needed to pay more attention. She'd always been that way.

She went into the main doors, following the crowd. Good thing most of them were just shopping and not going to the signing. She ran for the stairs and tripped over some guy's rolling backpack, which was nearly invisible in the crowd, goddamn it. She stumbled but regained her balance and bounded up the stairs. By the time she made it to the second floor, she'd caught up with Heather.

They joined the end of the line, which the staff closed off four people behind her.

Lily stood there, breathing heavily. She looked down at her shin and saw it wasn't bleeding badly, just a trickle. But it would be a nasty bruise. Luckily her jobs for the near future were modeling outdoor wear. Her legs would most likely be covered.

She felt like a huge bedraggled giraffe. Except that giraffes were probably graceful.

Her cold, sopping wet clothes stuck to her and she busied

herself with unsnarling her hair from the straps of her huge bag. She was still breathing hard.

Heather, on the other hand, was breathing normally. She was a runner. Her long auburn hair waved in Lily's face. She'd always wanted hair that color, but it didn't work with her skin tone. She was tired of dumb blond jokes. Soon enough though, her hair would turn gray, no one would hire her, and she'd have geriatric jokes to look forward to. It was okay that she looked like a tall, blond amazon now, but a tall, gray haired amazon was just too scary for today's culture. No one wanted older women to be or look powerful.

Heather bumped her and said, "Told you we could make it."

Lily nodded and looked around. The line up here on the brightly lit second floor was outlined with purple ropes and golden metal stands. It snaked around isles of books, then wrapped around the mezzanine. The smell of coffee wafted up from below making her want some, but she didn't want to risk leaving the line and losing her place.

She couldn't see him yet, or even the beginning of the line where he signed, but she knew Sean O'Neill was here. People in the far corner held up cell phones and she could see flashes going off. There were a few professionals with real cameras, standing on chairs. Were they paparazzi? How awful to be stalked all the time. Someone always wanting your autograph, a photo, a piece of you.

She watched as the staff tried to get them off the furniture, but as soon as the bookstore employee moved on, they were right back up there.

Rubbing her leg, trying to wipe off some of the blood, she noticed her capris were ripped. When had that happened? Her t-shirt was clinging to her like she was in a wet t-shirt contest. At least she'd worn a bra. Although red probably wasn't the best choice. It had been her only clean one. Now her nipples stood out from the cold. And then there was chocolate stain. She moved the bag over to her hip to cover it. She felt guilty about the girl's cone. She hoped all the rushing had been worth it.

She ran her fingers through her hair; at least she could make that look decent. Maybe.

She'd dressed down for work today. The photographer was always hitting on her. She had hoped that her everyday clothes would discourage him. At least until she put on the dresses for the shoot. Her strategy hadn't worked. He was such a sleaze bag. Why couldn't a nice guy ask her out?

There were lots of nice guys around, supposedly. But they didn't make themselves known to her.

She looked around at the people in line. Teenagers who were probably in love with his action-adventure flicks. Middle age, art house types who liked his whimsical, critically acclaimed films. A few dark, moody people who must be fans of the Nick Drake movie. She'd heard Sean O'Neill made something for everyone.

As the line moved forward, she caught a glimpse of him sitting at a table with two female bookstore employees hovering over him.

His brown eyes seemed warm, inviting. And those full lips. My oh my. He actually looked better in person than on film. His hair, just a little long, curled around his neck.

She'd seen only a couple of his movies and knew he had a prolific career, but he'd never appealed to her as a lust item. Lily had always gone more for musicians than actors. Bree and Heather lusted after him, ravenously.

Most people carried his latest book, *Adventures in Kuala Lumpur; the making of Flight from the Wind.* That was the one she needed to buy for Bree, who'd gone home earlier in the day, puking her guts out and broken hearted about missing the signing.

Heather turned around, "He's so gorgeous." She rolled her eyes in ecstasy. "Have you seen *Shadows* yet?"

"No, I've been too busy apartment hunting." Not that she would have necessarily gone. It hadn't looked that interesting.

"I thought you've only lived there a year? Moving already?" asked Heather.

"Yeah. They're tearing the building down to make condos."

"Bummer. Well, you'll find something. You live alone, it'll be easy," she said, turning back to drool over Sean.

Over by the calendars, she heard clanging metal. Lily couldn't see what happened. Sean leapt to his feet and rushed over. He disappeared from her sight, then reemerged with an elderly woman on his arm. He took her over to the table and gave her his chair to sit on while she recovered, leaning on one of those four pronged walkers, which weren't supposed to fall over.

The lady looked a little confused. She stared at him.

Sean stood, signing books and chatting with people in line, as well as with the old lady, who Lily guessed hadn't been in line. She was still clutching a calendar. The staff brought him another chair.

The lady eventually recovered, stood and put a hand on his shoulder, patted him and said something, then walked away with her calendar.

Lily felt a sharp pain in her back as the boy behind her accidentally jabbed her. The air felt warm and stuffy, maybe her clothes would dry and she could stop shivering. She was so distracted by everything, she hadn't even realized her arms were covered with goose bumps. She shuffled a little farther forward.

The signing was supposed to end at six and they'd arrived and five-thirty. The clock on the wall said seven. Only five people remained ahead of her. She could smell the enchilada someone on the staff must have brought him. She'd overheard the conversation where he insisted on staying to sign for everyone.

Heather said, her eyes never leaving him, "Do you have the CDs and DVDs of the movie about Nick Drake and his other one *Songs of the Soul?*"

"Nope," said Lily.

"That's the one about Ian Shayne and this band. They didn't really exist, but in the movie they revolutionized music in the late '90s. Sean did vocals, played acoustic guitar with the band and actually wrote *all* the music and lyrics while in character. He's so brilliant. You've seen it right?"

"Uh, no," said Lily.

"Lily, it's amaaaaazzzing. You have to rent it. Or buy it. I wish I'd brought mine for him to sign. Poor Bree."

Lily shook her head. "I don't understand it, if he's so smart then why is he so stupid about women?"

"What do you mean?" asked Heather.

"Nina Vicente? Weren't they together for years? She's such a viper," said Lily.

"Okay, definite bad choice. I think he just needs to find a good woman." Heather sighed and returned to Sean watching. She held up her cell to get another photo.

Only four people left.

Sean had dimples and even a cleft in his chin. His brown eyes looked kind. He wore a green, plaid flannel shirt and jeans. She had expected some swanky suit. Wavy brown hair drifted over his forehead as he bent his head to sign. He shook hands with everyone who wanted to. He was perfectly charming. Rugged, yet gentle. Not airbrushed or perfect. He looked human.

Lily watched him with Heather as she turned up the charm, flirting with him. Poor girl, all she'd get would be an autograph and a smile.

Lily's turn came. She grabbed a book off the pile and handed it to him, fumbling it. He caught it and their hands touched. Her fingers felt as if they'd been asleep their entire lives and now they lit up like candles. Sparks shot through her entire body.

"What's your name?" he asked, smiling.

"Lily, Lily Toureau. But it's not for me. It's for my friend Bree. She's sick and couldn't come."

He looked into her eyes and Lily felt as if she were melting into a giant primordial blob.

"So you braved the elements to help her out. That was very kind of you," he said.

Lily felt sure it was a reference to her wet t-shirt. Her cheeks felt hot, but she said, "Thanks."

Just in case he was sincere.

After Sean finished signing the book, he handed it back. Her hand touched his and their eyes met. He looked amused. She felt dizzy as he looked at her and her head tingled. The sensation traveled down her spine, then became overwhelming until her entire body resonated with it. She felt herself wilting to the floor.

When she came to, Sean knelt over her, along with one of the bookstore women and Heather.

"Lily, are you all right?" Heather asked.

She nodded, sure her face must be on fire with embarrassment.

"I just got dizzy."

"Can you sit up?" asked Sean. He took her arm and helped her sit up. She still felt dizzy and nauseous, but was able to move to a chair. Sean returned to signing books, but glanced at her occasionally, his forehead wrinkled.

Heather knelt beside her, whispering, "He's awesome, isn't he? Are you going to be okay? Can you make it to your car?"

"I'll be fine," said Lily, not sure it was true.

"Did you eat lunch today? Oh yeah. I remember you ate a huge lunch. A slice of pizza and a yogurt. You always eat and never gain anything. Well, if you're okay. I've got to run. Promised to meet him in five minutes, down the street. See ya." She hugged Lily, then disappeared down the stairs.

Lily slowly stood, the nausea dwindling. She felt so flustered. She had never fainted. What was up with that?

Sean asked, "Are you sure you're okay?"

"I'll be fine, thank you," she said, picking up her book and walking over to the far side of the mezzanine. Moving made her feel better. She stood near the calendars and watched him talking to the staff for a few minutes.

Her head reeled. Nausea came in waves, but she couldn't seem to stop staring at him or leave where he was. She leaned against a column for support. Then it came to her that she wanted more from him, but she felt confused as to what that might be.

She picked up a calendar, trying to look less like a drooling teenager or pathetic middle aged addict. But she felt like both. She glanced at the calendar, 'Hot Babes & Hot Cars.' So not her type of wall decoration.

She gazed at him again and found him staring at her. She felt such a jolt of energy and the tingling began again. Was he checking her out?

In her dreams maybe.

She began trembling until the entire calendar section, which wrapped around the center of the mezzanine, was in danger of collapsing.

She wanted to get closer to him.

But that would be even more embarrassing. She needed to leave. What was wrong with her? She put the calendar back, then went to the elevator, not trusting herself with the stairs.

Downstairs, she walked towards a cashier to check out, but stopped at a table of books which caught her eye. She flipped through a book on new archeological discoveries in Ireland. It would be perfect for Mom. She put it down, trying to decide whether to get it and looked up. Across from her was Sean looking through a book. He'd been there when she walked up to the table.

Unbelievable. She turned to head for the cashier again. She managed to make it this time and pay for the book for Bree. She got a thick plastic bag for it, so it wouldn't get ruined by the rain.

Sean was standing just past the cashier, looking at a table of remaindered books. With great effort, she walked past him and headed towards the stairs to go out the back door, but instead of going up, she went down to the art supplies. She just couldn't seem to make herself leave.

He came down the stairs and looked at pens. He probably went through a lot of them.

What was she thinking? She fled up the stairs and still couldn't make herself leave the store. She dawdled in the gifty section for a while, still nauseous. Then she went back down to the art supplies. He was gone. She searched for him through all three floors of the store, including textbooks. But he was gone.

She felt a sense of loss that threatened to swallow her up like a huge black hole. Finally, she gave up and was able to go out the back door to the parking lot. Her body still tingled and she felt nauseous. She must be getting sick or something. Hopefully, it wasn't what Bree had.

The rain had been replaced by a cold breeze that cut through her still damp clothes. She shivered and now the goose bumps were obvious. It was dark out, even with the lighting casting long shadows over the cars that filled the parking lot.

Woodsmoke drifted past her nose, mingling with the scent of wet earth and fallen leaves.

She stood for several minutes trying to figure out where she'd parked her car, before she realized it sat in the lot a block away. Shaking her head at the stupidity, she started walking in that direction.

Then she saw him. Leaning against a white car, talking on his cell and staring at her.

She dug into her bag, searching for her keys, stalling for time. Glancing up, she saw him put his phone away. It's now or never. She took a deep breath and walked towards him. He moved towards her. Or was it the dizziness? It made her weave slightly.

They both spoke at the same time.

"Wait," he said, "you first."

"Hi, I'm Lily. I don't know if you remember me from the signing."

"Of course I do."

"I know, how could you forget? Probably not many women faint. Or maybe they do. I feel like a complete idiot and I don't really know how to do this, but I was wondering if you'd like to get a cup of coffee or dinner or something."

"I'd love to, but I can't. Tonight."

"Oh," she said, feeling completely deflated. Now would be a good time to go crawl under a pile of wet leaves.

Sean touched her arm and said, "My twin sister made dinner for me and I'm known in the family as the one who's always too busy to make these gatherings. If I don't show, no matter how late, and I am late, she'll string me up by my toes and throw dinner at me, dishes and all."

"I see." Her head spinning, she tried to think of a way to leave gracefully. It wasn't coming to her. He touched her arm again and the spinning stopped.

"I'll still be in town tomorrow. Are you free for dinner tomorrow night? I'd really like to find out who you are."

Lily felt so stunned she could hardly reply. Finally, she croaked out, "Yes, I'm free."

"How about if I pick you up at seven?"

"I'm working tomorrow and may be home late." She felt torn between jumping up and down and screaming or just falling over. She'd never reacted like this to a guy. All the tingling as if something deep inside her was waiting to erupt. Her skin, her entire body was on fire and it felt as if she'd be burned up with the heat.

"8:30?"

"That'd be perfect."

She gave him directions to her apartment and her home phone number. He punched them into his phone, then got into his car and drove off. Without staff, a bodyguard, a chauffeur. Or paparazzi.

Lily slowly staggered back to her car, feeling wonderful and horrible at the same time. Her head whirled. She felt even more nauseous. But tomorrow she had a date with an amazing man.

Things just couldn't get any better.

SEAN

THE DAY AFTER HIS SIGNING AT THE BOOKSTORE, SEAN DROVE his rental car to Wallingford. He pulled into the Food King parking lot, looking for Casey's PT Cruiser. Between the wiper swipes on high, he finally spotted her, leaning against the purple car and underneath a cartoony umbrella. He parked in the last empty spot, down the row a bit.

Getting out, he said, "Nice umbrella," and dove under it to get out of the driving rain. The air smelled so fresh. He pulled the collar of his khaki raincoat closer, since he couldn't get all the way under the small umbrella.

"I can't find mine. Don't ever have kids. They steal all your stuff," she said.

He laughed. His twin was one of the funniest people he knew. He hugged her, "God, I've missed you."

"Show up more often," she teased him.

"Are we walking or driving?"

"Wimp. We're walking," she said, starting off.

The umbrella pulled out from over him, Sean pulled his hood up.

"I see you still have parking karma," she said.

"And I'm ever grateful for it." Casey had observed for years that he could almost always find parking spaces with ease. He didn't know how or why, but parking always magically opened up for him. When it didn't happen immediately, he found from experience that it wasn't a place he should be going. A shopping experience which turned out all wrong, a party where he had an encounter with someone that ended badly. He'd learned that it was best to pay attention when he couldn't easily find a place to park.

Sean followed her to the crosswalk, his head pounding. He'd had the nasty headache all morning. Thank god for sunglasses. Even the dim, gloomy light of a rainy, November morning in Seattle hurt.

A block away, they entered the Indian Restaurant. Spices floated through the air: cardamon, cumin and other curry ingredients. Casey plunked down in a red vinyl booth and Sean slid in across from her, unzipping his raincoat and sliding out of it. The restaurant felt cozy, with heat coming from the kitchen and warm turmeric colored walls. They were the only customers. At two in the afternoon they'd caught the lull between storms of lunch and dinner. The waiter brought menus and water.

"You look good today," Casey said.

"Good, how?"

"You're sort of beaming."

"Ah, it's the charming company," he said, not wanting to bring Lily up.

"Flatterer. So, how's your day been?" Casey shook our her navy raincoat and put it on the bench beside her.

"Busy. Lots of interviews. Publicity is really hard work. And repetitious. And I've had a raging headache that won't go away. Aspirin didn't help."

"I've got something," she said, digging through her purse.

"What is it and is it legal?" He glanced at the menu and quickly decided on paneer and peas with rice.

"Of course it's legal," she said, taking an orange pill out of her pill case. "I'm a mother. I carry a pharmacy in my purse. Want a cough drop? Having an asthma attack?" She pulled out a bag of cough drops and an inhaler.

Sean swallowed the pill.

"Are you going to keep wearing those sunglasses? It's a gray day. This isn't California," she said, perusing the menu, her lips tight.

"Sorry," he said, taking off the glasses. The light still hurt his eyes, but he knew Casey thought sunglasses inside were rude. She'd once observed that when you can't see someone's eyes, it's as if they don't want to communicate with you.

"So," he said, "how has your day been?"

The waiter, a short, thin Indian man with a mustache, came and took their orders, collected the menus, and left.

Casey said, "Oh, same old stuff, getting the kids off to school and James off to work. Moved some stuff around in the garden."

"In the rain?" he asked.

"Best time to move plants around here. In the fall, in the rain. They don't get so stressed," she smiled, impishly. Casey's brown hair curled around her shoulders from the rainy weather and her chocolate colored eyes sparkled with mischief.

He missed being around her. His twin had the amazing gift of being able to juggle ten million things in her mind at once. He could give her seemingly disconnected words and she'd find the connection. She was a genius in his eyes.

"And I got a call from Marcia. She apologized for not coming last night. Got hung up with clients. But at least they bought the house." Casey paused and looked at him.

"And?"

"And she's got a sweet condo for sale in Fremont. Just finished three months ago with great views, a cute deck, gas fireplace and a jetted tub in the bathroom."

"Casey, ..."

"I know. We're not pushing, but you might consider having a second home at least. Mom and Dad aren't getting any younger. As a matter of fact, neither are you and I. I want to spend more time with you before I die."

"Are you planning on going soon?" he asked. Was she just thinking or was something really going on?

"Having kids is great, but they also kill you sooner. But no, I've got too much to do to die and there's nothing wrong with me, but there is with you." She stared at him.

He drank his water, feeling the ice cubes clink against his teeth. He took a deep breath and tried to will the headache away. It had been a grueling morning doing the interviews while wishing his head would simply explode and get it over with. He felt exhausted.

Last night's dinner at Casey's, with most of his huge family, had flowed smoothly. Now he knew why. She'd been saving up her energy for lunch. He'd be under fire until she said what she needed to. He just wished his head would stop hurting. At least he had the date tonight to look forward to.

He sighed and said, "Okay, shoot."

"Well, since you asked. Let's start at the edges. Mom and Dad getting older, me getting older, you getting older, my kids getting older and they don't even know my twin brother except from what they see on a screen. Then there's the main part of what worries me. Just what are you doing with your life? You know I don't mean your career, that's fabulous and I'm proud of what you've done there. I'm talking about your personal life."

"It's coming along," he said.

"Okay, I can understand not dating for three years after what Nina did to you. But if 'coming along' means dating twenty-something starlets for a week or two, maybe even a month, before moving on to the next one for two entire years and then now there's nothing, well, that is *not* 'coming along'." Casey glared at him in silence as the waiter brought their food.

Sean stirred the sauce with peas and homemade cheese into his rice and took a bite. The sweet, spicy flavors mingled in his mouth as he tried to think of a witty reply and failed.

"I get your point. I was never serious about any of them; I doubt they were about me. I was much too old for any of them. It was a business arrangement, sort of. My publicist wanted me to prove I'm still man enough and popular enough to get the hot young things, that I wasn't emasculated by Nina. And they got publicity and attention they wouldn't have gotten on the arm of a less famous man. I finally got frustrated with the charade and quit.

"You turned your romantic life into a business strategy? You are way more messed up than I imagined. Sean, your romantic life should be private."

"My romantic life hasn't been private since Nina walked into it. No way could the paparazzi resist two megastars together." He rubbed his eyes. The headache wasn't leaving. It would be a long day.

"Well, I understand that. However, it needs to be private from now on. No more dating bimbos."

"I'll have you know that I have a date with a very respectable woman, who's at least out of her twenties, this very evening," he blurted out, instantly regretting it. He took a bite of his food. It was too soon to talk about Lily. He didn't know her well enough, even though his attraction to her felt overwhelming. He *needed* to be with her. But he couldn't figure out how to explain that. To anyone.

"Is she an actress?"

"No, well not that I know of."

"Blond?"

"Yes, blond. Many people in this world are blond. Are you that bigoted?"

Casey gave him her patented 'you idiot' look. "How did you meet her and when?"

"Last night. At the signing."

"So you only met her last night? You don't know anything about her."

"She's not a twenty something starlet."

"However, she's not someone to settle down with, is she? She just thinks you're some hot movie star."

"I don't know what she thinks of me. You can't figure that out from one short meeting. And I don't get a chance to meet many women who are unaware of who I am."

"Touché," said Casey, toying with her lunch. She set her fork down and looked at him.

"I want you to find your soul mate. As far as James can tell from his research, the Gift doesn't simply skip one half of a pair of twins. I want you to find the right woman and start attracting kids. I just really want you to meet someone you can be happy with. I know you're not right now."

"I understand you want the best for me, Sis. That's why I haven't thrown you through the beautiful glass door of this establishment," he said, not wanting to talk about the Gift. He felt so mixed about the whole thing. He was in his forties and it still hadn't appeared in his life. He desperately wanted to find his twin soul and start a family. Because the Gift hadn't shown up yet, he was equally afraid that he'd missed his chance somewhere or that it simply wouldn't happen to him.

"You'd never be able to throw me through the door. I can take you," she said, sipping her water.

"No, but I'm sorely tempted to try." He rubbed his temples and pushed the plate away, half uneaten. "Are you sure you can take me?"

"Sure of it. I'm in shape. I have teenage boys to wrestle with, remember?"

He insisted on paying the bill. They walked to their cars. The rain had momentarily stopped, leaving the streets and everything else intensely sparkling. The sunglasses went back on.

"Headache still there?" asked Casey.

"Yeah. No change."

"I'm sorry. But you get to rest this afternoon, right."

"No, I have to make a few phone calls. Business to attend to," he smiled, grimly, remembering the message Nina had left.

"It sucks to be you. Daniel thinks you're a god, you know. He wants to grow up to be you. You need to hang around him more often, so he sees the downside of his uncle's life."

"I really will think about what you've said. I would like to spend more time with my family. I need rejuvenating. I've got a lot to sort out."

"Well, call Marcia if you want to see the condos. I love you, little brother," she said, hugging him and getting into her car. "Take care of yourself."

"Yes, big sister, I will. Take care of yourself as well."

"I always do. Put the oxygen mask on myself first, kids second."

He laughed, got in the rental car and drove to the hotel, feeling desperate for his head to stop hurting. In the elevator, he checked his messages. His agent had texted. 'Urgent, call me. Nina replacing Lillian to play opposite you. Lillian injured.'

Sean's heart dropped to the floor. He loved Lillian Anderson's work. It was one of the reasons he'd chosen to be in the upcoming film. Nina had left a gushing message earlier in the day, telling him the same thing. Nina. Rage poured through his body as he walked down the hall to his room. Rage at her, rage at his pounding head, rage at feeling powerless to change his life.

Inside the beige suite, he kicked off his damp shoes, tossed his raincoat towards the closet, drank some water and pulled the gauzy layer of the curtains shut. He sat on the carpet and did some stretching and breathing exercises. Only then did he call the director of his next film. The one that started shooting next week.

"I'm sorry, Mr. O'Neill. Mr. Nicholls is on another line. Would you care to hold or shall I have him return your call?" asked the assistant, whose syrupy voice on the other end only made him want to put his hands around her throat and strangle her.

"I'll hold," he said. He put his phone on speaker, and paced back and forth around the room, trying to calm down and think of a useful way to voice his objections.

Finally a male voice came on, "Sean, how are you?"

"Not great. How are you?"

"I'm running a mile a minute, as always. What's up?"

As if he didn't know. Bloody bastard.

"I don't want to be a pain in the ass, but I agreed to do this picture with Lillian Anderson as my costar."

"You agent told you that Lillian has been in a car accident."

"I understand that, however, I will *not* do a love scene with Nina, if in fact she does replace Lillian. I won't budge on that. Isn't there any way to postpone shooting? I really want to work with Lillian."

"Sean, we didn't choose Nina to spite you. She was the only actress available, who could give us the performance we need, at such short notice. They can't give us a time line for Lillian's recovery, even if we could postpone. Which we can't. Our lead time is too short and the other actors and tech people have other commitments."

"I won't do a love scene with Nina. You can release me from the contract and find a different actor if you need to." Sean's head throbbed and he sat on a chair, laying his head on the nearby table.

"Sean, I don't want to do that. You and Nina set off fireworks together on screen. And we need that love scene. It's crucial to the story. You know that. Can we compromise here?"

"I'm not a good enough actor to do a love scene with her. I'm not even sure I can be on the same set as her without strangling her. What other compromises did you have in mind?"

"I don't know. I just don't feel good about letting you go without trying to work something out. We had to scramble to find Nina. Time's running short. We've already started shooting. We'd need to rethink costumes and makeup, again. Maybe we can do something with body doubles. I don't know. Let me meet with everyone to see if we can find a solution. Give me a chance to work with this."

"I'll give you a chance, but no love scene," said Sean.

He hung up and ran water in the bathtub. He hadn't handled that well. Damn, he was a mess. Now he'd get a reputation as a prima donna.

He walked to the door and clicked on the 'do not disturb' sign and switched his phone to vibrate. It was six. He poured a scotch from the mini bar and drank it. How could he possibly go on a date tonight? How could he do this movie with Nina in it?

Part of him wanted to call and cancel the date. Another part held out hope that the amazing electricity he'd felt when meeting Lily last night, meant something. He wouldn't give up that chance for the world. She might be the one.

He undressed and sat in the hot tub with the lights out.

In the darkness his head throbbed. And his mind went back and forth between Nina and Lily.

LILY

Lily dangled from the orange Fremont Bridge, held only by a purple bungee cord. For three hours. In the pouring rain.

She'd accepted the booking for the sportswear shoot months before. Gerard, the photographer, shot from a boat below, then on land, then above on the pedestrian walkway and lastly, leaning over the bridge.

They should have pulled her up to take a break, while he moved around. But they didn't. They should have prearranged a signal for her to use if she needed to come up. But they didn't. She should have thought of that. But she didn't.

She'd been too excited anticipating her big date with Sean to think clearly.

Normally, heights didn't scare her. After the first hour of swinging in the cold breeze and streaming rain, her arms and legs went numb, except her bad knee which ached from the cold. At least she had water. All she had to do was stick out her tongue to get fresh, cool water.

She looked down on the ship canal, watching the boats

move past below, half hidden by the rain. Occasionally, the awful smell from their engines drifted up to her. It was almost as bad as bus exhaust.

Would she ever be able to move her limbs again? Losing control of her body made everything else more frightening. She tried not to focus on the fact that only a purple string kept her from plunging into the freezing cold water. Instead she kept her attention on the fact that the money was good and would give her enough to get by for a few months.

Twisting in the downpour gave her plenty of time to think as her body slowly atrophied. She stuffed thoughts of her hot date to the back of her mind. It felt too important and she didn't want to think about it, somehow afraid she'd jinx it.

Trivial stuff, that's what she needed to make herself stay present. What part of the city did she want to live in? The cheapest were far north or far south.

Cold water ran down her sides, beneath the loose fitting sweater.

Damn.

The coat leaked. So did the helmet. It must be a cycling helmet with vents. She hadn't really seen it before they'd strapped it on. The urban chic sportswear was not impressive. It might look hip, but it sure wasn't warm enough for this weather. She felt as if the wind blew right through her.

Lily heard sirens above and looked up to see the lights. Police.

Finally, they closed down the shoot. She'd overheard the crew speculating when they started on how long it would take.

Gerard had said, "No, no. Do not worry pretty little heads about zis."

He called everyone pretty.

"All ze permits are in order."

His assistant had stood behind him, shaking her head.

Which meant there were not permits. Gerard, or someone higher up the food chain, would get a rather hefty fine for holding up traffic.

That they had no permits should have been her first signal that she should bail.

After the police arrived and she was pulled up, Lily changed into dry clothes and took her lunch break in her car, the failing heater on full blast. She alternately drank hot coffee and hot soup that one of the assistants brought, staring at the rain-blurred windows.

As her body thawed out, she relived the previous evening at the bookstore in detail. Sean had been amazing, thoughtful and kind. She'd never had a man like that in her life. Other than Dad.

Her first choice for a partner had seemed kind, but he started drinking and turned cruel. The marriage ended in divorce, years ago. She wanted to find someone who could really care for her, as she was willing to care for him. Sean was out of her league, but he was a good start in looking for the right man. A warm glow surrounded her as feeling returned to her arms and legs.

The next phase of the shoot involved an outdoor climbing wall at the UW. Still raining, harder this time.

Lily stood waiting for her turn. In dry clothes. At least for a while.

Jennifer scrambled up the wall first and hung there, waving her arms and whooping like a frat boy. Sam went lower and to her right. Lily scaled the wall directly beneath Jennifer. Michele came up below her. They formed a rough parallelogram.

The rain increased in volume and Lily silently thanked her gloves and shoes for their grips as she clung to the wall, moving ever so slightly to keep her body warmed up.

She smelled magnolia flowers. There were a few trees across

the way, she didn't know what kind. But they weren't flowering. And it was November. Didn't magnolias lose their leaves in the fall? She didn't know. Someone must be wearing heavy perfume. Otherwise how could she smell it during a downpour?

She started sneezing from the fragrance. The wall was slippery from the deluge. How could Gerard even see to shoot?

Her mind wandered back to the date. She just needed to think of something intelligent to talk about. To impress Sean that she wasn't a dumb blond model. Even if he wrote her off, she'd still have one evening with that luscious man.

Gerard pranced around in his warm, eggplant purple coat with red, faux fur around the neck.

He said, "You must envision yourself fighting for your place wiz nature. Life is a battle and you must be ze vinner. Ze Fierce line of clothing is about having mastery over oneself and one's environment. You must feel zis to ze core of your beings!"

Above her, Jennifer whooped and hollered.

Lily felt miserable and wanted to haul off and belt either Jennifer or Gerard. She caught the overwhelming scent of magnolias again. It was so powerful, that it made her feel nauseated. She fixed her concentration firmly on the glove in front of her on the wall. Why did she smell magnolias? It couldn't be Jennifer. She wasn't that close. Neither was anyone else.

Across the grass, a boy with longish brown hair and one shoulder raised to support a heavy backpack stood watching the shoot. He was close enough that she could see him rolling his eyes, but at what? Then he smiled at her and her heart melted.

Just then, Lily felt Jennifer slip and hit her. It took forever to fall just a few feet.

The next moment she lay on the ground, her back spasming. The pain took her breath away. Then Jennifer landed on top of her. Lily pushed her off and the nymphet bounced up unharmed. Lily's back was out. It throbbed as if elephants were tap dancing on it.

The boy came running over, "Mom, are you okay?" he asked, his face wrinkled with worry.

Had she hit her head in the fall? Who was he?

"Are you Lily's son?" asked Michelle.

"Yeah," he said. "Are you okay, Mom?" he asked again, touching her arm.

"My back's out, I think." How could she have forgotten a son? It didn't make any sense. Still, she knew his name was Teddy, he was fifteen, hated school and loved music. She slowly moved to a sitting position, breathing hard at the pain shooting up her back.

She watched Jennifer and Sam climb up the wall again. Gerard and his staff ignored her, probably terrified she'd sue them.

"We've got to get you to the ER," said Michelle.

"No. My back's just out. There's a clinic by my apartment. I've been there before."

Michelle turned to the boy. "You're Teddy, right?"

"Yes."

"Well Teddy, we've got to get your mom to the clinic. Can you help me get her up?"

"No problem," he said, dropping his backpack.

"Gently now," said Michelle.

She tried to stand, but it hurt too much. She ended up crawling back to her car, through the puddles, which soaked through the rain pants. The cold wetness chilled her skin.

Michelle walked alongside grumbling about Gerard. Teddy carried Lily's bag.

The shoot continued on with Sam and Jennifer. They hadn't even stopped to see if she was okay. She felt furious about that, but her back hurt so much it distracted her from throwing Gerard into the climbing wall.

She tried to crawl mainly on the grass, instead of the sidewalk. Until they got to the parking lot. Then it was all asphalt. At least she wore gloves. Too bad the Fierce climbing pants didn't have knee pads. The didn't hold up well to crawling through parking lots. Pathetic climbing gear.

By the time they got to her car, she could stand. Sort of. A stooped stand. She didn't think she could sit. Teddy put the back seat down and folded a spare blanket for a pillow. She crawled in through the tailgate and lay down, breathing hard into the pain.

Teddy sat beside her, tears streaming down his face, although he tried to hide them from her. He held her hand.

Michelle drove them to the clinic in Lily's car, after getting the directions.

Michelle said, "That incompetent, pretentious imbecile. I'll never work for him again. And more than that, I'll make sure to tell every model I know, and that's a lot, how shoddy and dangerous his working conditions are. This should never have happened. You don't shoot in this kind of rain. How many indoor climbing walls are there in the area? The only thing the big boob can do is take photos."

Lily could only get out a mumbled, "Uh huh."

"Don't worry. Word about him will spread. He'll have to pack it in. Too bad photographers don't have licenses that can be revoked. He'll probably just set up shop in another city. That's it, I'll start a website for models to go to. We can put the word out about jerks like him."

Lily stopped listening and tried frantically to find a way to relax her back muscles as she rolled around the car, feeling like a piece of abused luggage. She appreciated Teddy's quiet presence as he held her hand, but she couldn't figure out who he was. How could all this happen on the day of her big date?

After the clinic, Michelle ran into the pharmacy across the street. She was back by the time Teddy had helped Lily crawl into the car. Lily finally got some medication at about four.

Then Michelle drove them to Lily's apartment. Teddy and Michelle helped her up the stairs. Lily groggily wondered what she'd do about Teddy, when she noticed an unfamiliar bed in the second bedroom of her apartment. Her desk had been moved to the living room. Teddy walked in the tossed his backpack and wet coat on the bed as if he'd always lived there.

They got Lily's shoes off and tucked her into bed; she refused to try to get out of her wet clothes. Lily heard Michelle ask Teddy if he'd be okay.

"Yeah, I'll look after her. We've got food in the fridge, so I can nuke us some dinner."

Michelle left to catch a bus.

After that Lily drifted off quickly.

She jolted awake and saw the clock read 7:48. Sean would be here in forty-five minutes. Still groggy, she climbed out of bed and hobbled into the bathroom as fast as possible with the pain. A blue bruise stood out on her cheek and her hair had dried so one side lay all scrunched up and the other went out straight.

Lily quickly took a coldish shower in an attempt to wake up. She brushed her hair. None of which made her feel any better. A massive bruise on her hip clinched it. No matter how well the date went, she wouldn't be sleeping with Sean tonight.

Coffee. She needed coffee.

Slipping into her robe, she limped into the kitchen. With a shock, she saw Teddy at the table, reading a music magazine and listening to his iPod. The remains of a frozen pizza lay on the table beside him.

She'd completely forgotten about him.

When he saw her, he took his headphones off. "How are you?" he asked.

"My back hurts so bad, I can barely think straight," she said, trying to stretch a little, while getting some espresso brewing. The elephants had stopped tap dancing, but now she felt as if kangaroos were boxing her spine. The pill hadn't helped enough. She took another.

She turned back to Teddy and asked "Why can't I remember you from before yesterday?" Then immediately realized what a horrible question it was.

"Dunno," he said, looking unconcerned. "Maybe you *did* hit your head. I only came here night before last."

"How?"

"I flew in and the airline helped find me a cab who brought me here."

"Where did you live before that?" she asked.

He shrugged, "I bounced around a lot, can't remember all the places."

"But, I'm not your mom, am I?" She couldn't make any sense of this. Knowing his name and who he was. Michelle knowing his name, the new bed.

None of this was normal, but she knew it was real.

She *was* his mom, now at least, although Lily couldn't understand how that could be. She'd had always desperately wanted two things in her life, to find a soulmate and to have a child. She just hadn't envisioned having a teenager drop in on her. She didn't know what to do with that.

"You're not my biological mom, no. Please let me stay. I don't have anywhere else to go," he said, green eyes pleading, close to filling with tears.

Lily tried to figure out what to do about her date with Sean. She couldn't leave Teddy alone. She had a sense he'd gotten in real trouble before, which was why he'd bounced around so much. And she couldn't call Sean, because she'd been so flustered at being asked out, getting his number hadn't even occurred to her.

There was knocking on her door. And giggling. She hadn't heard the gate down below buzz.

Lily opened the door, pulling her bathrobe closed more tightly.

"Hi honey," said her mom.

"Mom, Dad! What are you doing here?" She gingerly hugged them, her back screaming, and they followed her inside. Hugging hurt enough to bring tears to her eyes. She turned away to grab a coffee mug and wipe the tears away.

"Oh, we were in the neighborhood, coming back from Canada, so we thought we'd surprise you," said Dad, pushing his unruly black and silver hair out of his eyes.

He saw Teddy, now standing, and his eyes lit up. "Teddy my boy, how are you?" He shook Teddy's hand and hugged him at the same time.

Teddy looked thrilled to see him.

Her parents had the skill of making everyone feel included and valued. Her dad, Nick, was the same height as Teddy, but soon Teddy would be taller. Dad wasn't handsome, probably never had been. She always thought he looked sort of goofy; he usually wore a silly expression on his face. At sixty-seven he looked fit, muscular and twenty years younger. He'd always acted younger, claimed it came from teaching teenagers. Both her parents were retired and spent all their time traveling.

"You two know each other?" asked Lily.

"You are so silly sometimes, my dear," said Mom. "Of course we know your son." She smiled and her brilliant, blue eyes glistened.

Her mom, Susan, was plump with short, gray hair and her

eyes always saw more than she let on. She used to teach elementary school.

Lily opened her mouth and closed it again. She made an espresso.

"Can I offer you two something to drink or eat?"

"Nope," said Dad. "We ate on the road and good thing, since it looks like someone else has almost killed the pizza! We just dropped in to say hello." He ruffled Teddy's hair and sat at the kitchen table. Then, almost as an afterthought, grabbed the last piece of pizza.

"Did you hurt yourself, honey?" asked Mom.

"I fell at work."

"She got knocked off a climbing wall today by one of the brainless, who then fell on top of her. We had to take her to the doctor," said Teddy, putting the empty pizza box in the garbage. He picked up his magazine and iPod and took them to his room, followed by Nick.

"What an eventful day," said Susan.

"It's not over yet. I have a date arriving in fifteen minutes."

"So, your back's not hurting enough to keep you from going?"

"It hurts terribly. But I really want to go." How could she explain what Sean made her feel? The separation since last night felt unbearable. Worse than her back pain.

Lily said, "I just don't know what to do about Teddy. I can't leave him here alone."

Susan said, "Situation solved. ALL HANDS ON DECK! I'll help you dress. Go get started. Teddy, you pack some clothes and PJ's. We're staying in a hotel tonight. I need a break from the RV. We'll go to a movie, use the hotel swimming pool and hot tub. Maybe even work out. No, probably not. But we can catch up with you, find out what music you're listening to. 1,2,3, GO!

Teddy and Nick returned to Teddy's room. Lily put down her now empty cup and shuffled back to the bedroom, followed by Mom. She opened the closet and her world spun around.

She felt so grateful for her parents. Mom and Dad knew Teddy, they said he was her son. How could she not remember? She remembered seeing him just before the fall from the climbing wall, but not before that. She'd always wanted kids. But how could she possibly take care of him? She couldn't even take care of herself; what kind of a role model was that? She didn't know how to be a mom.

Susan looked through her closet and asked, "Is this a dress date or a pants date?"

Lily tried to focus and said, "It better be pants. I have bandages on my knees, had to crawl to the car." She flashed her wet-from-the-shower bandages at Mom. "Jeans and a sweater, I guess."

Susan picked a purple V-neck sweater and a pair of plain jeans, while Lily painfully slipped on panties. She decided against a bra, it would hurt too much. She got the sweater on, but Mom had to help with the jeans. By the time they were on, she was sweating so much she had to towel off again. She ended up putting on a blue sweater, instead. The whole process of getting dressed had been an ordeal and she hurt even more.

"That sweater matches your beautiful eyes. A much better choice," said Mom, looking in the closet. "Now what shoes? Do you have any flats?"

"I think just running shoes and sandals. Can't wear those. I'm moving soon, so I purged my closet and haven't had a chance to replace anything. There might be a pair of heels in the back. But I don't have any flats."

Susan dug around in the closet and stood back up.

"Will you be able to walk in heels?" Susan said, holding up a pair of red heels.

"Guess I'll have to, at least I'll be able to get them off tonight by myself."

"You're welcome to come to the hotel and I'll help you undress," said Mom, laughing. "I hope he turns out to be worth it. He must be something special."

"I hope so too," said Lily, slipping into glittery, red heels. Might as well take it all the way, she thought, grabbing a gaudy, red necklace.

She put the finishing touches of her makeup on without any problems and went into the kitchen. Mom, Dad and Teddy sat around the table. Teddy had a duffle bag at his feet. He and Nick were arm wrestling.

The buzzer sounded, startling her.

She spoke into the intercom, "I'll be right down." She pulled on her black leather jacket, got her purse and phone. Her back still hurt, but now the pain felt like a dull roar.

"Okay, let's go," said Nick. "I don't know what hotel we'll end up at, but call our cell when you get up in the morning and we'll bring breakfast over. Or lunch," he said, winking at her.

"Or call if you need any help, okay honey?"

"Okay Mom. Thank you, you two are such gems."

Teddy said, "I'll see you in the morning, okay?"

She hugged him and said, "Yes, you will. We need to go apartment hunting."

"Can we come?" asked Nick.

"The more the merrier," said Lily. She loved her parents. And they might have to drive.

They walked down ahead of her, trying to pretend they weren't with her.

Lily found that between her back and the heels, she couldn't walk down the stairs normally. So she turned around and crawled down them backwards, hoping they were clean and she wouldn't get her jeans dirty. She ignored her sore hands and bandaged knees.

"We'll cover you," whispered Nick. He started singing, 'Yellow Submarine' as the three of them walked down the stairs in front of her. Susan joined in and tried to teach Teddy the words. They stopped at the bottom until Lily caught up.

She dusted off her knees, stood slowly and turned around, her head spinning. Nick, Susan and Teddy opened the gate and walked out, pretending they didn't know her.

Sean stood watching them dance away, smiling.

Lily stared at him and said, "Hi."

He wore gray slacks, a sport coat, and a yellow ochre colored shirt that showed off his tan beautifully. And a tie. He'd dressed up. And she hadn't. He exuded sexy.

"You look beautiful," he said.

"Thank you." She didn't believe him, but Mom taught her never to turn away a compliment.

"I don't know if you have a restaurant you'd like to go to." He hesitated.

She didn't know what to say. Her mind was filled with too much pain to think.

He continued, "My sister told me about a new place, Wind and Sea. Over on the Sound."

"That would be wonderful," she said.

Why couldn't she think of anything to say? She'd heard of the restaurant. Very trendy. She wasn't dressed up enough. But the thought of herself in a dress with bandages on her knees made her want to laugh hysterically. She had to work hard not to laugh. Finally, the thought of crawling back up the stairs to change clothes, knocked all the humor out of her brain.

Her mind ran a mile a minute, but her mouth couldn't catch the words to say them.

Should she tell him about the accident? Best not to point

out her clumsiness. He'd find out soon enough. She'd always been graceless, teased about it all the time in school. She just couldn't keep track of her lanky body. At least this accident hadn't been her fault. She certainly couldn't tell him about Teddy. Not until she got things sorted out. She didn't even remember Teddy coming to her house the night before. How could she be his mom?

Sean took her arm. Lily felt surprised to find him a few inches shorter than she was. She hadn't noticed that the night before. If it bothered him, he didn't say anything.

She walked as smoothly as possible in the heels, to the car. Why had she gotten rid of all her flats? Obviously, she hadn't planned on a back injury. Silly her.

Lily was close enough to smell him, subtle and musky. Was it aftershave or just him? She inhaled the scent deeply and felt goose bumps on her back and shoulders. Was he wearing a pheromone cologne?

Getting into the car was relatively easy. Her back simply screamed with pain during the entire process. She did her best to smile as he waited to close the door.

As they drove, he talked about his book tour and the beauty of Seattle. She tried to listen, but found keeping track of his words difficult. She envisioned them as colorful speech bubbles, like in a cartoon, but on string. She worked really hard to follow the string, but always seemed a few words behind. Finally, she gave up and admired his chiseled chin, wanting to touch his lips with her fingers and nuzzle into that warm, tan chest. Lily shifted in her seat and the pain came to the forefront. She wasn't sure if the pills weren't just making things worse. It didn't completely kill the pain, but it certainly derailed her brain.

Traffic was more terrible than usual. The rain only made it worse. The only intelligible comment she could come up with was, "Seattleites don't know how to drive in the rain." There were accidents everywhere.

Sean's hands gripped the steering wheel, his jaw muscles grew tighter. In one of the few films of his that she'd seen, his character did just that before he killed someone or maybe was attacked by aliens. She couldn't remember.

They had to park at the back of the lot. The asphalt was uneven and it was dark, making walking even harder. Cold rain poured from the sky, mingling with a shivery breeze. She pulled her coat tight around her neck. Should've worn a scarf.

Puddles seeped into her shoes, chilling her bare feet.

"I wore the wrong shoes for walking," she said, trying to walk and shake the water out of them at the same time.

"Your shoes are fine," he said, taking her arm. "I'm always in such a hurry that I walk fast all the time. Sometimes I need to slow down."

"I just had a really bad, hard day. I'm so tired."

"I'll do my best to keep you awake," he said, smiling a devious smile.

At least it looked devious. She shivered with delight.

The restaurant walls were glass from floor to ceiling, bound together by warm colored wood panels. Long metallic sea-green streamers wafted in the breeze from the air circulation system. She took it all in as Sean got them a table.

A tall, long waterfall stood at the entrance, not noisily gushing, but trickling and making a melodic, tinkling sound. Red, orange and yellow fish swam in the deep pool. She sat down on a tall boulder and dipped her fingers in the water, mesmerized by the swirling colors of the fish. Her eyelids drooped as her body swayed with sleepiness.

Sean came over and took her arm. She felt a strong tingling run through her body. She stood and they followed the host, who led them to a table next to a window.

The storm outside pounded the glass. There would have been a spectacular view of the sound if the rain hadn't been falling like molten steel.

A menu appeared before her and Lily sat gingerly in the chair, then picked up the menu. Sean pushed her chair in, which was good because she was unable to.

"Can I get you something to drink?" asked the Host.

"I'll have a scotch. Laphroaig, if you have it," said Sean.

Lily thought for a moment, unable to come up with a reason why she shouldn't drink, although her mind wasn't functioning very well. Her brain felt like a marshmallow, a toasted, melty marshmallow. Maybe some wine would help the pain in her back go away. "I'll have a glass of white wine."

"Chardonnay?" asked the Host.

"Perfect," she said.

The host smiled, nodded and walked away.

Looking around, she felt completely outclassed. All the women here were *dressed*. Stockings, heels and jewelry. Sean had also dressed up, although he would have looked fantastic in a garbage bag. She felt so uncomfortable.

"What looks interesting to you?" Sean asked.

She looked at the menu again and the room began to reel. She tried to focus on the words, but they kept moving. Her imagination flew wildly around the room, she was close to hallucinating and it was all she could do to stare at the menu and pretend she was thinking.

The drinks came and the waiter left the bottle of wine. She drank her wine quickly, out of nervousness. What must he think of her not talking? Boring, boring, boring. She hadn't said much on the drive over either. She couldn't seem to say what she was thinking. But maybe she *shouldn't* say what was going on in her brain right now.

Just let him do the talking. He didn't seem very comfortable either. She looked at the menu again, but still couldn't make sense of it. She could pick out a few words here and there, but couldn't connect them to any food she knew of.

"I can't decide. Why don't you surprise me and order for me?" she asked, smiling at him.

He looked at her strangely. "Are you sure? I don't know what you like."

She nodded and her head began to spin again.

The waitress came to the table. "Hi, I'm Sonya," she said, tossing her long red hair back over the shoulder of her sleek, little black dress and peering out from under those chic bangs, with sultry eyes. Lily noticed that she smiled a long time at Sean. She might as well have said, "Hello, I'm Sonya. I'll be your waitress tonight and when you've finished dinner, I'll warm your bed."

Sean and Sonya had a little discussion, that Lily couldn't really follow, about the specials of the night. At one point Sean asked Lily if she liked salmon and she told him yes. He finished ordering and Sonya left. By then Lily had finished another glass of wine.

She felt uncomfortable with the silence. Sean looked out the window at the rain as he drank his whatever he'd ordered. He rubbed his forehead as if he had a headache.

Lily decided to try to start a conversation. "I have a joke for you. You're in Seattle, it's 52 degrees out, gray, drizzly and depressing. What day of the year is it?"

Sean smiled and asked, "What?"

"Any day."

He smiled again.

God, he was polite. But so withdrawn.

Well, she tried. It was a bad joke, but oh so true.

Her poured her another glass of wine and she drank more, just to be doing something. Was this her second or third glass?

He gazed at her and said, "So you said you had a bad day?"

She listened to the quiet chatter of the people surrounding them and the gurgling of the waterfall. She didn't really want to describe how awkward she felt about having gone from having fair potential as a model to being an aging model reduced to working with flaky photographers in order to pay the bills. Lily just sat there, staring into her wine, not knowing what else to say.

"I'd like to hear about it."

She began to tell the story quietly, then her mouth wouldn't stop. She felt outside herself and watched, horrified, as her body described the Fremont Bridge shoot in great detail complete with gestures. People at nearby tables stared. Did they recognize Sean or was she talking too loud? But she couldn't stop and the audience just made her more nervous.

He looked at her and made sympathetic noises.

The food arrived and she managed to eat part of it while continuing the story.

"So there I was, hanging upside down from a purple bungee cord attached to the railings in an orange jumpsuit thing with a pink helmet in the pouring rain. They kept trying, but finally couldn't even get a shot off it began to rain so hard. The colors were all wrong too. And it was lunch hour, so traffic got all tied up. The police cars came. Five of them, sirens and all. It was a fiasco."

She made a grand gesture, her back spasmed again and she managed to knock both their drinks off the table.

Lily dove to catch the glasses, inadvertently tackling a passing waiter who carried a large tray loaded with plates. Crashing plates and breaking glass deafened her.

Somehow, everything landed on Sean. Waiter, plates, food and all.

She fell off the struggling pile and sat on the floor, her back exploding with pain. For some reason that she couldn't fathom, Lily began to laugh. Sean looked great even covered with salad and dressing dripping down his face. She couldn't stop. She tried, but the combination of tension, drugs, caffeine and wine made it impossible to control herself. Finally, she was laughing so hard her emotions went over the edge and turned to tears.

Sean and the water had a contest of apologies. The waiter, along with another waiter and a bus boy tried to clean off Sean. His red face and look of deep embarrassment told Lily how he felt.

She saw him look down at her on the floor, crying, and he said to the waiters, "I think it's time we left."

As Sean pulled her up she felt his strength and how much control he had over himself.

Pain pushed sharp little knives into her spine. She clenched her teeth.

He extracted his jacket from one of the waiters, who was trying to clean it. Sean pulled the wallet out of his pants and dropped several fifty and hundred dollar bills on the table, much to the waiters' protests and began to walk towards the door with her in tow, just as she grabbed her purse and coat from the chair.

The little knives turned into swords slicing through her muscles. She gasped in response. No longer crying or laughing, she wiped tears off her face and saw a mascara smear on her hand. She tried to keep up with Sean. The searing pain in her back felt overwhelming and she needed to stop. Wrenching her wrist free of his hand, she accidentally threw Sean off balance.

He tripped over a metal pole. She watched, unable to move or speak. He rolled over a boulder and into the fish pond.

Lily felt appalled at what she'd done.

The fish dove for the depths. Sean sat glaring up at her, neck deep in water lilies, in the shallow end of the pond. He slowly stood and tried unsuccessfully to disentangle himself from all the plants and climbed out of the pond without saying a word.

The entire restaurant had stopped and fallen eerily silent. The staff stood frozen. Sean walked towards the door, trailing long rope-like foliage and creating pools of water.

Snickers began to emerge from the restaurant guests. Flashes from phone cameras came in a flurry amid what quickly became howling laughter. Sean turned around, bowed to the audience, then held the door open for her.

Speechless, she slowly followed him to the car. She watched as his shoulders rose higher with each step. He stood by the now open passenger door in the cold pouring rain, waiting for her with a grim look on his face. A few people had come out of the restaurant to stare.

She felt furious. She hadn't done any of this on purpose and his rabid glare infuriated her. Well, damn him. Mr. Famous Movie Star. Who did he think he was, treating her like this?

"Get in the car."

"No."

"Do you do this often?"

"What?" she asked. He was treating her exactly like her ex-husband did. That realization made her even more angry. She suddenly felt completely sober and sane. In complete control.

"Ask guys out, get completely stoned and drunk, then embarrass them? No, I've heard about people like you. You're a stalker. Or a paparazzi set up artist. Is that it?" Sean waved his arms.

Definitely losing control. He's raving.

"Is that what you think?" she asked, cooly. Fury roiled around deep within her belly.

"I'd be happy to hear another explanation," he said.

"Well, I'm not going to give you one, if that's how badly you think of me." She limped closer to him, slapped him across the face, hard, then turned and walked toward the bus stop down the street. If he was going to treat her like a child, then she was going to behave like one. Damn him anyway.

"Lily," he said.

She kept going.

She heard the passenger door slam and then a minute later the other door shut and the car started. She walked as gracefully as she could despite the pain, drugs, alcohol and heels. She felt enraged. It was a good thing she'd only slapped him with her bare hands, which unfortunately weren't lethal weapons like some ninja.

As his car passed she heard him gun the motor and race by. Spoiled movie star. He wasn't nearly as good in person as in the movies. Rude and insensitive. Good riddance.

She sat at the bus stop, suddenly sober and clear. What were her options? Take the bus, but where did this one end up? Call a cab? She couldn't call Mom and Dad. That would simply be too embarrassing. She was thirty-eight and should have her life together by now. Then she began to cry.

A few minutes later, a car pulled up to the bus stop. She heard the window roll down. She didn't look up until a voice said, "Lily, I don't care what you've done to me. It's not right to leave you here alone. At least let me drive you home. You don't have to talk to me and I won't talk if you don't want me to. Just let me make sure you're safely home."

She looked up at him, confusion filling her mind.

SEAN

Sean lay in his trailer on the set of *Red Sunsets*. The artificial smell of its newness hung in the air. He'd left the windows open in an attempt to air the thing out, but was hot, smoggy air any better?

He glanced at the clock. An hour before he needed to be at makeup. He pulled the blanket back over his head, trying to block out the light. His head felt like someone was pounding on it with a rock and his mouth tasted like something had died in it, months ago.

It had been that way for a week. Ever since he met her. The date from hell. At least that's what the tabloids had called her. His head hurt too much to decide if he agreed.

Even after she drank too much, or maybe she'd taken something before the date, dumped food all over him, pushed him into the fish pond and then slapped him, after all that, when he tried to take her home, she told him to 'go to hell'. The bus had come and she'd gotten on it. He hoped it was the right bus.

He stupidly felt responsible for getting her home safely and had called a couple of times since, just to make sure she was okay. She hadn't answered. The last time he called, it said her number was no longer in service.

That night everything had felt off. That was the first day of his never ending headache. Clearly, she had problems too. But he'd felt something that never happened to him with any other woman. A sort of attraction, an electricity, a connection. He thought she was the one. That he'd finally found her after years of believing the Gift had passed him by. And he thought she felt something too, at the signing.

Someone pounded on his trailer door. He got up, turned lights on and smoothed his hair in the mirror before answering.

He opened the door to find Nina standing there.

"Hi," she said, her voice silky and sexy. "Can I come in?" she asked.

"I'll come out, let me grab some water. Want some?" He might as well get this over with. He hadn't seen or talked to her in years.

"No thanks," she said.

He got a bottle from the small fridge, slipped his sunglasses on and went out the door. On the side of his trailer was a little awning to create shade. Beneath it sat a couple of lawn chairs and a small table.

Nina lounged in one. She wore a crimson paisley dress out of a slinky material which enhanced her curves and whose colors made her hair flame. She'd slipped off her sandals, her feet resting on the asphalt as if they could feel the dirt beneath it. Very earth mothery and sexy all at the same time. An appealing exterior that hid the viper inside. How did she do that?

He sat in the other chair.

"Hello Sean."

"Hi Nina."

"You look like hell."

"Thanks. I feel like hell."

"I heard the studio sent you for tests. Any results?"

"Nothing useful. After a couple of days of tests, I don't have migraines, a brain tumor, parasites or some weird disease from somewhere I've filmed. I have a hard time dealing with light and noise and they haven't found anything to kill the pain. I'm considering a guillotine."

"Oh, is it really that bad?" she asked.

He nodded, instantly regretting it as misery washed through him. He tried not to show it.

"How did you find out so quickly. You just got here, didn't you?"

"I'm seeing Manuel these days."

Manuel was Sean's nemesis in the film. Quite a nice guy, actually. Poor kid, if he was with Nina.

"He's a good guy," said Sean.

"You're just saying that," she said.

"You're right. I'm really just an insensitive bastard. So, I'll say what I think. He's too young for you."

"You're just jealous," she said.

"Of what?" Sean asked.

"Of his muscles and his height." Nina smirked.

She had to work hard to come up with that one.

"Thanks, no. I quite like my body the way it is. I don't need to be taller, or look like a body builder."

She sighed dramatically and brushed her hand across his cheek. He pulled away.

"I'm worried about you. You know I never stopped caring for you," she said.

She really was incredible.

"I stopped caring though. After the public disaster you made of our relationship," he said, coolly.

"It wasn't my fault. If you hadn't pulled away, ..."

"You drove my away, with all your affairs. But that's all water under the bridge. I'm doing fine, except for this headache thing," he lied. "And here comes Manuel. You'll want to be leaving."

Manuel had come out of his trailer. Muscular and wearing black leather biker pants and a blue silky shirt unbuttoned halfway down his tanned chest, he waved at Sean and Nina.

Nina waved at him and blew air out between her lips. Her gesture of annoyance.

"Sean, I need to know if we can work together on this film."

"Doesn't seem like I have much choice. I know it's not your fault. I'll be a professional about this. Not guaranteeing anything though. Not with these headaches. But I'll do the best I can do for the film. Just stay out of my hair. I don't want to revisit the past with you. We're done with that. Deal?"

"Deal," she said, nodding and sighing.

She clearly had hoped for more.

Nina slid out of the chair and sauntered off, as only Nina could. Sean tried not to watch them kiss, not because he felt jealous, it was more of a privacy thing. Then they took off on Manuel's Harley.

Poor guy. He didn't know what he was in for, Nina would date him for a month, maybe two, before dumping him for someone new. Sean's friends told him that was her current pattern. The friends who never tired of trying to hook him up with someone.

He got up, went inside and got his iPad, then went back outside and sat again. He opened the script and tried to work on learning the newly added scene. After a few minutes of gazing at it, he set it on the table.

Drinking some water, he gazed off down the mostly empty road, towards the desert. Normally, he loved being out here in the desert. Now, it was too bright. Even under the awning. But the air smelled fresher than in his trailer, it was just foul in there. Even worse than the smog outside. He got up and opened the trailer door to add some more airflow and then sat back down under the canopy, pondering Nina's visit.

She may or may not have come to make peace. The whole 'I never stopped caring for you' was an indication she wanted more than that. They'd lived together for five years. But during the last year of their relationship, he found out about all her affairs. Apparently, he was too boring for her. On the night he won Best Actor for *The Way of the World*, his first, and so far only, Oscar, Nina tore their lives apart.

Thinking about her led him to mull over the disaster in Seattle. It was just a week since the date with Lily. His intuition told him that, despite appearances, he'd made a major mistake about her.

He didn't think she really set him up for the paparazzi or that she stalked him. That was only the first explanation that leapt to his mind. The rational part of him wondered if Lily had done it intentionally, to humiliate him in public. Nina, who was clearly a pro at it, had done a more thorough job.

Sean stood and picked up the iPad, stuffing it inside the trailer. He looked at the clock. Half an hour till makeup. He locked the door and walked down the road, carrying his bottle of water.

He angled off onto one of the nearby trails, watching the sun sink lower on the horizon, but growing seemingly brighter. The air had gotten cooler and the evening birds, which he didn't know the names of, began calling. He loved the pinks and oranges which colored the few clouds in the sky.

Why had Lily not responded when he accused her? Did it mean guilt or innocence? The whole humiliation theory felt like leftover baggage from the relationship with Nina. Had he misread Lily completely?

He stopped and stretched his arms, shoulders and neck in a vain attempt to get rid of the headache. The wind picked up a little, kicking up swirls of sand. He smelled the dry air. It had a strange scent to it this evening. Almost as if there was rain on it. He missed the rain of Seattle, even while enjoying the desert. The moistness, lushness of the Northwest made him feel as if all things were possible, growth and change could arise from the damp soil.

The logical part of his brain told him to let the whole thing with Lily go. But it felt like letting go of a dream, one in which he carried the family Gift. He'd felt so sure that Lily must be his partner in this. He'd never felt anything like that touch in the bookstore.

He should have tried harder to understand what was going on with her. With the raging headache and his paranoia about being humiliated, he'd let it go too easily.

Last night, he'd tried to write her a letter, apologizing for his behavior. He'd obviously hurt her enough that she slapped him. And she'd never gotten to the end of her story about the bad day at work. Had she been fired? Her cheek had a bruise under the makeup. She'd talked about hanging from the bridge with bungee cords for hours. And the police. Had she been hurt or what? He never finished his letter. Instead, tearing it up and burning it. If a woman goes to all the trouble of changing her number so he couldn't contact her, what hope did he have that she'd read his letter?

He stopped and looked reluctantly at the sunset. Then turned and walked back the other direction.

Time to head for makeup and get on with things. He only had a few more days of shooting and then he'd dive into figuring out this headache.

If he could just hang in there a little longer. Not bungle any more scenes. He'd cost them too much money already. And he didn't want people to think he was screwing up just because Nina had replaced Lillian.

He made it to the makeup trailer and opened the door only to be blinded by the bright lighting. Taking a deep breath, he stepped inside and sat down.

He had to overcome this.

LILY

LILY WOKE FROM A NEAR COMA TO FIND HERSELF SLEEPING ON the hard floor, the top sheet and blanket wrapped around her. She lay for a moment staring at the wood flooring illuminated by the faint glow of her alarm clock. She'd been dreaming about Sean.

What time was it? It was still dark outside, she could see through her window shades. Why was she on the floor? What day was it and did she have to be anywhere?

She raised herself slightly and groaned. Her back screamed at her. It was six. Presumably in the morning.

It seemed to take her forever to sit up. She was still in her clothes. Sweater and jeans. Which were damp. Just like the sheet and blanket. Why? And why did her back hurt so much?

Then some of yesterday came rushing back into her brain and she covered her face with the pillow. What an incredible mess. She spent several minutes pounding on the pillow in frustration.

She wanted to go back to sleep and forget yesterday ever

happened. But her back wouldn't shut up. She needed to get her drugs.

It seemed to take an eternity to untangle herself from the covers and get to a position where she could stand up. Finally, she was able to use the bed and nightstand to balance herself and stand.

She gingerly stepped over her boots and walked to the bathroom. Even her legs hurt. It felt like she'd been run over my a steamroller. Only her hair didn't hurt.

At least she didn't have to go to work today. Michelle had called the agency for her. Shuffling through the messy living room, Lily smelled an unusual scent that she couldn't identify. Blue suitcases and cardboard boxes lay strewn around. She ignored them and closed the bathroom door. At the sink, she rubbed her face with cold water, trying to wake up fully.

Which would kill her first, the throbbing of her back or her head? Why had she drunk so much wine last night? Why did she have wine at all? Shouldn't have, not with the drugs.

She didn't remember much about the night. Something about feeling massively insecure and insulted at the restaurant. And slapping Sean in the parking lot. Taking a bus home. The rest of it was a blank. Which made her feel even worse. What had happened?

Pulling a brush through her long tangled hair made static fly through the air. It must have gotten really cold overnight. She gave up on the tangles and set the brush down on the counter. There sat a bottle of apple shampoo and cucumber lotion she didn't remember buying.

It was then she realized the scent she'd smelled earlier was of roses. She opened the bathroom door and walked out. Her apartment was filled with the aroma of roses. That was strange. She hadn't burned candles or incense lately. She hadn't bought flowers. She didn't wear rose lotions or perfumes.

The smell was so overwhelming, she felt nauseous. Or was that from the hangover? What happened last night anyway? An image of Sean, smiling at her and trying to make small talk came to her mind.

She sighed and went back to the bathroom, tying her hair up in a pony tail. She smoothed some of the cucumber lotion on her face.

A noise came from the living room. Rustling followed by a dull thud. Then a cough. Someone was in her apartment.

She quickly shut and locked the bathroom door, trying desperately to think.

How could someone have gotten in? Had she forgotten to lock the door last night when she came in?

If they were a burglar, wouldn't they have just taken her purse and left? What did they want? She should call 911. But her cell phone was in her purse. And where was her purse? Kitchen? Living Room? She'd have to go past them to get to it.

She looked down on the floor and saw the rolled up umbrella. It had been in the bathtub to dry and tossed out of it last night before her shower. She could use it as a spear or whack someone with it. It was the only weapon she could find in the bathroom.

Silently she unlocked the door and opened it as quietly as she could. She stood ready to spear someone.

Lily barely registered the warm glow coming from the table lamp near the couch.

A young girl with shoulder length brown hair lay face down on the couch, propped up on her elbows and reading a magazine with large photos of a soccer game. She was dressed in turquoise sweats. The girl sat up at the sound of the wood floor creaking, and looked curiously at her.

The scent of roses flooded her senses.

"Oh, hi Mom," the girl said. "I woke up early and didn't want to wake you. I didn't know you were in the bathroom."

She could think of nothing to say.

"Are you okay?" the girl asked.

Lily lowered the umbrella, not knowing what to do or say. She must be hallucinating. Then it hit her, the boxes and suitcases she'd seen earlier weren't hers. The girl hadn't broken in, not with all that baggage.

She walked to the front door and saw that the dead bolt was still closed and so was the chain lock. She flicked on the ceiling lights. And there were no broken windows.

In the kitchen Lily took her pain meds and started up the espresso machine.

Finally, she turned to the girl, who'd followed her into the kitchen, and asked "Where did you come from?"

The girl winced, as if in pain, but covered it quickly with an expressionless face.

"Don't you remember? Gram raised me cause Mom was doing drugs. And Grandma Myrna died last week. Grandpa Arnold said you were her niece and called you. He said you agreed to adopt me. I got here last night. You had just gotten home and were drenched and really upset about something, so you probably don't remember. You got me some blankets and a pillow. You weren't sure if Teddy was in his room or still with your Mom and Dad. Then you went to bed." The girl plunked down at the table.

Teddy. She'd forgotten about him. Again.

She glanced towards his room. The door was shut, but he must still be with Mom and Dad. They wouldn't have dropped him off and left him here alone.

Lily walked to the door, knocked and after silence, she opened the door and looked inside. A couple of comics lay on the bed, the curtains were open and a couple of big bags sat on the window seat. He hadn't unpacked. Maybe he thought he'd be kicked out again. Poor kid. She closed the door and returned to the kitchen.

What was happening in her life?

She sat down at the table, waiting for the espresso to cool a bit. As she did, the umbrella burst open, scaring both of them. They laughed. Lily closed the umbrella, her heart pounding.

She didn't remember the girl coming last night. She didn't remember an Aunt Myrna either. Despite the unlikely story, she knew the girl believed the story.

Had all this happened and she just couldn't remember because she'd been out of her mind from too much wine and the pain killers?

She knew the girl's name was Tracy. And that she was nine.

"Tracy remind me again, how old are you?"

"Nine," she said."

Lily nodded. "You like soccer?"

Tracy rolled her eyes dramatically and smiled. "I *live* for soccer."

"I guess we'll have to find a team for you to play on."

"Yippee," whooped Tracy. She ran over to the couch and pulled a ball out of a large pink bag. Then threw it up in the air, bounced it gently off her head and caught it, several times.

Lily smiled. That was all it took to make this girl happy. Life sure wasn't that simple for most adults. They needed a phone with a camera, ten million apps, a computer that did everything, a TV that took up an entire wall of the house and had a gazillion channels, the car of their dreams, a house large enough for a third world country, a stimulating job, masses of friends, oodles of money and they still weren't happy. For most people there was always the next big thing to want. Electric cars with auto pilots, self exercising bodies, energy on demand.

Lily asked, "Do you like school?"

"Sort of. I like P.E. and reading. I don't really like math."

"What's your favorite food?"

"Indian fry bread."

"That is sooo good. We'll have to try and find some." She got up from the table and made more espresso, putting cream in it.

"I almost forgot. I was supposed to call Mom and Dad. They said they'd bring breakfast." And we should straighten up a bit.

"I'll go make a neater pile of my boxes," said Tracy. "And get dressed."

After she made the phone call, Lily changed into clean clothes and dragged her blankets back onto the bed.

She sat at the table drinking her breve. After breakfast, she'd look at the advertisements and call about seeing apartments. With Teddy first and now Tracy, they'd need a three bedroom apartment. She hoped she could afford it. Her income wasn't exactly increasing these days.

She pushed away the realization that she'd already known Tracy's answers to the questions before Tracy had replied. Lily didn't understand how she knew all this. It was simply there in her mind, a piece of knowledge, the same way she knew if a color would look good on her or not.

Her buzzer went off and Lily got up and pushed the button, so the gate down below would open for Mom, Dad and Teddy. She heard their laughing before they made it up to her door.

"Come in, everybody," she said.

Mom and Teddy smiled and entered, carrying two big, white boxes.

"A grand estate you have here, my dear," said Dad, pulling a newspaper out of his coat and handing it to her, along with a plastic shopping bag.

She kissed him.

"You're letting the cold air in and the warm air out," said Mom, pulling Dad inside the door.

He pretended to fall on his face, catching himself just in time on the couch.

Everyone laughed, except Mom who rolled her eyes.

Teddy tossed his bag into his room and shrugged out of his jacket.

"How was your date?" asked Susan.

"So awful I don't even want to talk about it," she said, setting the bag on the kitchen table. She pulled out a big jug of blueberry juice and a gallon of milk.

"I used to have dates like those," Susan said.

"Then she found me," said Dad, hugging Susan. "Now she has them everyday!"

Lily laughed.

The bathroom door opened and Tracy came out quietly. Looking a little timid.

Teddy saw her and called out, "Tracy!" He gave her a big puppyish hug.

She smiled and hugged him back. "I heard you were here."

They were immediately swarmed by Mom and Dad. Lily smiled, but didn't really want to join in the fray, for fear of hurting her back hurting more.

Inside one box were a couple dozen pastries and in the other a bacon quiche, which smelled divine.

Nick and Susan set the table. Teddy poured beverages and Tracy rounded up an extra chair.

Lily sat and smiled. She loved having this many people at her table. Even if she wasn't sure why a couple of them were there.

After breakfast, she looked at the classified ads, trying to decide which ones were worth calling about.

Teddy was helping Tracy find places for all her boxes.

Lily asked, "Why don't I remember Aunt Myrna or Uncle Arnold? And who was Teddy staying with?"

"His Grandpa Ralph. We never made it down to Arizona to visit my brother Ralph, so you never met him. Or out to Indiana to visit your dad's sister Myrna and her husband Arnold. I don't see how we could have missed two entire states. We went everywhere else on our travels."

Nick and Susan were restless souls. Now retired, they took the RV and constantly traveled. It had been on one of their trips, adventures they called them, that they'd found her, an abandoned baby, and stuck around long enough to get custody and then, finally, adopt her.

"But how am I going to do this? I have no idea how to be a mom. And now, two at once."

"I know it's a lot to ask of you, but I think you'll do fine with both of them. You've wanted kids your entire life."

"I know, but I'm afraid I'll screw up."

"You'll do fine," repeated Susan.

"But why don't I remember you or Dad even talking about them?"

"Oh dear. We have been remiss," said Nick, peering over the top of the paper he was reading. "We're such bad relatives. The scourge of the family."

They'd seen three apartments by lunch. Absolute dives. Then after fast Mexican food they saw two more. One was way too small, the other came with a bidding war. Lily was outbid by a couple with a baby. The fifth and last, was just north of Gasworks Park and overlooked Lake Union. How could it not be a mess of an apartment, in a great neighborhood for such a low price?

The manager showed them in and said, "It's actually a sublet, for only six more months. The person who was subletting it had a medical crisis in the family and had to move out of town. This is a condo and the owners have gone on a cruise.

Three decent sized bedrooms and no mildew! It was clean and felt spacious.

Teddy and Tracy looked at her eagerly.

The deal was made and since it was empty, she made arrangements to move in immediately. Six months would be enough to find another place.

"The trucks are almost at our door to tear down our current apartment building," she said.

"We can get you moved today," said Dad.

"No, really, it'll take a couple of days," she said.

Mom stood with her hands on her hips. "No, we can do it all today. With the four of us? All you have to do is supervise, sit, rest your back and made a few phone calls, to close or transfer accounts.

They went straight back to her apartment and she set people to work, after taking another painkiller. Mom & Dad took her car and went to rent a small van. Teddy and Tracy packed.

In the living room, the message light from her land line was flashing.

She listened.

"Hello Lily. I'd really like to talk to you about last night. I behaved abominably. Please call me." Sean left his number.

She erased the message. It would have to freeze in hell before she called him. She slid onto a chair, watching Teddy and Tracy pile boxes by the front door. Something bad happened last night. She hadn't had a moment to breathe and think about the date. To try and remember what happened.

Lily spent the afternoon dealing with cable, internet, mail, electric and phone services. She decided to drop her land line and use the money elsewhere. The kids would need cell phones, probably.

When Mom and Dad got back with the van, Dad, Teddy and Tracy loaded it up. Mom packed her stuff.

"Ha, this is payback for you packing food for our trip the summer you turned thirteen," Mom said.

"Hotdogs and s'mores are the perfect food for every meal," Lily said. She cocked her head, suspiciously. "How is this payback?"

"You'll have to unpack every single box in order to find everything," Mom giggled.

Groceries, of which there wasn't much, got packed in an ice chest of Mom and Dad's.

"Tomorrow, we'll come back and clean and then you'll be done," said Mom.

They left everything by the door, for when Dad, Teddy and Tracy came back with the van. Then took Lily's car to get some more groceries and go to the new apartment.

They picked up a cartful of food and Mom insisted on paying. Lily stood at the checkout stand looking at magazines. She caught sight of one of the tabloids, then noticed that each one had a similar version of *Sean O'Neill's Date from Hell*.

She quickly grabbed one of each and paid for them in another line. "It'll save time," she said to Mom, hiding the covers.

"Do you read those?" Mom asked.

"No, crosswords. They have great crosswords."

She paid and stuffed them in her huge purse as they left the store.

She dropped Mom off near her old apartment, so she could fire up the RV and park it near the new one.

Mom said, "Don't you dare unload the groceries. I'll do that when I get there. You go lie down on the couch."

"Promise," she said. It was awful to feel like an invalid. And everybody else was working. But she wanted her back to get better. This was the only way.

Lily sped across town and parked in her new parking space. The van was gone, they must have gone back for the second and last load.

It was dark, but thankfully, the rain had stopped. Lily went up to the apartment. Boxes were piled everywhere. Dad or Teddy had plugged in the TV and other electronics and hooked everything up. The couch sat in front of them complete with pillows and the heating pad, which had been found in a closet, as they packed.

She hung up her coat, turned on the heating pad and turned the TV on. It was 6:30. Time for the end of the news. She called and ordered pizza for everyone.

Then, she pulled the tabloids out of her bag and sat down, adjusting the heating pad to deal with the porcupines which rolled up and down her spine.

In most of the photos, her long blonde hair hung over her face. In all of them, she was, thankfully, a blur. Most of the photos were focused on Sean who dripped with what looked like salad. Then there was one of him sitting in the pond at the restaurant. One of him dragging her out of the restaurant. The last photo showed her slapping him. She remembered so little of what happened.

One story claimed she was drunk, tackled a waiter, screamed at Sean, pushed him into a pond, slapped him and stormed off. He drove away 'to lick his wounds' and hopefully rethink his choices in women.

One reporter compared their date to the public humiliation Sean received from Nina Vicente.

The others told similar stories. The only good thing about

them was they didn't mention her name. They didn't know who she was.

Her face burned with heat. How could she have done such a thing? Clearly the drugs and the wine she drank didn't mix well. If she had the courage, she'd call him and apologize. They had both behaved badly.

But she didn't have the courage.

And she'd erased his message, containing his phone number.

She heard noise on the stairs and stuffed all the tabloids back into her bag and sat there, pretending to watch tv, as Dad, Teddy and Tracy came in with another load.

The next three days flew by. Her old apartment got closed out. Her new one came to life as things got unpacked and put away and furniture arranged. Mom and Dad helped with everything, including getting Teddy and Tracy into school.

"I've never seen anything move so fast in the major bureaucracy that makes up a school," said Dad. "Magically, both their school records have arrived and now their education has been set in motion." He took Mom's hand and they bowed.

Lily almost choked on his joke. He really didn't know that the school records arriving was magic.

Mom and Dad left for parts unknown. One of them usually closed their eyes, pointed to a map and off they went.

Her schedule slowly began to coincide with school hours and she, Teddy and Tracy settled into a routine. Thanksgiving came. Mom and Dad came back. She and Teddy fumbled around in the kitchen trying to cook a turkey.

She felt blissful. Everything was going along perfectly.

She had never felt so happy in her entire life.

SEAN

Sean walked down the concrete stairwell of his hotel. The cold grayness made him feel glad for the warmth of the brown plaid sports coat. Even indoors, it was as gray in here as it was outside in the rain. December in Seattle. He also had his beard and long hair to keep him warm. Maybe even unrecognizable.

He glanced at his watch. 4:00. Right on time to meet the private investigator, Ned Hanley.

He opened a door and entered the lobby. The dark wood everywhere made the room feel warm and maybe even respectable.

Off to the right was the bar. A sign outside the door announced a lingerie show. Today. Now. He grumbled, but went inside. He didn't want to see women parading around in underwear. All he wanted was to meet Ned and see what he found out.

He took a table near the back, far from the stage, so he and Ned wouldn't interfere with the show. When the waitress came he ordered a double black stout. Maybe he'd just drink his beer and when Ned arrived they could go to his room or someplace else quiet.

The bar looked like it had been decorated in the velvet era. Maroon velvet curtains surrounded the stage and draped across walls, walls which were made of cream and burgundy flocked fleur-de-lis wallpaper. There was an aroma of stale alcohol and staler cigarette smoke, even though the bar was now a smoke free one and had been for years. Some things never went away. Burgundy and black velvet chairs surrounded the black tables. All the velvet would probably be hip again in a few years.

The floor ramped down like an amphitheater, tables on every level, all the way to the stage. Quite a few tables were filled, mostly with men. The lights dimmed a bit and the show started. A short woman with lacquered hair stood at a podium that was almost taller than she was. She must have been in her seventies and wore an enormous amount of makeup, spackled into her wrinkles. Enough so he could see it across the room.

Sean leaned back, savoring the richness of the beer and scanning the room, keeping an eye out for Ned.

The first model was followed by a spotlight. She reminded him of an actress he dated a couple years ago. Maia something. He dated a lot of women after Nina.

He sipped his beer again and felt relieved that his head wasn't throbbing. That hadn't happened much lately. The doctors still hadn't found anything. One of them suggested he lower his stress level, take some time off from his hectic lifestyle.

He lived in fear of when the next attack would come. Which made him alternately angry and depressed. Fear was so not useful as a way of life.

He felt so badly about his pathetic performance on the last film that he didn't want to line any more work up for a while. He hated disappointing people.

The first thing that had to happen was to get his health back.

He decided to move to Seattle. Spend time hanging out with his parents, siblings and their ten million kids. Spend time relaxing and just living. Get to the bottom of these damn headaches.

And most importantly, find Lily. Find out who she was. And what really happened that night.

He heard the name Lily and she magically appeared.

His mouth dropped open and he almost dropped his beer.

She stood onstage wearing turquoise lingerie. He couldn't take his eyes off her for fear that she'd disappear. His blood raced and a roaring filled his ears as the throbbing inside his head began. He started to get hard at the sight of her, but the oncoming headache killed the erection.

Closing his eyes, the pain pounded behind his face and moved through the back of his head and down into his neck. Even his eyes ached with the pulsation, the darkness gave him no refuge.

Sean tried to take deep breaths and relax.

Maybe she wouldn't recognize him. Well, what if she did? What would be the harm in that? Why didn't he want her to think he was following her, when in fact, he'd hired someone to do just that?

He watched as she walked through the audience, smoothly and casually. When she reached the top level, her eyes met his, but he saw no sign she recognized him.

She tripped on the stair next to his table and he reached out to steady her. She nodded a casual thanks to him and looked away quickly. No more than a woman might who was being ogled by a complete stranger. She continued moving between tables with the spot following her.

His fingers tingled where they had touched her arm.

He took in every movement, absorbed her walk, her hair and that luscious body. He'd only seen her fully clothed and this was a revelation.

She went back to onto the stage, turned and paused for one last look from the audience before disappearing behind the velvet curtains.

It was only then that Sean realized he was holding his breath and gripping the sides of the small table as if it were a steering wheel and he was bracing for a crash. The realization slapped him upside the head. He hadn't really hired Ned just so he could find Lily and get an explanation of what happened that night. That was just the justification he'd given. And he'd believed it at the time.

Now he knew better. He wanted all of her. Mind, body, heart and soul.

His brain pounded against the inside of his skull, making everything more confusing. It felt like wading through a swamp to get some clarity, to find the truth.

First he needed to find out if she had intended to humiliate him. To find out if she was worth wanting. His intuition said she was.

A flash of blue went past him and a man sat down at his table.

Ned Hanley held out his hand. Sean shook it.

He was drinking a martini and wearing a royal blue silk shirt and black leather pants and jacket. Younger than Sean expected, Ned had dark hair and a mustache.

"Sorry, I'm late. I got tied up in traffic."

"Not a problem."

"I see the show has started," said Ned, nodding towards the stage.

Lily was back on again, a vision in fluffy pink. She walked through the audience again.

He watched her, hungrily, not caring what Ned saw. Even the headache almost disappeared. Almost.

When she went off stage, Ned asked, "Are you ready or do you need a cold shower first?"

Sean laughed and took a sip of his beer. Inside he felt annoyed at Ned. Or any man looking at Lily half naked.

"Okay, what have you got for me?"

Ned pulled a folded paper from the pocket of his leather jacket and handed it to Sean. He unfolded it and began to read about Lily.

Single, two adopted children, ages fifteen and nine. Both newly registered in the school district within a week of the signing. Thirty-eight. That was a surprise. He'd pegged her at early thirties. *Worked various modeling jobs. Lived in north Seattle, in an apartment. Address and phone number,* which was different than the one she'd given him.

"That's all I have right now. There's more to come, but I thought you'd want to know she was working here at your hotel today."

"Thanks, great. I'd love to see more."

Towards the end of the show, Lily came out wearing a simple black and red teddy. His eyes locked with hers; he felt strangely victorious. She looked away quickly and continued walking between the tables. He felt sure she didn't recognize him. Not with the long hair and beard.

He would conquer the headaches, find a great place to live and possess this woman. He just didn't know how yet.

After the show, he and Ned went out to the parking garage. They casually waited for Lily to show up. Eventually, she and the other models came out of the hotel.

Lily wore a navy raincoat and jeans. She carried a child in her arms. He pulled the paper out and it read that she had three children 15, 9 and 2. That hadn't been there before. Not the two year old. His mouth nearly dropped open in amazement.

It was a little girl, squirming to get down and move on her own. Lily buckled her into a car seat in an old blue Subaru station wagon. Ned leapt into his silver Honda, ready to follow her.

Sean watched her drive away and then went back into the hotel, wearing a huge grin.

So, she had three children now. And all of them arrived since he met her.

He liked where this was going.

LILY

Lily parked in the hotel lot before work and lay her head on the steering wheel. She felt tired. They'd all been up way too late, helping Teddy on his science project. Painting and labeling. But it was done.

The kids had only been there two weeks. Getting Teddy on track was the biggest challenge. He had a long ways to go to get up to his grade level. She sighed and got out of the car, grabbing her bag.

Most of her money was coming from this job. The lingerie show. It was an old fashioned sort of thing. Executives buying lingerie for their wives and girlfriends. Although sometimes women came in and ordered things as well.

The kids were at classmates' houses. Hopefully, the shows would move to lunchtime soon. Jeannie had said they would. It would make childcare easier.

She entered the sea green dressing room behind the stage. Chaos itself. Six models trying to cram themselves into thongs, bustiers and negligees. Three assistants worked to make sure the right lingerie ended up on the correct model along with matching jewelry, shoes, etc. Makeup and hair products lay strewn all over the long table in front of the mirrors. Shoes rolled around on the floor, threatening to trip people. Half a dozen conversations filled the air and the faint smell of sweat mingled with half a dozen different perfumes, scented moisturizers and makeup.

Lily dropped her bag on an empty chair and pulled off her raincoat, hanging it up in a space for the models' street clothes. She shoved her bag beneath the table and sat down in the chair and looked at the circles under her eyes. One of the assistants handed her an aqua bustier and thong. Lily sighed and stood, quickly changing into the lingerie.

Molly, next to her, put on eyeliner and didn't even pause. "So there's these things called chakras. They're like energy centers in your body."

Lily tried to fasten the bustier. "God, who invented this thing? It doesn't have a fast way to get in or out of it. What's sexy about that?"

"Now that's your problem, Lily," said Molly, talking while she held her mouth open to put on eye shadow. "You're still living in your lower chakras."

"What?" She pulled her stockings on and attached them to the bustier.

"Well, the lower chakras are about survival: sex, food, security. That kind of stuff. You need to move into your upper chakras: love, communication and spirituality."

"I'll add that to my list of things to do," said Lily, thoroughly annoyed. She did think about sex a lot, probably because her only partner was a vibrator. As for food and security, well, duh. Now she had kids to feed and clothe. She slid her heels on.

Molly continued, "If you don't make the step yourself, the universe throws things in your path to force you to change and grow. It's not very pleasant."

Lily sat down and did some touch ups on her makeup. Not much she could do to improve things.

"Lily, you're up next," said Josie, the stage manager.

She did a final check of her hair and went onstage. Heather walked past, coming offstage, rolling her eyes with boredom.

Lily moved near the podium where Jeannie, the show organizer and dictator, announced the merchandise. Slinky, sexy Brazilian music that made her want to dance streamed out of the sound system.

"Now, here's Lily wearing a beautiful aqua bustier and thong by Satine. Notice the way it highlights her curves."

Lily stood for a moment, then stepped down the stairs into the audience and walked through the tables. She'd done this a lot when she was younger. It used to make her nervous to model underwear and swimsuits, until she convinced herself that her job was simply to show off the clothes. A million bodies better looking than hers existed in the world and five hundred million more computer enhanced ones graced the pages of magazines. The realization helped ease her worries about her own imperfections.

The audience was mostly men. Suits and ties. She did notice one guy in back with a bushy beard, long hair tied back and wearing an appalling brown plaid suit. Scary, stalker looking material.

She made it to the top level and as she looked at him, she tripped. Her adrenaline rushed. He reached out and grabbed her arm to steady her. She could feel the strength in his light touch.

Lily nodded a thanks to him and as he met her eyes, she felt as if he could see straight into her mind and understand everything about her. As he let go, she shivered. He reminded her of a cat who just caught a mouse and was trying to decided whether to play with it or devour it.

She continued walking the circuit through the audience and back onstage. Pausing for a moment to give the audience one last look and another thrilling bit of Jeannie's commentary, she saw the guy in back again. Definite stalker material.

As she left the stage, Lily felt dizzy and nauseous. The overwhelming fragrance of hyacinths overcame her as she stumbled a little on her way back to the dressing room.

Once there, she quickly peeled off the bustier and began putting on her next outfit, a pink negligee with fluffy pink feathers on the bottom and pink fluffy heels.

"Lily, this girl is so cute, no wonder you couldn't resist her. Who would abandon a sweet child like this?" asked Heather.

Lily slowly turned and noticed the other models clustered in the corner, cooing.

In the corner stood a two year old girl with blond ringlets wearing a ruffly purple dress and laughing at Molly, who was making funny faces for her. Emily, that was her name and she had been abandoned, then a foster child. And now she was Lily's.

"Yes, she's just the cutest thing on two wheels, isn't she?" said Tanya.

Lily stood there, trying not to hyperventilate. She was really scared now. Three kids. And two years old was practically a baby. What did one do with a baby? And why did this happen? Had she opened up some hyper-fertility wormhole that was drawing these kids out of the ozone? Or was she truly losing her mind? And if she was, did that mean the kids didn't exist or that she just couldn't remember them arriving in her life?

No one seemed to notice anything unusual. No one. Her coworkers acted like she had a childcare problem and had to bring Emily to work with her. She knew her parents would come to visit and act as if nothing out of the ordinary happened. Neither would the other parents at school.

No. It must be her. Maybe she had a brain tumor. Or memory loss.

The show went on. She did the pink number. Then a black and red teddy. Stalker guy was sitting with a sleazy mustachioed guy wearing a silk shirt that was a little too shiny. Looked like a stalker too.

The show ended. Lily took Emily to her car and almost gasped to see a car seat in the back seat.

"Now where did that come from?" she asked Emily.

Emily babbled at her.

"Where did you come from?"

Emily babbled, then started giggling. She was clearly a happy toddler.

What if the kids came in response to some need from her? If they had she better figure it out quickly, before more came.

The apartment only had three bedrooms. And her carseat space was limited. So was her time and money for that matter.

What would happen if there were more kids?

SEAN

Sean stood staring out the window of his hotel room. There was nothing new outside. Gray, drizzly rain and low clouds cloaked Seattle. It felt oppressive to him. But then he hadn't left his room in days and had been living on room service and delivery food.

He ran his fingers through his damp hair, trying to dry it a little more. At least he'd gotten up. At least he'd taken a shower. The combination of immobilizing headaches and depression had hit him like a two by four to the face.

He hadn't even called Casey to let her know he was in town. He knew vaguely that Christmas crept ever closer, he had no idea what day it was. The headaches had left him feeling so helpless that he'd retreated into himself and been swallowed up by depression and hopelessness.

When he opened a window, the rainy, clean air wafted in. The coolness chilled him. Still, he was grateful this was an old enough hotel that the windows still opened, if only a crack.

There was so much to do. All his belongings sat in storage, waiting. For him to find a place to live.

He needed to go for a walk. Or maybe drive around and make a decision about what part of town to live in. Maybe check out the condos his sister, Marcia, emailed the listings for.

He looked around at the available food in his room, settling on a two day old croissant. It tasted pretty good compared to the pizza delivered last night. He scratched the bushy beard and looked in the mirror, grimacing. Turning away he ran water into the coffee maker near the sink, hoping he'd gotten all the coffee flavor out. He liked coffee, just not in his tea.

Sean felt like he had one foot on a boulder and the other on a different boulder with a huge abyss in between.

Behind was L.A. and in front, Seattle. He couldn't go backwards, only forwards. Or fall into the pit. Somehow, he'd become paralyzed in the middle, unable to move.

The only hopeful thing today was that the headache had faded. He felt almost human.

The downside was that he knew one lay in wait on the path up ahead, but around which curve he couldn't say. And there was no way he could commit to another film with that looming. He needed to be doing something. Waiting was hell.

His cell rang. Sean picked it up, looking at the caller I.D.

Nina.

He put the phone back down. He didn't want to talk to her. Word had probably gotten out. His house went on the market today.

He didn't want to talk to anyone, except Ned.

"Enough of this bullshit."

Sean stuffed the food, wrappers, cans and bottles into the garbage and recycling. He picked up all his clothes, except what he was wearing and stuffed them in a hotel laundry bag, then set it by the door.

Better.

He scrolled through the emails on his phone to make sure

he still had the address for the condos. Then grabbed coat and car keys and headed out the door, flicking on the *maid service please* sign.

The next two days whizzed by and Sean drove to his new condo to meet Casey. He felt thrilled that things had moved so quickly. The power of cash, even this close to Christmas, was amazing.

It also felt good to have a permanent place to live outside of L.A. His life had dramatically slowed down. His difficulty to saying *no* to all the parties and business lunches back in L.A. meant nothing here. It wasn't even an issue since he didn't know anyone here to network with.

Now, he had space for his family and a real relationship. Everyone thought he was lucky with women, but the reality was bleak. He hadn't slept with anyone since Nina. No one interesting had come along. Until now.

Sean parked in the condo garage and took the stairs to the third floor at a run. He could hardly wait for Casey to see the place. Unlocking the door, he went in and looked out one of the south-facing windows. Mount Rainier wasn't out today, but even so, it was an incredible view. Overlooking Fremont, an old artsy section of the city which had gone upscale, and Lake Union.

The place needed painting. He hated white rooms. It was small, a thousand square feet with a bedroom, office, bathroom, living room with a gas fireplace, dining room and kitchen, as well as a balcony.

Terra cotta and chocolate. That's what he'd paint most of it. With interesting accent colors. Something warm for those gray, Seattle days. He looked forward to getting furniture and decorating the place.

The buzzer rang and he unlocked the metal entrance gate below. Opening the front door, he went outside and leaned over the wrought iron railing, waving at Casey as she climbed the open air stairway.

"Hi Case."

"Hiya." She trudged up the last flight of stairs, her dark eyes smiling. Her skin, tanned from daily gardening, peeked out from under the raincoat.

She hugged him. "Great location, but I'm way out of shape."

"Come in," he said, ushering her inside.

"When did it close?"

"Yesterday," he said, proudly.

"And you haven't moved in yet?" she said, sarcastically, walking into the kitchen.

"I want to paint first. And I got rid of all my furniture."

"I think it's gorgeous. What an amazing view," she said opening the door to the balcony which would have a perfect sunset view of the Olympic Mountains. It stayed dry from the large awning, despite the rain. "Marcia did a great job finding it for you."

"It's awesome, isn't it? Nice to have a sister who's a real estate agent."

They stood staring at the mountains, barely visible behind a shroud of clouds and rain, in silence the way only two people who are comfortable with each other can. He had missed so many moments like this by living so far away.

After while she said, "I'm so glad you've moved up here. I missed you."

He put his arm around her. "I missed you too, sis."

They left the condo and walked up the street through the drizzle to a cafe, for coffee. As they dried off in the cozy warmth of the small dark room filled with the aromas of coffee, cinnamon rolls and bacon, Sean sighed with relief that his head wasn't pounding.

"Casey, in James' research about the Gift, did he find anything about headaches?"

"No idea," she said. "You don't think your headaches are connected to the Gift, do you?"

"Could be," he said, stirring cream into his coffee and taking a sip. The bitterness was blunted by the richness of the cream. "I've been to so many doctors, had so many tests, tried different things, but they don't respond to medication. And there's really no pattern to the headaches, so I'm beginning to think it's possible."

"I left my phone in the car. I'll give him a call when we get back. So who is she?"

"I only have a suspicion," he said. "No proof."

Is she in L.A.?"

"Seattle."

"Well, that's good. At least you can keep an eye on her. I thought it wasn't going to happen to you, that somehow the Gift simply skipped you and zapped me. How many kids have arrived?"

"I'm not sure. Maybe three, at last count. I'm having her followed."

"Not a PI? Sean how could you stoop so low?" she asked, in mock horror.

"Had to be done. She moved and I didn't have her address or phone number."

"She didn't give it to you? You're slipping, Casanova. Didn't you send roses after you met her or something?" she asked, teasing him.

"She wouldn't even answer the phone after our date, or return my calls," he said, nearly chugging the rest of his coffee.

Casey looked shocked and asked, "No...she wasn't your date from hell?"

Sean nodded. Casey had set him the copy of one of the

tabloids as a joke. She'd drawn in dozens of broken hearts and written a new caption. 'The Rake gets his comeuppance from the Spirit of Broken Hearts left lying beside the road'. Sean knew she hadn't realized how frustrated he'd been.

"Oh, my god. She really hurt you, didn't she?"

He raised his eyebrows at her, "Duh."

"I'm sorry, if I'd known I would never have teased you about it." She reached out and touched his arm in apology. "Well, that's interesting. Your date from hell. So, you haven't talked to her since, have you?"

"No."

"Do you think she understands what's happening?"

"I have no idea."

"Oh man. Have you got your work cut out for you."

"Yeah."

Casey finished her coffee and they walked back down the street. The rain had stopped and the sun tried to peer through the clouds. Most people's gardens were filled with scraggly looking bushes of bare branches. She stopped at one that had a small tree with tiny spidery looking flowers and made him smell it. He got a faint scent from it, but mostly a nose full of water.

"Witch hazel," she said. "Lovely to have flowers in December."

At her car, they stopped. She picked up her cell from the front seat and called James at work. Sean stared at the landscaping for his building. It looked new compared to the nearby gardens of houses. The plants hadn't spread out, there were big spaces between them that was just bare soil.

"Okay, well see ya later love, bye." Casey snapped the phone shut. "He thinks there might have been a few cases of headaches. He'll find out for sure when he gets home."

James, Casey's husband, had spent years doing genealogical histories for his family and Casey's. He tried to find patterns on how the Gift had affected them down the generations. It did seem hereditary, although many of the records had been lost or the lineage information left blank, often because of people cutting connections and hiding. They changed names, even countries. There was a great deal of secrecy and mis-education, occasionally a suicide from someone being unable to handle how such a thing was happening to them.

Sean sighed. He didn't want to have to wait. To be patient. He'd waited his entire life.

LILY

IT WAS A FREEZING, BUT SUNNY, LATE AFTERNOON AS TEDDY, Tracy, Emily and Lily stood in the Christmas tree lot. Everyone was bundled up with puffy coats, gloves and hats. The scent of fir trees filled the air, reminding Lily of past Christmases with her parents.

She smiled, watching Tracy and Teddy discuss the merits of each and every tree on the busy lot. Lily held Emily by the hand. Emily kept putting her face into the lower branches of the spiky trees, then shaking her head and pulling it out. Then she'd look up at Lily and giggle as if it was the biggest joke in the world. Lily laughed along with her.

Tracy and Lily had gone to see Sean's new movie *Dahlia's Dream* that morning. A lovely fantasy set in Victorian England about an eighteen year old girl's flirtation with Death, Tracy had begged to see it; otherwise Lily would never have gone. She wanted nothing to do with him.

However, the movie was wonderful. Sean played Death, very sexy and charming, with a lovely accent. She couldn't help but watch him and feel an attraction to him. She felt embarrassed that he could get her so turned on. He certainly knew how to play at a good seduction. Even the thought of a kiss from him sent tingles up her spine.

After Teddy and Tracy had examined every tree, they decided on a huge Douglas Fir. Lily wasn't entirely sure it would fit in the living room without moving all the furniture, but it was the only tree they both agreed on.

While they waited in line to pay, the kids picked out an ornament each. Lily grabbed a tree stand and dug in her bag for the money. An image of the love scene from the movie shot through her mind. She shivered, imagining herself and Sean together. Then shook it off.

What was he doing these days? What film was he working on? She'd read somewhere that he'd been ill, but the article contained no details. She'd never get another chance to know him. That made her feel a tug in her chest.

A strong floral scent overpowered her. Lilac. So strong it made her nauseous. She looked around, trying to see who would be wearing so much perfume at a tree stand.

Someone pulled on her coat. She dropped her gaze to see a young boy, age seven, tugging on the bottom of her coat.

"Mom, I'm sooooo bored," he whined. "Can't we go now?"

She didn't know what to say. Looking around for the child's parents, she saw no one looking at her or the boy. He must be talking to her. It felt like Teddy, Tracy and Emily all over again.

Tracy said to the boy, "Just wait Jim. It's almost our turn to check out."

Sandy brown hair curled around the collar of his hooded jacket and freckles covered his pale skin. She knew he could program everything in the apartment with ease, while most of it remained a mystery to her. Jim was one with all things technological.

"What's your name?" she asked him.

He looked at her strangely, then said, "Jim Toureau. What else would it be?"

"Just checking," she said, suddenly flooded with memories that she knew couldn't exist. Her high school friend, Maria, had died in a car accident and Lily had been named the guardian of her son in the will. Except she had no such friend.

Lily used her glove covered hand to tuck her hair back under her hat and out of her face. She closed her eyes and sighed. What was happening here? She had to force herself to take deep breaths. Teddy was first, then Tracy second, Emily third and Jim fourth. Four children in a little over a month. There was a place in the car for him. And he could share a room with Teddy. But why was this happening?

And could she afford to feed him? Her head spun at the thought there might be more. No. No, that's just not possible.

By the time they hauled the tree to her car, she noticed another booster seat in the back. They hefted the tree on top and tied it on. Jim climbed in and buckled up as if he'd always been there. Teddy, who'd always ridden in the back with Tracy, climbed into the front instead.

They wrestled the tree up the stairs and into the living room. Lily stood on a chair and cut a foot off the top of the tree with a pair of scissors, so it would fit beneath the tall ceiling. The smell of fir now filled the apartment and the tree took up most of the living room. Teddy found a tape measure and determined the tree had an eight foot spread. They ended up cramming all the furniture along the wall on one side and voted to bury the TV behind the tree and do without it for the holidays.

"Wow, that's a big tree," said Jim.

"I've never had a Christmas tree this big," said Tracy.

"Me neither," said Teddy.

Lily went to the storage closet to dig out Christmas

decorations. What had their past Christmases been like? Walking past Teddy's room, she noticed a second bed. More clothes hung in the open closet. On a battered desk models of airplanes, cars and spaceships sat beside a laptop. A bamboo privacy screen divided the small room in half.

She shook her head, still trying to understand what was happening in her life.

They tied the tree to the wall, just in case, and decorated it with colored lights and glass ornaments she'd bought years ago in a thrift store, only breaking a few of them. It didn't bother her much. The bottom part of the tree, within Emily's reach, was left for unbreakable ornaments. And they each hung up the new ornaments which they'd chosen. Emily had wanted a plastic rocking horse, but she wouldn't relinquish it to put on the tree.

How wonderful it felt to be celebrating Christmas with a family, instead of alone.

That evening they sat in the glow of the tree, drinking hot spiced cider.

Tracy said, "This is going to be my best Christmas ever."

"Mine too," said Teddy.

"Me three," said Jim.

"Really?" asked Lily.

Tracy nodded, "Grandma and Grandpa never bought a tree. They always said it was too expensive in Arizona. Mom was always too stoned to think about it."

"Everybody I've ever lived with hated Christmas," said Teddy. Emily sat in his lap, chewing on a plastic toy pony.

"It was always just Mom and me. She was always too busy working to do much," said Jim. Now, I've got a real family," said Jim, hugging her.

She realized, once again, how tough their lives had been.

She put her cup down and knelt, swallowing them up in one big hug. The kids slowly melted in her arms.

"You can talk about your lives with me anytime you want," she said. "But the past is through. We can all make our lives become whatever we want it to be now."

"I just want to play soccer," said Tracy.

"I want to make websites," said Jim.

"I don't know what I want to do," said Teddy, sadly.

"Well, we'll have to work on that then," said Lily.

After the kids went to sleep, Lily tried to read a book. It didn't catch her. Thoughts of Sean making love to her kept streaming through her mind and the more she pushed them away, the more they invaded her brain.

Finally, she got up and went into the kitchen, did some dishes and called Mom.

"Lily, it's good to hear from you. We're doing great here. Your father has decided to take up cycling. I decided to join him, I need some exercise. So yesterday we bought bicycles. We're having a ball riding around the campground. How are you dear?"

"Mom, I think I must be going crazy."

"What's wrong?"

"Well, last month Teddy and Tracy appeared out of nowhere. Then earlier this month, Emily showed up. And today, Jim. Again, out of nowhere. He said I'd adopted him. I don't understand any of this."

It felt hard for her to admit the possibility of being insane, but she didn't have any other explanation. Happily insane, though.

"Lily dear. You're working too hard. Of course you adopted the kids. They needed a stable home and you're a good mom. I know Teddy has been a handful in the past, but with you around, I'm sure he'll turn out fine. Myrna did the best she could and Tracy's a gem. And you're an angel to take in little Emily. As for Maria, she was always so nice. I can't wait to meet her son."

"Mom, there was no Myrna, Maria or Ralph. These kids just appeared out of nowhere." She could feel her heart beating faster and her breathing speed up.

"Oh dear," Mom said. "We were planning on coming up next week. Do you want us to come sooner? It sounds like you're overwhelmed. Have you been under a lot of stress at work? Have you had a physical lately?"

Lily knew where this was going. Nowhere. Mom couldn't see what was going on at all. "Yeah Mom, I guess I've been a little stressed out. Next week will be great."

"Why don't you put on some relaxing music and go take a long, hot bath?"

"I think I'll do that. You guys have fun cycling."

"Cycling, that sound so adventurous. See you soon."

She got up and paced around the small kitchen. Mom's solution to all the world's problems was always a long, hot bath. She could almost hear her say, 'If everyone would take some time to soak in a steaming tub and relax, the world would be a nicer place. The pace would slow down and there'd be so much less stress. People would treat each other and themselves with more respect and kindness. That would go a long way to helping them communicate.'

A hot bath wasn't going to solve this problem. But holding her head under water just might.

She took a hot bath anyway.

Over the next week, which was school break, everyone locked themselves away and made secret presents for each other and for Grandma and Grandpa. They gathered in the evenings and drank hot chocolate with marshmallows and played games.

Lily made a stab at baking gingerbread cookies from a tube. The only prepared frostings she could find in the stores were pink and orange. Teddy, Tracy and Jim got more on each other than on the cookies.

Jim ate the leftover frosting and said, "Those look like mutant snowmen cookies."

The following week Nick and Susan came back to town, parking their RV on the street near their apartment. They greeted Jim and Emily as if they'd always known them.

"Jimmy, Jimmy, Jimmy," said Dad in his best Cary Grant imitation. He picked Jim up and swung him around, which made Jim shriek with laughter.

"Hello dear hearts," said Mom. She hugged Lily and the other kids, ending up with Emily, who she picked up and put on her hip.

"Teddy, good to see you again," said Nick, shaking Teddy's hand. "And Tracy, give me a high five." They slapped hands.

Again, her parents acted as if everything was completely normal.

After lunch Nick took the kids to a nearby park to play soccer in the rain. Emily went down for a nap. Lily sat down with Mom and drank coffee.

"But why can't I remember even hearing about Ralph and Myrna? I know I didn't have a friend name Maria. And why can't I remember Tracy even arriving? I just woke up one morning and there she was, in the living room."

"I don't know dear. Are you sure you aren't working too hard?"

"No, I'm not. Jobs have been dwindling all fall, I'm getting older. And the holidays are always the slowest."

"Maybe you can't remember, because it's just not important where they came from or how they got here. They're here and I can see you're doing a fine job parenting them."

She sighed.

"I mean, look at you. There Nick and I were, playing our usual game of close your eyes, pick a place on the map and drive. So I was driving and we stopped at a rest stop. We found you, bundled up at a picnic table. No one else around. We used the pay phone and called the police. No one ever claimed you and we arranged to foster you, then adopt you. There was no explanation as to why you were there or where you might have come from. But you were there and we've never once regretted finding you."

Lily hadn't looked at it from that perspective before. So perhaps the universe was playing a grand cosmic joke on her. And she was enjoying it thoroughly. Although she did worry about having enough money.

The holidays continued. Nick and Susan treated them and they went to see the Nutcracker one night. Christmas ships the next, standing in the freezing cold and dodging the blowing smoke from the bonfires.

It was the best Christmas Lily had ever had and her parents had often managed spectacular Christmases. Mostly, she enjoyed watching the kids experience new things.

Finally, just after New Year's her parents drove off to parts unknown.

"We're driving south and who knows where we'll end up. We'll call you and let you know," said Nick, hugging them all goodbye at once.

"Take care all of you," said Susan. "Call us on your new phones if you get a chance."

"Grandma and Grandpa are so cool," said Teddy.

"Yes, they are," said Lily, grateful to have such parents.

Never again would she let herself get so rattled as to doubt her sanity. She hadn't felt so peaceful since, well, ever. Life was good.

SEAN

They found him.

He was on his way back to the condo from the paint store. He stopped for coffee and the next thing he knew a car full of paparazzi was stalking him.

The rain was driving down hard and cold. It was nearing 4:30 and already dark. As their SUV pulled up on his left, the flashes blinded him. He waved and smiled anyway. No sense in being grumpy about the whole thing.

Not going back to the condo though. Not with them following. He wanted to keep his new home a secret for as long as possible.

Sean turned right at the next corner, knowing they couldn't, but he wasn't hopeful about losing them yet. He took two more rights and got back onto 45th. St., heading towards the freeway.

There were so many white SUVs around, he couldn't tell if any was theirs. Once on the I-5, he headed towards the mall. He'd get some Christmas shopping done, along with the rest of the crowds.

Once there and parked, more of a challenge than he'd

anticipated; he walked through what was now drizzle, getting his pants wet from the puddles. He should have worn better shoes too. But he'd just been going to buy some paint.

Inside, he hit store after store, buying mostly gift cards for his eleven siblings and nieces and nephews. And Mom and Dad. It was so much easier than trying to figure out what everybody wanted or needed. Casey was the only one he could make the right guesses for. He'd already gotten her a gift certificate to her favorite nursery.

He was at a bookstore when the headache hit. Standing in line. By the time he'd finished the transaction, he could barely stand. He hobbled back to his car and sat in the darkness, rain pouring down so hard it sounded like hail.

Waves of pain came and went, pounding his head so hard, he almost cried. Finally, it eased enough to drive home. As he drove down the street and began to turn into the garage, he noticed a white SUV parked across the street. Damn. It would be really difficult to escape them now.

He hauled the buckets of paint upstairs. Stupidly. But he wanted the car unloaded now. He didn't want to have to leave the condo until this latest headache was gone. They seemed to last about a week. And he didn't want to run into the paparazzi in the middle of this mess. The headaches left him so incapacitated and he felt too vulnerable to deal with the media.

Once unloaded, he hung his dripping coat on a kitchen chair as well. Then he threw his soaked shoes in the bathtub to dry and his wet clothes in the laundry. He pulled on some sweats, drank a gallon of water and curled up on his couch with the gas fireplace burning. And slept.

The next three days weren't any better, but on the following day, he was able to get up and cook eggs and sausage for breakfast. He savored the rich flavors, grateful for his new refuge, even if the paparazzi were parked outside. He drank coffee and read the news online. After showering and shaving, he looked at the calendar. Today was Christmas Eve. Crap. This month had flown past.

Tonight he needed to show up at Casey's. He sighed, thankful that he'd at least gotten the shopping done.

He spent the day wrapping gift cards. In the afternoon, he wandered down to the mailbox to pick up the mail. The SUV was still there. He grabbed his mail, before they could get out of the car, and sprinted back upstairs.

Two more gift cards had arrived in the mail, so he wrapped those as well. Then checked the list again. Yep, everything ready. He'd arranged to pick up a couple of cakes at a bakery this afternoon to bring as his contribution to the potluck.

Maybe he could lose the paparazzi then. He could never do it in L.A. They knew the town better. But here in Seattle, …

His phone rang. Ned. Sean picked it up and said, "Hi Ned."

"Hi. I've got a little more information for you. Not much yet. I'm going to spend next week following a couple leads."

"Great, what've you got?"

"Well, she's still in the Wallingford apartment. It's a condo, she's only got about four more months there. It's owned by a couple who are traveling and they'll be back. So, she lives there with her four kids. An older couple, I'm guessing parents, are staying in an RV parked on the street. Doing lots of holiday stuff. I talked to the old man, friendly guy. Sounds like he and his wife travel a lot. They're from California, Bay area."

"Wait, did you say four kids?"

"Yeah, wasn't that the info I gave you last time?"

"I only remember three," said Sean. Had she gotten another child in the last few weeks?

He heard paper shuffling and Ned came back on the line. "Yep. She has four. A 16 year old boy, 13 year old girl, a boy 7 and a girl 2."

"Tell me about the 7 year old," said Sean.

"He arrived this week. An old friend of hers died and Lily had been named guardian in the will. Name's Jim."

Sean didn't say anything.

"That's about all I've got for now. She doesn't seem to be working much, but it is the holidays and she has guests. Maybe that's normal for the modeling biz to take December off."

"Thanks Ned."

"Want me to keep going?"

"Yeah, if you think there's more to find out."

"There's always more. I'll get back in touch early in January."

"Great."

Sean had known Ned wouldn't have the information he sought. He needed to know if she'd intended to humiliate him on their date. Or if it had just been an awful night.

He looked at the clock. Time to get on the road.

After changing he gathered up his gifts in a plastic bag and went down to his car. He had two parking spaces. Perhaps he should consider getting a second car. But that wouldn't fool the paparazzi for long.

He sighed and got into the Prius. As he approached the exit, the gate opened. He'd used the exit not in view of the SUV, but knew they'd have a lookout. Which they did. The guy moved to cross in front of his car, but Sean curved and sped out onto the street around him.

At the next block, he turned left, then right again, left again and heading to the next main street. Then turning right at the next large cross section. He zigzagged down the two lane streets, through the rain until he was far enough away to lose them completely. He hoped.

Then drove across town to the bakery and picked up the two large cakes. He hadn't wanted to drive quickly with two cakes in the car. And he certainly didn't want the paparazzi to find out where his family members lived. He wasn't bothered by them much anymore. He didn't have much to hide. But his family was private. Maybe moving to Seattle hadn't been such a good idea after all.

It was nearly five thirty before he made it to Casey's. He brought in the cakes one by one, trying not to drip everywhere. Casey waved at him and went back to the stove. James slapped him on the back and asked, "Can I help you unload?"

"No. I got it."

Finished unloading, he put his wet coat in the mud room to drip, making a note to himself, that if he ever bought a house in this area a mud room was a necessity. He really wasn't used to this much rain. How did people ever dry out?

James took him aside and they went into his office and closed the door.

"So, headaches," said James. "I've found a few references to them. And one really good documentation, done by one of us who was a scientist. I found a copy of his journal, which had been handed down in my family. I'd never read it before. He was able to connect his debilitating headaches to the arrival of a child. He'd been watching, okay stalking, a woman who he was obsessed with. He came from money, she didn't. His parents were dead, he lived with an aunt and uncle who would have been horrified if he'd told them about her. Children kept showing up in her life, she was dirt poor. He anonymously left money for her, until he connected the headaches and the kids. He'd finished his studies and they eloped, with all the kids. And sealed the deal. No more headaches. No more unusual kid arrivals. He established his career in Astronomy and life went on."

"Wow. Great story. Well, that's good. I just found out she

got another child last week and I had a major headache at the same time."

"How many has she got?"

"Four."

"You better get a move on. Unless you're looking for a huge family."

"I'm working on it," said Sean.

He took a deep breath and joined the party. It had been decades since he'd been with his family at Christmas. There were Mom and Dad, all eleven siblings, all their kids, an occasional in-law and anyone else who didn't have somewhere else to go. Casey needed a bigger house, he decided. But even though everyone was squished, he loved the coziness. And there was always a niece or nephew looking for a lap. Usually he played with them, but with his lingering headache, he was happy just to sit and cuddle with someone.

What was Lily doing right now? Cuddling the two year old. Emily. He longed to be part of her family. To have a home, not a house. He didn't even have a Christmas tree. Next year would be different.

Every flat surface was filled with bodies as they ate the amazing turkey that Casey made and the salads and side dishes everyone else had brought. Casey made turkey just like Mom. It took him back to his childhood.

While cleaning up all the plates and silverware, Casey turned to him and said, "I'm really glad you're here, but you look like shit."

"Headache," he said, shrugging.

"Did you talk to James?"

"Yeah. He confirmed what I suspected. Headache equals new child."

"So what are you going to do about it?"

"Call her or meet her somewhere."

"When?"

"I'm not sure."

"Well, don't wait too long. She may be having a nervous breakdown. How many kids has she got?"

"Four."

"Oh my god. I started melting at two. By the time there were four, I was a complete mess."

"Okay, I'll do it soon."

Somehow.

LILY

THE COOL AIR CHILLED LILY. WHY DID THEY KEEP GROCERY stores so cold? It was January. Freezing outside with a threat of snow. And here she was looking at watermelons. Craving summer.

She thumped the watermelon again. It sounded sort of hollow. Did that mean it was rotten or ripe? It sort of smelled like a melon, so she picked it up and carried it to the cart, where Emily sat in the top, playing with her stuffed cow.

That's when she saw him.

On the other side of produce by the end cap of Easter candy. Why was Easter candy out already? Valentine's Day was still a couple weeks away. So annoying.

She tried not to stare, but couldn't help herself.

Sean seemed fascinated by the Easter candy. He wore a puffy jacket and plaid flannel shirt, hiding what she knew were washboard abs. His baggy jeans concealed a gorgeous ass. And the Mariner's baseball cap flattened his curly hair. She completely lost it over the dimple in his chin.

She hadn't expected to see him there. Anywhere for that matter. He shouldn't be there.

She felt self conscious wearing ripped leggings and a truly gross sweatshirt. Emily had thrown up on it as Lily pulled her out of her carseat. Just before entering the store. Her gray roots showed and dark circles lived under her eyes from a constant lack of sleep. Had she even brushed her hair this morning?

He could only have been looking at her and wondering why he'd ever asked her out.

He walked towards her.

She felt embarrassed about standing there gaping at him like a teenager. No, a teenager would have been much cooler about it.

Turning to put the watermelon in her cart, she tripped over her own feet. The watermelon bounced off the cart and went flying. At least she caught herself before hitting the terra cotta floor.

The watermelon wasn't so lucky. On its way to the floor it took out the entire tarragon white wine vinegar display.

By the time she stood up, he'd vanished.

The thin faced Manager came over and had a fit. Apparently she'd broken over five hundred bottles. He stood there complaining and she stood there apologizing, as everyone in Food King within smelling distance was slowly asphyxiated.

He was huffing and puffing and supervising the cleanup of a couple harried looking young boys. He must think she was crazy.

But just what was the vinegar display doing next to the watermelons anyway? They were just asking for trouble.

Feeling frustrated and angry, she gathered her wits together and headed for the checkout line. Emily just watched the Manager and giggled. Her cart overflowed with groceries and the lines were long. She could swear the Manager stood behind her somewhere, his beady eyes burning holes in her back.

The line got longer behind her and the very friendly checkout clerk, who was probably trying to make up for her boss, checked and bagged the entire cart and almost one child. Lily only then remembered she needed to cough up some money and dug around in her huge shoulder bag.

Complaining noises came from the cute young thing in line behind her. The clerk gave her the total of $397.28 and waited. Lily found no wallet in her purse. No cash, no credit or debit cards, no checkbook and she'd been driving without her license.

One of the kids probably emptied her purse and forgot to put everything back in.

She tried to explain. There could be no graceful exit. She offered to put everything back.

The Manager came up and reveled in a new found opportunity for viciousness, threatened to have her arrested for malicious mischief. He then called security to escort her out of the store.

At that moment Sean appeared again. He squeezed past her and stood next to her cart, leaned over it and said, "Allow me." He swiped his card and stood smiling at the Manager, who recognized him.

"Is this woman a friend of yours, Mr. O'Neill?"

"Yes, she is," said Sean.

"My sincerest apologies, Ma'am," he said, then walked off and berated another clerk who stood watching the entire scene.

Lily stood speechless and embarrassed and angry. Her face flamed with heat and she clenched her fists around the handle of the grocery cart. She wanted to kill the suck-up Manager and take Sean out as well.

After he finished the transaction, he moved forward and she was free to wheel the cart out into the pouring rain and escape.

She unlocked the car and put Emily into her carseat, buckling her in.

"Here, let me help," said Sean, grabbing a bag of groceries to put in the back end of her wagon.

"I don't want your help," said Lily. "I don't need your help."

Except that clearly she had needed help. She stopped, sighed, lowered her shoulders and looked at him.

"Thank you for what you did in there. If you give me your address, I'll send you a check."

"You don't need to pay me back," he said, touching her arm."

Even through her coat she felt such a rush of sensation from his touch, it was difficult to form words.

"I need to pay you back."

"Okay, if you really need to."

An expression she couldn't decipher crossed his face. He shrugged, took out a notebook, scribbled his name, address, phone number and email, then handed the page to her. She pushed it into her purse, then continued loading groceries, while he watched with an uncomfortable look on his face.

Finished, she closed the tailgate and pushed the cart to the return, while he followed her.

"Lily, could I talk to you?"

"This isn't a good time," she said, returning to her car. Looking down at her running shoes, she noticed they had brown stains on them. Chocolate milk.

"Well, you choose a time then," he said.

"I'll call you." She just wanted to run away.

"When?"

"I don't know. My life is complicated right now."

"I'll be waiting for your call," he said, looking a little dejected and touching her arm again. Then he turned and walked to a green car and got inside.

She got into her own car and sat in the front seat, waiting until he drove off. She buried her face in the steering wheel and began to laugh uncontrollably. Emily always the one to follow along, began to laugh in the back seat as well. Lily howled until she began to cry. People on their way out of the store looked like they were trying, unsuccessfully, not to stare.

She drove towards home, vowing to torture whoever was responsible for her missing wallet. Her one window of opportunity for grocery shopping almost blown. But worse, now she owed him. And she didn't want to owe him anything.

Yes, she'd spent the months since she met him fantasizing madly about him. Because fantasy lovers don't tell you you're too old, you need to lose weight, you need to improve your mind or you have bad breath. Fantasy lovers don't leave you with no job, no prospects for one, a month's worth of rent due, bills to pay and an empty bank account at tax time. Like her ex-husband did.

She couldn't remember if Sean had treated her badly on the 'date from hell'. She couldn't remember any of it, but she knew it felt safer to have him only as a fantasy. Reality was too menacing. Especially now with the kids to think of. Even if she didn't have to explain that all the kids just 'arrived'. And who knows, he might be the one person on the planet who didn't just accept that the kids were a normal part of her life.

She glanced at the clock on the dashboard. She had an hour to get home, put groceries away and get everybody ready for Tracy's first soccer game. Hopefully, that would include a change of clothes for her. Her face warmed at how he'd seen her dressed like this. How embarrassing. Her life really was complicated now.

She didn't want to wonder if Sean would be another bad choice, like all her past relationships, while trying to keep him separate from the kids until she felt sure he was reliable. She didn't want them hurt by disappearing or jerky boyfriends.

It was easier to keep going as she had, reading steamy romances, substituting her name for the heroine's and Sean's for the hero's, watching his movies, collecting photos of him in her bedroom. Nude photos from an upscale magazine lived in the drawer of her nightstand.

He might have been a jerk in person, but he was a great lust item. Was he a jerk? After reading the tabloids, she still wasn't sure what happened that night. Did she behave badly because of the drugs and wine? She'd never know unless she asked him. And she'd never do that. It was too embarrassing.

She'd send him a check and that would be the end of it.

She pulled up in front of the house. Emily had fallen asleep in her car seat, so Lily got out of the car and closed the door very quietly. She opened the back door and stealthily unbelted Emily, maneuvering her out of the carseat and carried her towards the house without waking her.

Her house. A rambler painted sky blue, it looked like the typical Ballard area house on a treeless lot. Who would've thought Ballard was once a forest?

The house had six bedrooms on the main floor and a full basement that didn't leak. A rare thing in Seattle. Someday there would be a rec room down there for the kids.

Mom and Dad cosigned the loan and made a hefty down payment when Emily came along. The condo owners wanted to come home early and it was too small for all of them. She could just make the house payments, but wasn't sure about keeping the appliances running and the roof from leaking. Now she needed to learn how to be an electrician, carpenter and plumber.

Inside, she lay Emily in her crib. Thankfully, Emily stayed

asleep. Lily covered her with a blanket and slipped out of the room.

As she unloaded four bags of groceries, she held an imaginary conversation with Sean.

"Do you believe what one of the little darlings did?"

"With your wallet?" he asked, smoothing her hair.

"Yes, amazing. I'm going to kill whoever it was."

"Good thing I showed up," the imaginary Sean said, as he helped her carry groceries inside.

She searched through piles of papers, clothes and toys on the kitchen table looking for her wallet/checkbook combo, as he walked in to check on Emily.

He asked, "You little devil, you didn't do that, did you?"

She heard Emily squeal and giggle in reply.

Lily found her wallet, two rooms later, on the couch under some pillows. As she continued to clean and put groceries away, she and Sean carried on a long conversation about the meaning of life, the manner in which black holes sucked up finished homework and where the kids came from.

He said, "I think they've come to you because they desperately need love and nurturing. You're able to give them that. Perhaps they're the lost souls of children who've died of neglect."

"You may have a point. They all have a deep insecurity about them, no matter how they try to cover it up."

As the kids trickled in from various schools, all thoughts of Sean vanished like chocolate ice cream at a birthday party. The kids talked about the excitement of their days. Backpacks and papers flew everywhere. Emily woke up and ran in circles around the kitchen, shrieking and bouncing, pretending to be Tigger.

Tracy immediately confessed to hiding the wallet.

"It was for my homework. We needed to find out the

birthdate of our parents and then research what happened that day and make a collage about it. As a surprise."

"But you didn't put it back in my purse."

"I'm sorry. Jimmy came and hit me with a pillow and after I chased him outside, I guess I forgot."

"Please, don't do it again. I almost couldn't buy groceries for us today."

"I'm so sorry, Mom," said Tracy, hugging her. "I'll be more careful."

She took the kids out for Mexican fast food and then to the video store, since no one had homework. Sean remained in her thoughts. Why had he been at Food King? Had he moved to Seattle? Had she made him appear with all her fantasizing about him?

She'd seen his movies dozens of times. All since the date from hell. Even owned a couple. The store had a five day checkout policy, so everyone got a movie and she had veto power.

Lily chose Sean's film, *Twilight Magic*, a new release this week. He directed and starred in it. Teddy got a music DVD from his favorite band, Chrome Island. Tracy chose *Chariots of Fire* and Jim wanted to see the newest James Bond flick. Emily was too young to make a choice, but she'd sleep through anything after dinner. As an afterthought, Lily grabbed *Winnie the Pooh; the Piglet Movie.*

After they got home, the kids drew a name to see who got to watch their movie that night. Tracy won. Lily started popping popcorn and the kids set the DVD up.

She looked forward to seeing Sean's movie. His dark eyes stared at her from the DVD case. Gazing at that husky, shirtless chest made her warm. How could he look so gorgeous?

As the popcorn popped, she caught a strong whiff of strawberries. She looked around, trying to find the source. The scent was so strong it almost made her sick. She hadn't bought strawberries lately, not in the middle of winter. The dish soap was lemony and there was no food out, except the melting butter and the popcorn.

Crying came down the hall from Emily's room. But Emily was playing on the floor of the living room. Lily, warily walked down the hall. It couldn't be. Not again.

She found Katie, age one and a half standing up in a second crib, holding her arms out to be picked up. Lily sighed and picked her up. The crying stopped immediately and Katie started cooing while being rocked.

Lily tried to push the confusion and worry from her mind.

Looking up, she said, "Okay, this isn't funny anymore."

She walked back to the kitchen, carrying Katie.

"I guess you need some dinner, huh?"

She set her in Emily's high chair, strapping her in. In the fridge, she found some creamed corn with ham that Emily had eaten half of. Tracy came in and took over feeding Katie, and Lily finished the popcorn.

Afterwards, Emily and Katie sat on the floor, playing with plastic animals, while the others ate popcorn and watched the movie. Teddy, Tracy and Jim didn't act as if anything was unusual. It was as if Katie had always been there.

Lily felt almost relieved that they didn't notice. Or react badly to their growing family. She still didn't understand any of this, but she could handle it. She hoped.

They watched *Chariots of Fire* for the gazillionth time. Tracy would either turn out to be a soccer player or a distance runner when she grew up. Or maybe she was getting activity out of her system and would turn out to be a couch potato.

Afterwards, she spent a couple hours putting the kids to bed. Then she sat on the lumpy old couch alone and watched Sean's movie.

She imagined herself watching the movie with him, wrapped in his arms.

It was a sweet film, set in Ireland, about an American traveling through the countryside who gets waylaid by fairies and comes to terms with his grief left over from his wife dying of cancer. He gradually learns to love again and returns to Boston, refreshed and ready to start his life over again.

She cried at the end and Sean kissed her.

"You are so beautiful and sexy," he said.

"Not as beautiful as that red-haired fairy you made love with," she said.

"More beautiful. You're real. And I never much cared for redheads. I always kind of went for blond amazons," he said.

As she walked into her bedroom and closed the door, she pretended that he unbuttoned her shirt and kissed her neck.

He added, "I kept waiting for you and you never showed up."

"I was busy doing other things."

"Ah, with other men," the imaginary Sean said.

She pretended his fingers dipped into the upper edges of her bra, imagined him grasping her hip with the other hand, pulling her back towards him.

"Yes, I mean no. I don't know what I mean."

Her breasts ached for his touch as she unfastened her bra in the front and rubbed her nipples, her body tingling. Her other hand slipped beneath the front of her jeans and she imagined it was his hand. Her breathing came more quickly as her pants unzipped and slid down along with her panties. His hands slid down her belly and between her legs. She could feel his hardness against her buttocks. She felt close, oh so close, so wet. She wanted him badly.

"Mom," came a yell from down the hall, then a knock on her door.

Jimmy. Lily pulled up her pants and zipped them. Fastened her bra and buttoned the shirt.

"What?" she asked.

"Mom, I forgot. I have a field trip form that needs to be signed tonight. It's for Microsoft. I have to, have to go!"

She opened the door and said, "Okay, but in the future, please give them to me when you get home from school." She tried to keep her voice calm, although anger and frustration roiled around inside. She rubbed her arms, feeling energy flow off her skin.

"I know. I forgot," he said, handing her the piece of paper.

She took it into the kitchen, found a pen and signed it, then handed it back to him, hugged him and sent him off to bed.

She sat at the kitchen table. All desire for sex had passed.

She ignored the panic that tried to surface about Katie's appearance.

Sean. She didn't know whether she wanted to kill him or have mad, hot sex with him. Or both.

SEAN

Sean backed his green Prius into the parking place in front of the cafe, letting the line of traffic pass him. Parking karma again, which was good since he was almost on time for the interview. Rain flooded the windshield as he turned off the wipers, causing the world outside to become a blur.

It had taken him quite a while to evade the single SUV full of paparazzi who had staked out his condo. Traffic had been particularly bad today. Maybe because of the late winter deluge.

He unbuckled the seatbelt and was about to open the door when his phone rang. He looked at it to decide whether to answer or just go into the restaurant. It was Ned Hanley.

"Ned, how are you?"

"Good, good. I've got more information for you."

"Great," said Sean, pulling the notebook out of his sports coat.

"The little lady has a new address and phone."

"Okay," he said, writing them down.

"Seems like she was married in L.A. They were together ten years. Divorced a couple years ago. No kids from the marriage.

I don't think they've had any contact since the divorce. It wasn't exactly amicable and he's left a trail of unpaid bills behind him wherever he's been."

Sean felt stunned. He hadn't pictured Lily as having been married. He also felt a little jealous.

Ned continued, "She moved up here and has been making her living modeling here and there. The first kid came to her from the death of an uncle. Another from the death of an aunt. The next came from the death of a high school friend. The two year old was an abandoned foster child. The paperwork for that adoption seems to be almost magically flowing around all the normal roadblocks, a friend in CPS tells me. Lily has fabulous marks as a foster parent, considering she's working part-time and single. The fifth has already been adopted."

"Fifth?" asked Sean, surprised. In December Ned had told him there were three children. Two months later, Ned didn't seem to notice the disparity.

Sean sighed with relief. He didn't want anyone to notice the kids' arrivals.

"Yeah, a little girl, one and a half. I don't know how she qualified as a single parent and with her income and four kids already. She must have a nest egg somewhere. I'll keep looking for the money source. I know she's not making that much modeling. It's not like she and the kids live lavishly. Their splurges seem to limited to thrift store shopping and movie rentals. Maybe she's getting money from her parents. I'm having a difficult time pinning them down."

"When did the adoption go through?" asked Sean.

"About a week ago"

That was when he'd seen her at the grocery store. The day of his latest headache. He'd received a check from her two days later, but no phone call. He must be the catalyst for the kids.

Ned continued, "She seems to spend her free time doing

Mommy things. Driving carpools, going to her daughter's soccer games, grocery shopping, jogging around Green Lake, etc. Doesn't seem to have a life outside of work or her kids."

"No boyfriend?"

"Not that I've seen any indication of. She's buddies with a neighbor lady, seems to be her only close friend. She's friendly with people she works with and parents at the soccer games, but doesn't seem to do anything with them. Only with her kids. I wouldn't expect anything else from a single mom with five kids who works part time. Beats me how she can even squeeze work in."

Sean felt relieved there was no other man in the picture. He felt very territorial about her. He wanted to be the catalyst. He wanted no other man around her. He didn't want to have to worry about being betrayed again.

"Thanks Ned. I don't think I need to know any more. I'll take it from here."

"I'll fax you the specifics of what I've found. It's been a pleasure doing business with you, Sean. Call me if you need anything else."

"Will do." Sean closed the notebook and returned it to his pocket, set the phone to vibrate and slid it into the pocket as well.

Interesting about two new kids. Something tickled the back of his mind. He couldn't quite figure out what. Well, if it was important, it would come back.

He got out of the car and rushed through the rain in through the door of the cafe, trying not to get too drenched. Opening the door, he was greeted by the sweet smell of cinnamon and sugar from the just baked cinnamon rolls that the cafe was famous for. Following that came the scents of coffee and lastly onions from quiche. His stomach rumbled and his mouth watered.

He spotted his interviewer, Julia Montgomery. She stood out in her red dress. In fact, she was the only woman in the cafe wearing a dress. Seattle was much more casual than New York. She stared at him. He waved.

Julia was tall and black. When she smiled warmly at him, her face lit up. She had a reputation for integrity, which was why he'd allowed the interview. That didn't mean it would be easy, or that he could trust her.

He walked over to her table and she rose, holding out her hand. He shook it.

"Sean, it's good to finally meet you."

"Hello Julia, you're even lovelier in person than your voice is over the phone."

They'd done a preliminary interview a couple weeks ago and he'd admired her warm voice.

"Thank you."

He could tell she meant it. He liked people who could accept a compliment.

They stood in line at the counter to order. He chose the feta, artichoke quiche with chai to drink. Julia ordered a green salad and ice tea, whipping out her company credit card to pay.

Sean waited for his drink, admiring the display decorations. Baskets of Easter eggs dyed with natural colors. They had patterns from ferns and leaves on them. Very tasteful. Easter must be coming soon. He'd have to see if Casey, James and their kids were doing anything. It would be fun to have an Easter egg hunt. Or were high school kids too old for that? What if the eggs were filled with gift cards?

The barista handed him his chai and Julia her iced tea. They sat at the table waiting for the food to come. A vase of daffodils and paper whites graced the table. He lifted it to his nose and inhaled the sweet fragrance as Julia organized her notes. Casey was gradually teaching him the names of flowers, hoping somehow to convert him into a gardener. Last week had been sunny. He was excited about the upcoming spring with all the flowers and new life coming after the bleakness of winter. He wanted to enjoy it with Lily and the kids. He hadn't figured out yet how to make that happen. But he did think of them as 'their kids', not 'her kids'.

"So, how do you like living in Seattle?" asked Julia, as she set up the recorder.

It had been a long, hard winter moving up here. He'd left all his friends behind and felt lonely and depressed about the debilitating headaches. He spent a lot of time with his family, they were probably sick of him by now. The days, so much darker here than L.A., with rain for months on end was difficult to adjust to.

Still, when the sun shone, it felt like joy bursting out everywhere. Everyone in town seemed to take the day off to celebrate.

Okay, answer the question. Sound spontaneous.

He grinned and said, "Oh, I love it, but don't print that. I don't want to be held in any way responsible for the next wave of immigration to Seattle. The natives get a little testy about all us strangers moving in."

She laughed at his lame attempt at humor. He needed to up his game here.

"All right, then I'll move on to the big question. What's going on with your headaches?"

"Well, they're hanging in there and so am I. The doctors still don't know what's causing them. We're working on that. I don't want to be put into a position of dealing with one on a tight shooting schedule, so I'm taking this time to make a few lifestyle changes. You know, what office workers call personal days."

"But aren't you afraid if you take too much time off that

people will forget about you when the next hot script floats around?"

She was going straight for his jugular. He worried about being passed over. A lot. God, why were actors so damn insecure? It's why he fit in so well.

He replied, "Not really. It would be worse if I took a part and royally screwed up a film. I won't do that to my fellow actors and everyone else who puts so much hard work into a film. Or to my fans who have high expectations."

"I've heard there were some issues on the set of 'Red Sunsets'. What happened between you and Nina?" she asked, flashing the concerned reporter mask across her face.

Another shot at the jugular. But he'd been deflecting these kind of questions for years. All he had to do was blather along and most reporters would consider the question answered.

"Nothing happened between Nina and I. She and Manuel were dating. Nina and I got along fine. The problem on the set was me and the bloody headache I got during the last days of shooting. I couldn't deal with the lights on the set, they made an already incapacitating headache worse. And I felt worried, not knowing if it was a headache or a brain tumor or what. And the drugs they gave me, to try to mitigate the effects, did nothing, except make me sleepy. So, all in all, that was a really tough time and I'm glad it's behind me. Which is why I said, no more films until the headaches are gone or I've found a way to deal with them."

He leaned back in the hard wooden chair and sipped his chai, the spices rolling across his tongue. A look of annoyance crossed her face and she was about to speak when a young redheaded girl, face covered with freckles and wearing thick glasses, brought their food.

"Thank you," said Sean.

The girl smiled shyly and quickly returned to the kitchen.

Julia asked, "But how did you and Nina do the love scenes? I've seen a preview of the film and I find it hard to believe that there wasn't something going on between the two of you. The love scenes are, well, hot."

"Well, thank you. They were meant to be. We had a fabulous cast and crew, not to mention director. Both Nina and I are seasoned actors. It's our job to act and do it as well as we are able at any given time. I know you understand that during love scenes there's half a dozen or more crew people hanging around messing with cameras and lights. Not exactly a romantic atmosphere, even if I had a costar I was interested in. Which wasn't the case on that film."

Sean took a bite of his quiche and smiled as the sharp taste of feta, the basil and buttery crust mingled in his mouth. Someday he'd have Casey teach him how to cook.

Julia looked unhappy as she crunched on her salad.

She swallowed and said, "So, you're telling me, that you and Nina are really over?"

"Yep," he said. She was angling for a story that wasn't there and he felt annoyed by it.

"So, who's the woman in your life now? The last one who made a big splash in your life was the 'date from hell' that all the tabloids covered. Who was she?"

He shook his head. "A one night date, which was clearly a disaster. You read the tabloids."

She raised an irritated eyebrow at him and kept pushing.

"No name for us?"

"Nope," he said.

"So who *are* you seeing?"

"No one at the moment. I'm hanging with my family. Catching up with them."

"But since you're not working, that leaves you with a lot of spare time."

"And I'm loving it. Hasn't happened at any time of my adult life."

"So you finished two other pictures last year that are about to open. Which would you like to talk about first?"

He had another drink of chai and took a deep breath and let it out. Back on comfortable territory.

"Well, I'm most excited about *Around the Edge*, because I discovered the script and directed it as well. It turned out to be the most challenging film I've ever done."

"Why? It's such a simple story, few characters, few settings?"

"That's part of what made it so difficult. I was on-screen for nearly the entire film and it was all about interior, emotional stuff. Self discovery. It's rough to do that and keep the tension up. If you go too far, it's boring. Even with the brilliant cast and crew I had."

Sean took another bite of his quiche, savoring the snappiness of the artichoke hearts. He could smell the sun dried tomatoes. These days his life felt too short and he'd become determined to learn to enjoy it. To squeeze all the richness out of every single day.

Julia shifted in her chair. "The film was anything but boring. Everyone who's caught an early screening has loved it. There's great intensity of emotion and the fascinating love story woven around this wounded man's recovery of his emotions simply blows people away."

She crossed her legs and her dress slipped just enough to reveal the tops of her stockings and a little flesh. She leaned forward.

It took a moment for him to process her conscious or unconscious body language. She didn't adjust her dress. Whether she was aware of it, or not, she was coming on to him.

He drank more chai, shifted in his chair and politely said, "That's very kind of you. I know it will appeal to the more impressionable among us, but a lot of the guys who I've talked to, you know the men's men, not the sensitive new age guys, thought it was sooo borrrrrinnnggg. They'll like *Spectral Veins* better, I'm predicting."

She sat up, catching his more formal tone.

"So, you're still trying to be everything to everybody?"

"Oh, low blow. Yeah, I'm guilty on that one."

"Well, since you brought up your other film, how was *Spectral Veins* to work on?"

"It was an incredible experience. Glad I didn't direct it though. I always love doing SF films. The imagination it takes to envision a completely different world always astonishes me. It felt great to work with John as a director and the cast was so innovative. Makeup and costumes were, as you probably heard, extreme. But to get across the idea of aliens who communicate through subtle changes of color, body temperature and movement, well the silence alone felt intense. We're a species who chatters away and we surround ourselves with constant noise. To sit in a movie theater and hear silence for as little as five minutes is profoundly uncomfortable to us. What a challenge. And John pulled it off brilliantly."

"You know people who've seen previews are talking Oscars about both those films."

He laughed. "Yeah, like I said, people like to chatter away. Anyway, none of that's in my control. It's a great honor, but it's never had anything to do with why I chose to do a film. I'm in there for the challenge and because I love the work."

"Last week when you won an Oscar for *Twilight Magic*, you talked about the power of having a dream to work towards and you thanked Lily for being your dream. Who's Lily?" Julia asked. Her eyes pierced right through him.

Forget the jugular, this one was a blow straight to the heart. He'd wondered when someone would get to that question. He'd been able to duck the question at the press conferences. Shifted the attention to his costars or upcoming films. But, she wasn't going to give up.

He'd been caught out. Mentioning Lily in a moment of hopelessness in his acceptance speech at the awards had been a mistake. As soon as the words left his mouth, he regretted it. He was hoping she'd seen it and be impressed. He even considered sending her a copy of it, anonymously, of course.

The media were always hungry for details about his personal life. So far, he'd evaded it.

Well, here goes, this is going to be a whopper.

"This is pretty personal," he confided. "Ever since I can remember I've had this image of the perfect woman for me. I've daydreamed about her, changing her hair color or her possible interests or talents or whatever as I changed and grew. If you were being Jungian you might call her my muse or anima. She shows up at night in my dreams and when I'm working on a romance like *Twilight Magic* she's the one I'm falling in love with. Not the actress. I don't know if this is part of other actors' processes or not."

"So that's why you don't fall in love with your costars."

"Exactly."

Good, she was buying it.

He continued, "She's the feminine part of myself, I guess."

"But this must put a crimp in your love life."

"My love life has plenty of crimps in it already," he winced with exaggeration.

"But I mean, what real woman could measure up to that perfection?"

"Oh, she's not perfect, she's simply perfect for me. I'm afraid she's a bit of a slob; her house is a mess and she's not real attentive to her appearance, but she's beautiful to me. Her life is a little out of control and she's not exactly malleable."

"So you've thought about her a lot, this muse."

"Yes, probably too much. Someday, I'll find her in real life and if she'll have me, we'll settle down and raise a whole passel of kids," he said, nodding his head in the direction of the next table which erupted with shrieking from a toddler who bumped his head on the table. His mom picked him up and held him.

Sean finished his quiche, washing it down with the chai. Interesting combination, but probably not the best choice he could have made. The flavors battled it out inside his mouth.

"So, are you still happy with your decision to move up here and be closer to your family?"

"I love it. It's great to spend time with them and I'm working on my two other brothers who don't live here. Yet."

"You don't miss the social whirl of L.A.?"

"Not at all. I do miss my friends, but I get back there for business and I always work in some socializing. When I lived there I did a lot of empty socializing just because there was this party or that opening. My time is better spent here, developing new projects, exercising, reading, getting my nieces and nephews all riled up before their bedtimes and then going home," he said, winking.

"So, you *are* planning on having children?"

"I'd love to, but I can't predict the future. I love kids. I think that's the most important work any of us can do. Nurturing and teaching new life."

"So what's up with the paternity suit that's been filed against you?"

He'd known she wasn't going to bypass that piece of hot/juicy. And he needed it cleared up right away. Didn't want Lily to misunderstand it.

"Well, it was filed last week. It's preposterous. I'm not aware that I've ever even met this woman. I do know the child isn't mine. I'm fully aware of who I have or have not had sex with. I told my lawyer I'm more than willing to submit DNA as soon as the baby's born, or earlier, to confirm it. If the child were mine, I'd be the last one trying to weasel out of any obligation, but it just ain't so. The baby's not mine."

He paused for a moment, then said, "I love kids and big families. My parents had fifteen kids, many of them adopted, so I'm really comfortable with a large family."

"So you haven't moved up to Seattle to hide, like everyone says you are."

"Hide, from whom? The whole world, including the paparazzi, know I'm here. Who would I be hiding from?"

"Nina?"

He laughed and said, "Someday, the world will understand that Nina's water under the bridge for me."

Except that he obviously wasn't for her. She'd called him this morning.

Again.

LILY

LILY SAT AT HER DILAPIDATED KITCHEN TABLE WITH HER neighbor, Janice. She raised the cup of coffee to her lips and sipped the thick, bitter liquid. Nothing like the smell and taste of coffee in the morning. This was her third cup and she almost felt awake. She hadn't slept much last night. Katie had a cold and woke up a lot, crying. And then Emily would wake up.

She shook her head, trying to clear it.

Janice munched on a slice of the banana, chocolate chip and hazelnut bread she'd brought over. The smell of the cooked bananas wafted over to Lily's nose, making her mouth water. She grabbed a slice of the bread.

Lily said, "I think I've gained about ten pounds since I moved in next door to you."

Janice laughed and said, "Nobody could tell. You're so lean and lanky to begin with." She washed the bread down with some coffee and said, "But you know what the problem is?"

"No, but I feel sure you're going to tell me."

"You're panicked."

"Hell yes, I'm panicked. What would you be?" Clearly, Janice had no idea how terrified she felt. Lily took a deep breath and yanked her long, blue T-shirt back into place. Then crossed and uncrossed her legs, noticing a light stain on her black leggings.

"Oh c'mon. Stop and think for a minute. You've been fantasizing madly about this guy, this very, very famous guy who you went out with for one horrible date. He just happens to move to Seattle, partly because he has family here. Then he shows up in Food King, which is normal. It's a popular store. He also has a Fremont address, which is close to the store. And let's say he was staring at you and came to your rescue. What healthy man wouldn't stare at you? It's just logical."

"Men don't stare at me unless they're thinking 'she's a big giraffe, eh?'"

"Yeah right. That's why people pay you to model. And how do you know what they're thinking? Did you ever ask them?"

Janice rearranged the daffodils in the mason jar that sat on the table. She'd brought them from her garden.

Janice wiped her hands, wet from the flowers, on her jeans and continued, "Okay. So the real problem was the Oscar ceremony that I DVR'd and showed you, isn't it?"

Lily buried her head in her hands.

"God, I'm so embarrassed," she said.

"Well, nobody knows it was you. Unless you told them or unless he told them your last name. Right?"

"But why did he even mention me?" Lily asked.

Janice rolled her eyes. "He's got the hots for you. Well, maybe more than the hots."

"He doesn't even know me," said Lily.

And she didn't want him to. She didn't want the extra attention. And she especially didn't want him to find out about the kids. To look closely at where they came from. Even she was afraid to pay much attention to that. That might bring someone else's gaze to her family's origins. Questions might be asked. She felt desperately afraid of someone taking her family away.

"You're just afraid."

"Of what in particular?"

"You've made out your shopping list for the man of your dreams and he shows up. You're afraid of being happy," said Janice.

Lily's mouth dropped open. Janice was so far off base, she almost wanted to laugh. Well, maybe there was a little truth in it. Mostly, it was just about the kids.

"See," said Janice, misunderstanding Lily's reaction. "You need to work on believing that you deserve to be happy."

"Perhaps you're right, but I don't think so," said Lily. She drained her coffee cup.

They both jumped at the sound of the doorbell.

"Probably somebody selling something," said Lily. She got up to weave her way through the towers of legos and small plastic animals which covered the living room floor. Opening the front door, she found a short man in a white uniform. He reminded her of some comedian who had a sitcom on TV. The name escaped her.

"Lily Toureau?" he asked.

"Yes,"

"Grocery delivery."

Then she noticed the hand truck with four plastic crates filled with food.

"I didn't order any groceries."

He scrolled through his tablet and said, "They're for you. It says they're paid for and you're set up for a regular delivery. The person who paid for them wants to remain anonymous. You might as well take them. It's free food. I'm not allowed to bring them back."

"Sure," she said, completely puzzled. "Come in, the kitchen's this way."

She shrugged her shoulders and raised her eyebrows at Janice as he followed her through the narrow path among the towers and into the kitchen.

"Cool legos," he said.

"My sons built it last night and made me promise to leave them up."

"Very cool. Maybe they'll turn out to be architects," he said.

He unloaded the crates from the hand truck and said, "You can keep the crates until next week, I'll get them then. There are four more crates outside I need to get." He left to make another trip.

"What's all this about?" asked Janice.

"It must be Sean. Who else could it be?" asked Lily.

She began unloading the crates, realizing how eerily close he'd come to choosing what she normally bought. As well as a few luxuries she wouldn't buy, a couple of huge bouquets which she put into glass jars. She didn't even own a vase. When she finished unloading everything both the refrigerator and freezer bulged with food. She piled all eight crates in the garage.

Janice sat at the table, drinking coffee and snickering.

Lily felt floored. There must have been about six hundred dollars worth of groceries in those crates.

"That was sweet," said Janice.

"He's getting back at me because I said I'd call and didn't," said Lily. She was filled with mixed emotions. Torn between feeling grateful for the gift, angry at the presumption she needed help. Which she did. Annoyed and a little freaked out that he'd watched her closely enough to know what she usually bought at the store.

"How is this getting you back?" asked Janice, shaking her

head in confusion and pointing at the counters stacked with canned food, bread and cookies which Lily hadn't put away yet.

"Trying to make me feel guilty?"

"You don't know that was his intention. Maybe he just wanted to help. Maybe he's trying to impress you, get your attention since you won't call him back. Maybe he wants to ask you out again."

"If he's so interested in me, why did he get another woman pregnant?"

"What?" asked Janice.

"It's been in the news. The patrimony suit some woman filed against him."

"Just because a suit's been filed doesn't mean there's any truth to it," said Janice, leaning back in her chair and staring at her.

"It costs a fair amount to do the whole legal thing. I wouldn't go to the trouble unless I was right," said Lily.

"Everyone's not as rational as you. She might be gambling he'll settle out of court. She might be doing it for attention. Or it might be an old failed relationship."

"Or she might be right."

"Well, time will tell. You're really upset about this aren't you?"

"No," lied Lily. This just added to the confusion about Sean and his intentions. And her feelings about him. She felt all jumbled up.

"I don't believe that," said Janice. "So what are you going to do?"

"I know what I need to do. Stop fantasizing about that man."

"No, you need to work out your fears around relationships. So when the right guy comes along, Sean or somebody else, you'll be ready. Not every man's going to leave you for the neighbor's diaper delivery guy, like your ex did."

Lily sighed. That was a huge fear she hadn't dealt with. After twelve years of marriage, her ex husband, who she'd thought was happy with the marriage, and straight, came out of the closet and left her for a guy. The feelings of betrayal and pain from that abandonment had never healed.

She changed the subject. "But I can't take any chances with my kids forming attachments and then getting hurt," she said, scraping spilled blue acrylic paint from the table top with her fingernail.

"Well, that's true, but you won't be able to protect them from getting hurt forever. And they would benefit from having a dad. If he's a keeper."

"Maybe. If...."

"So you need to be ready to grab him if he shows up. Just in case Sean isn't the one."

Lily snorted.

She got up from the table and stood looking at the pile of groceries still to put away. She opened the cupboard doors and began putting the most used things away. She'd have to buy more shelves to find room for the rest. Until then, maybe she could stack the packaged food out in the garage.

She turned to Janice and said, "I'm so glad the soccer games start for the girls this week. They've been practicing so long. Is Ann excited?" Ann, Janice's daughter, was in the same grade as Tracy and loved soccer as well.

"Yes, she is. But changing the subject won't work."

"What is it that you think I should do?"

"Take a gamble. Call him."

Fear rose up inside her. She couldn't call him. She didn't really want a relationship.

Janet repeated, "Call him. Find out what he wants. Thank him for the groceries. That at least deserves a call."

Lily took a deep breath. Janet was right. She should call him, at least to thank him for the groceries.

Did she have the guts?

SEAN

Sean sat in his car across the street from Lily's house. She wasn't home, but he hadn't expected her to be. She was probably working.

He turned the key and glanced at the dashboard clock. Five till noon. He'd scheduled the appointment with his sister Marcia for noon. The pristine white house that he sat in front of was for sale and he had a plan.

If only his head would stop throbbing, another bad headache on the way. He popped some mint gum in his mouth. Sometimes the chewing helped. He'd finally decided to start chewing gum. All his jeans, including the ones he was wearing today, were getting a little tight from eating at Casey's so often.

He shifted, adjusting his green flannel shirt which stuck to the seat.

The stress of evading the paparazzi was really beginning to bother him. It was becoming more difficult to find ways to disguise himself or find new modes of transportation they didn't see coming. But he had to keep Lily and the location of his family member's homes a secret from the paparazzi.

A white jeep drove up and Marcia got out. Tall with blond hair, dyed to hide the gray that peeked out at age fifty-two. She wasn't his biological sister, but a 'Gift child' as Mom called all the kids who simply appeared. Of all the kids only Casey and Sean had been conceived and born the old-fashioned way. Mom and Dad treated all the kids the same though. There seemed to be some sort of amnesia with the 'Gift children'. They always said that they felt as if they lived their entire lives with the family. Sean and Casey hadn't found out about any of it until they became adults and the Gift surfaced in Casey's life.

Marcia was on her phone, trying to wrap up a conversation. She waved at him and shifted from one foot to another, impatiently. She wore a navy skirt and blazer, as if she'd just come from the office or from showing another property.

He got out of the car and walked around the front yard. A bush with salmon colored flowers peeked over the back fence, which was painted white of course. Quince. That's what Casey had called the bush. Daffodil clumps filled the bed in front of the house, some of which had an overwhelmingly sweet fragrance. And pansies.

"Hi Sean," Marcia said, slipping the phone into her purse.

"Hi Sis, good to see you," he said, hugging her.

"Sorry for being late. I showed a house up in Shoreline and there was an accident on the freeway."

"It's no problem. I had reading to do." Which was true. He had a script on his iPad, that he told his agent he'd look at. But he didn't really want to, so he was ignoring it.

"Are you okay? You look a little pale."

"Just another headache coming on."

"You haven't found what's triggering them yet?" she asked, touching his shoulder.

"No. One of these days," he lied.

"So, you're interested in the house, but I didn't have time yesterday to ask why. You just bought a condo."

"Well, I like the location. I've been talking to Bob. He, Melanie and the two kids have been thinking of leaving Eugene and moving up here. There's no work for him right now down there. I offered to buy a house for them. Part of my plan to get everybody to move here, to be close to Mom and Dad."

Marcia's jaw dropped open. "Wow, that's very generous of you, Sean."

"Well, it's selfishness, really. I just want to make up for all the lost years I haven't had time for family."

"Okay, let's go in then."

It didn't take long to tour the house. He took photos with his phone so he could send them to Bob. Everything was neat, tidy and repaired. In pristine condition.

As they walked around his headache came on full force. By the time they went back outside, his head felt ready to split like a ripe watermelon dropped onto the sidewalk. He put his sunglasses on.

"I wouldn't dawdle with a decision," she said. "I don't mean to pressure you, but the market's hot these days."

"Emailing as we speak," he said. "I'll get back to you later tonight. Are you going to Casey's on Sunday?"

"I'll be there. Might even get George to come and watch the kids hunt for eggs!" she said.

They hugged and she got into her jeep and drove off.

He stood by his car until she rounded the corner, then went to the blue house next door and rang the bell. There was no answer. From the house on the other side of the one for sale, his greeting was a small, yappy dog who only made his headache worse.

He crossed the street and saw the strangest thing. One minute Lily's porch was empty, the next a teenage boy with shoulder-length black hair sat on the steps. He had appeared out of nowhere. He was plugged into an iPod, listening to music and reading a textbook. Sean knew his name was Max.

How did he know that? Where had it come from? He also knew Max was fifteen and was gifted at drawing anime.

He'd stopped in the middle of the street to stare at the boy. Max glanced up from his book, smiled and waved, then went back to reading. Sean felt completely dumbfounded.

He kept walking to the house next door to Lily's, on the corner. He knocked on the door. Rhododendrons with blooms of pinks, red and even a limey green, threatened to smother the white house. He heard noise inside and the door opened. An elderly woman looked at him suspiciously through the screen door. He took off his sunglasses.

"Hello," said Sean.

"Hello," she said. "Can I help you?"

"I'm Sean O'Neill. I don't want to bother you, but I've been looking at the house for sale across the street. I think it's perfect for my brother, his wife and their kids. I was wondering if you could tell me anything about the house, the neighborhood or the schools."

"Oh," she said. She opened the screen door and stepped outside. She wore a navy blue sweat suit. "Well, the Nelson's were wonderful neighbors. They raised their two sons. I'm sad they moved away. He always spent his spare time tinkering with things around the house." She smiled at Sean. "He rewired the entire house a few years ago. I know he fixed plumbing and they had a new roof put on last year. He also kept up the yard. But they got tired of all the work and wanted to travel."

"What are the other neighbors like?"

"Well, Mr. Sullivan," she said pointing to the blue house, "he's retired and travels a lot. And Alice," she nodded towards the house with the yappy dog, "she works for Microsoft and is never home." She shook her head disapprovingly.

"What about the folks on this side of the street?" he asked.

"Well, Lily my next door neighbor, she's so sweet. She has kids so your brother's children would have someone to play with. They're nice kids, but she's go her hands full. And Janice and Tom on the other side of her have a daughter as well," she said.

"Doesn't Lily's husband help her out with the kids?"

"No, she's divorced. A single mother with that many children...still she does all right. She deserves a nice man to come along, but says she doesn't have time to date."

"Well, thank you very much for your time. I think this might be the perfect home for my brother."

"You're very welcome," she said. "I hope it works out."

He turned and saw Lily drive up in her battered maroon wagon. She got out and opened the back. A girl and boy went and pulled things out over the tailgate. A younger boy got out of the back door as well. Lily tossed her keys to the older boy who ran to the house, shouldering a heavy backpack. That must be Teddy. The girl was Tracy. The younger boy, Jim.

Lily pulled a red, canvas bag out and was handing it to Tracy. Lily looked over and saw him, then promptly dropped the bag, along with an open diaper bag. Bottles, pacifiers and toys rolled everywhere.

"Mommm," whined Tracy.

He couldn't hear what Lily said, but she handed Tracy a green bag, then knelt down to pick things up.

Max ran from the porch and said, "It's okay Mom, I'll pick it up."

Lily clearly hadn't seen him before. Her mouth dropped open and she stared as he lay down in the street, reaching under the car for an escaping bottle. Together, they hurriedly gathered the remaining diaper bag contents and stuffed them in.

Lily stood, dusting herself off, not making much progress with her now dirty, white T-shirt.

"Max, hurry or you'll miss 'Universe 2'," yelled Teddy from the doorway.

"I'm coming," said Max, cramming everything back into the diaper bag and running inside with it.

Lily's neighbor tapped Sean's arm and said, "Oh there's Lily now. Why don't you go meet her?" she asked.

"She looks a little busy," he said, watching Lily shake her head as she was half in and half out of the back seat, unbuckling a child. Jim, the younger boy unbuckled another child, the one Sean had seen at the grocery store, and walked her slowly into the house.

Sean wanted to vanish into the ozone. He really had been trying to avoid her.

"Oh, I'm sure she has a minute." The old lady waved to Lily and grabbed his hand, dragging him down the street. "Oh Lily," she said. The woman was surprisingly strong.

He couldn't break her grip without wrenching her arm. His face felt warm. He didn't embarrass easily. He tried to convince himself that this was all perfectly normal and felt the heat drain from his face. Mostly.

Lily picked up the child and walked towards them.

"Hi Arlene. How's James doing?"

"Oh, he's much better. That was a nasty flu. I'll be glad when he's up and around again. Your Max is such a thoughtful boy."

"Yes, yes he is," said Lily with a strange look on her face.

Had Max done something for Arlene or was it because he helped Lily pick everything up? Sean was at a loss to figure it out, but he figured Lily was too.

Arlene continued, "This young man, I'm sorry what did you say your name was?"

"Sean. Sean O'Neill," he said, holding his hand out to Lily.

She moved Katie, he was sure her name was Katie, to the other hip and shook his hand, an amused look on her face.

"This young man is thinking of buying the Nelson's house."

"Oh?" asked Lily, raising an eyebrow.

"Yes, for my brother and his family. They've wanted to move up here for some time. I'm trying to persuade them they need to be closer to the rest of the family.

"Oh, that's nice," said Lily, jostling Katie on her hip, trying to entertain her.

Sounds like I'm a meddling idiot. He felt stupid and inept. Unable to come out with the right words. His head was exploding with pain. This was all a bad idea. He should leave, but he couldn't stop talking.

"Our folks are getting older and the rest of the family's moved to Seattle. So I'm doing what I can to get my last two brothers up here."

"Big family?" she asked, not meeting his eyes.

"Well, yes. I have fifteen siblings. Some adopted, some not."

Lily looked at him. She had an undecipherable look on her face, but he could swear she was reevaluating him. Like a new pair of jeans that she'd bought, discarded and was reconsidering.

"Fifteen," said Arlene. "You must have kept your mom busy."

"Yes, we did. Now it's our turn to take care of her and Dad, although I'm not sure they'd agree with that," he laughed.

Lily moved a squirming Katie to her other hip.

"She must be heavy. What's her name?" asked Sean.

"Katie, and she's getting heavier every day, aren't you darlin'?

She remained focused on Katie, cooing at her. She was intentionally ignoring him and he desperately wanted to talk to her about something meaningful. How could he be at such a loss for words? He'd never had this problem.

"How many kids do you have?" he asked.

Panic flickered across her face, replaced by coolness.

Just then a white SUV roared down the street, windows rolled down, cameras flashing.

"Oh my," said Arlene. She began to wave, smiling at them. "I'm over here, boys."

Damn. They found him. And worse they found Lily.

"Looks like your entourage is here," she said, her lips drawn thin and her jaws clenched.

"I'm sorry. I really thought I'd lost them."

He turned to Arlene and said, "It was nice meeting you." She really was a cute old lady.

"It was nice meeting you," she said, winking.

What was that about? He shook his head and turned to his car. One of the paparazzi got out of the SUV and followed him to his car, snapping away. He kept his expression noncommittal and got in the Prius and drove off, followed by the SUV.

His headache was raging now. He'd probably completely blown it with her. And he had so many questions.

Did she know about the Gift? Where was her twin? The Gift always ran with the lines of naturally born twins, brother and sister. Each one had a soul mate, as well as a twin sibling, who carried the Gift. His brother in law James had discovered no other pattern.

And Lily was his soul mate. He'd actually seen Max come into being.

Smiling through the pain of his throbbing head, Sean turned onto the main street, heading towards home. He didn't feel up to trying to lose the paparazzi again today. Not that it had worked the first time.

He needed to go home and close all the curtains and sleep the headache off. Then call Bob, if he didn't call first.

Mostly, he needed to make a plan to capture Lily's heart. Although how that was going to work was anybody's guess. She hated him. But he couldn't let this drag out much longer. She already had six children. More would be coming.

LILY

LILY PUSHED A CLUMP OF WET HAIR OUT OF HER EYES AND
watched Tracy dribble down the soccer field. She played
midfield and wove around the defenders on the other team.
The teams were evenly matched and the game was intense and
no one had been able to score yet, even though it was the
second half.

Over to Lily's right a cluster of parents sat on cushions they
brought for the wet bleachers. There was no space left there,
but she hadn't gotten organized enough to buy a cushion, let
alone bring it to the game.

She wiped the rain off her face. Next time she'd wear a hat.
And rain pants. And boots. Her raincoat just let the water slide
off onto her soaking wet leggings. Maybe she should get some
La Fierce rain gear. She laughed, but then her thoughts turned
to the date, and Sean.

She had a sneaking suspicion that Sean noticed her growing
family, when no one else had. Not her parents who'd come back
to town last week, Janice or Arlene. But maybe it was just

paranoia. No one else noticed so, why would he? But he had asked her how many kids she had.

The whoops and cheers from the other parents brought her back to the present.

"Whoo hoo!" she cheered as Tracy's team scored a goal.

The other team called a time out to change a player. Tracy's team ran off the field in search of drinks and towels to wipe off some of the rain. Lily began to pour some sports drinks when she saw Sean walking towards her from the end of the field. She dropped the cup and the stickiness poured down her legging and onto her running shoes.

"Mom, geez, watch out," said Tracy.

Lily felt flustered. She picked up the cup, wiped it off on her leggings and poured more for Tracy. Her bare feet squished around in her shoes as she pulled a towel of out the bag beside her. Her feet now felt gooey, sticky and cold. Tracy downed the cup and gave it back to Lily, who handed the towel to her. Tracy quickly rubbed off some of the water, tossed the towel back and ran onto the field.

Lily tucked everything back into the bag and stood up to find Sean right next to her.

"Hi, how are you?" he asked.

Her face burned with embarrassment and she smelled like the fruity sports drink. Everything, the wet, the gooeyness, the unlikeliness of seeing him here piled up into one uncomfortable mess. She thought about trying to wipe herself off, but it was all just hopeless.

"Fine, just fine," she said, clenching her jaw. Where the hell had he come from? Why was he here? "I just spilled a cup of sports drink all over me. I suppose the rain will dilute it."

Sean laughed.

He thinks I'm funny. Or crazy. It didn't matter what he

thought. She couldn't figure out if she felt irritated or flattered that he came to talk to her.

"What are you doing here?" she asked, trying to make small talk. Why she didn't know.

"I was just getting some information from the school for my brother. I saw the game going on and thought I'd come over to look. I saw you and wanted to say hello. I don't know that many people in Seattle, outside of my family and the small horde of paparazzi I constantly try to avoid." He waved at the three drenched guys with cameras who stood nearby, taking photos and filming them.

He's lonely. How can a man with so much family and so many fans be lonely? She looked back at the field. The ref was talking to one of the other team's players. One of Tracy's team mates was lying on the ground. Maisie.

Lily glanced at Sean and sighed. They kept running into each other. Sooner or later they'd have to talk about that awful date. He was watching the action on the field. The muscles of his face looked tight, tense. Dark circles hovered beneath his eyes. Had he been sick? Were the headaches still bothering him?

The other parents yelled as the game picked up. Lily watched as Tracy got the ball, dribbled it, then passed it off to a teammate just before an opposing player went for it.

"Good job Trace," she yelled. She watched the game for a while.

"Your daughter's very good."

"Yes, she is. She eats, breathes and dreams soccer. I have to bounce the ball off her head repeatedly to get her to study," she laughed. "Is your brother going to take the house?"

"Yes, he is. It closed yesterday. He's coming up this weekend to teach me how to fix things."

"Fix things?"

"Yeah. The inspection turned up some slight structural damage. My brother's a carpenter and I'm completely clueless about these things. So he's going to teach me how to do things. I'm sure it's sort of a Tom Sawyer thing. I'll work and he'll watch."

"But don't you have movies to make, books to write?"

He ran his hand through drenched hair, the water only made it more wavy.

"Well, I'm still trying to decide between a couple of scripts. Neither begins shooting until next year. So I'm taking some time off to deal with my headaches. Luckily I'm at a place in my career where I can afford to do that," he said, with his rich, resonant voice. He looked her straight in the eyes and smiled that charming smile.

She almost melted. Almost.

She couldn't let him get close to her. What if he noticed about the kids? What if she lost the kids?

He said, "If I play my cards right and don't make any terribly stupid moves, then I can be in a good film every year or two and still get interesting parts offered to me. And have enough free time to get a life."

She blurted out, "Well, I guess you don't need the money," then instantly regretted it. She felt embarrassed again. How could she be so rude?

"The money doesn't hurt. Allows me to help people out when they need it. I don't lead a lavish lifestyle. If I wanted to retire today, I could. But I'm not working for the money. I never have."

"Lucky you to be in that place." That sounded bitter. And maybe it was. She hadn't worked for money either, until the kids started appearing. Now she scraped for it. She'd love to quit modeling and spend all their time with them.

She said, "I never thanked you for buying us all those groceries and having them delivered...."

"I don't know what you mean," he said, his eyes widening in surprise.

She didn't believe it for a minute. "I know it was you."

He shrugged and said, "I just wanted to help."

"Well you did, and thank you. But please cancel the account."

"Why?" he asked.

"It makes me uncomfortable. I can't possibly pay you back. I feel like you're trying to buy me." She watched the game go back and forth with the kids on the field getting muddier and muddier. Soon no one would be able to tell who was on what team.

"I'm not trying to buy you," he said. His mouth drooped with disappointment. "Like I said, I just wanted to help. You need the food and I have plenty of money. If I don't help the people around me, then what good am I?"

Now she felt like a heel. She was confused, wanted him in her life. Yet wanted him gone as well. She felt afraid of being exposed as a mutant child attracting magnet and didn't want him or anyone else to find out about the kids. But she did need the food. Grudgingly she said, "You're right. I need the food, but I can't pay you back and that makes me feel guilty."

"It's not a loan, simply an ongoing gift. You owe me nothing." He paused and shoved his hands in the pockets of his jeans. The constant drizzle became a downpour. It dripped off his hair and ran down his face.

She had an overwhelming urge to brush the raindrops off his face, to touch him. She dug through her bag, found the towel and wiped her own face instead. It felt dangerous to stand to close to him. He was intoxicating. She tried, but couldn't move off any farther. Unable to even lift her feet, she stayed still.

The sound of rain drummed on the earth around them.

He said, "I don't want to ruin what I've done as a gift. So, I'm not sure how to ask this. I wonder if you'd consider going out with me again. Giving it another try?"

She stared at him. Was he really saying what she thought? He just gazed back at her, waiting for her reply. Which she didn't have.

Taking a deep breath, she said, "I don't even remember what happened on the date we had. I had an accident that day at work. Hurt my back. Between the muscle relaxant, the pain killer, the espresso and the wine, I was a total mess. And I remember nothing."

"Well, it was a fine date," he said.

"Liar! What happened?" she asked, hands on her hips.

"Okay. It was the worst date I've ever had, but I did feel like you weren't all there or at least not fully responsible for your actions," he said looking away.

Lily glanced in the other direction as the ball went out of bounds. The other parents weren't watching the game. They were watching Sean and her. They recognized him. She felt very self conscious. He simply ignored them. He must be used to being stared at.

"Do you want the short version or the long?" he asked.

"Give me the short version, I'm not sure I could handle the long."

At that moment the ref blew a whistle. She looked to see that one of Tracy's teammates was down, but with all the mud, it was unclear who. The ref was giving someone a red card. One of the moms from the opposing team launched herself off their bleachers and onto the field.

She could see it was Violet who was down. Her mom, seeing her daughter get up from the ground and limp around, erupted from the parent's bench and ran onto the field, screaming her daughter's name. Other teammates' parents went along, trying to hold her back.

The opposing player's mom was swinging her fists wildly. The craziness on the field seemed to work as a distraction for all the parents.

"So tell me," Lily said.

"Well, I picked you up and blathered on about this and that. You were very quiet. I think you said about twenty words the entire night. I took you to the restaurant, ordered for you when you asked me to, tried to get you to talk. I was very uncomfortable. You accidentally knocked your third glass of wine off the table, dove for it, tackled a waiter who dumped an entire tray full of salads on me. You sat on the floor, laughing hysterically. I pulled you up, tried to wipe myself off and leave. I tugged you along after me. You twisted away and the force pushed me into the pond in the restaurant's foyer...." He stopped and looked at the chaos on the soccer field. She could see his jaw clenching, as if he was trying to control anger.

She felt mortified. The tabloid articles had been true. She'd thought everything was exaggerated. Heat flowed into her face. She wanted to disappear.

He continued. "I fell in and came up wearing all manner of slimy, smelly plants. And I lost it. I lost my temper and dragged you to the car and told you to get in. You were still laughing until you slapped me and walked to the bus stop. Of course people were taking photos with their phones and I wondered if you'd set me up. I drove around the block a couple times, then stopped at the bus stop, apologized for losing my temper and offered you a ride home. You refused, so I drove off. I tried to call you. The first time I got your answering machine. Then when you didn't return my call, I called again. Your number was disconnected," he said. He shrugged and looked down, as if resigned to failure.

He was hurt. It never occurred to her that she had hurt him. She felt an ache begin. It stretched from her throat to below her sternum and spread all through the back of her ribs. She didn't know what to say as her eyes welled with tears.

Gazing out on to the field, she watched the other parents trying to control the two erupting moms. Violet was huddled with her teammates, clearly incredibly embarrassed by her mom. The other player's mom belted one of the dads and he fell flat on the ground. She turned back to the referee who waved a red card at her. The woman reminded Lily of a mad bull.

The paparazzi were taking photos of the game as well as of her and Sean. Finally, she turned to him and said, "I felt embarrassed and angry. I couldn't remember anything about the date. I didn't know why. Only that you'd been unpleasant. Now I know why. I moved that week and dropped my land line. And I hadn't given you my cell number. I'd been planning on moving for a while, my apartment building was being torn down to build condos."

"You moved with a bad back?" he challenged her.

"My parents were in town. And Teddy and Tracy had come to live with me. Between Dad, Teddy and Tracy, I didn't have to lift anything heavier that a pair of shoes. And myself. They made me sit around. I feel awful about the whole mess that date was. I'm so sorry to have put you through that, I intended for nothing like that to happen."

"So will you go out with me again? I'm assuming you'll need someone to watch your children. I'd be happy to pay for that."

"I'm sorry, but this isn't possible," was all that she could get out of her mouth. The ache which had been forming turned into knots. This couldn't be happening. Her life had changed so much in the last five months. She didn't really want a romantic entanglement. Life was complicated enough and she couldn't risk anyone finding out about the kids' origins, especially all the paparazzi who followed him.

"Why?" he asked, calmly.

She didn't have an answer to give him. 'Because a child is likely to appear in the middle of our date.' She needed to say something. She could feel the tension of silence growing as he waited for an answer.

"I'm not looking for a relationship right now. My life is so complicated. Trying to juggle daily life is more than I can handle."

"Oh." He looked like she'd hit him. Had he never been rejected before? Then she remembered some big hoohaw about his public humiliation by Nina Vicente.

Lily felt guilty, she hated hurting people. But she couldn't let him get closer to her.

The ref finally got all the parents off the field, but the opposing team was one player short. And one parent short. The mom had gotten thrown out of the park. She grabbed all her stuff pulled her red-carded daughter along and stomped off to her car. The game began again.

The parents and paparazzi's attention was all back on her and Sean. How could he live like this? Under such scrutiny all the time.

Sean asked, "Is there nothing I can say or do to change your mind?"

"It's not you. I just can't date again. For years. Maybe decades."

He pulled a small notebook out of his jacket, wrote on it and handed her the piece of rain spotted paper. It had his name, phone number and email on it. "If you should ever change your mind, or just want to talk, please call me. But I have to warn you, I'm looking for a life partner, not a one night stand. I'm looking for a woman to marry and start a family with."

"I'm not who you're looking for. I've already got a full blown family," she said, looking at her huge freezing feet.

"I'm aware of that. I'd be more than happy to become part of your family."

"You don't even know me."

"And I never will if you don't give me a chance."

"I'm sorry, but no. It won't work," she said, looking back towards the game. She stuffed the piece of paper in her raincoat pocket.

"I don't want to pressure you," he said. "I'd better be going." He walked back in the direction he'd come, his shoulders drooping and head down. Drenched to the skin, he looked truly miserable. Followed by the trio of paparazzi who looked equally wretched.

She felt sad for him and for herself, but what she'd said was true. She wasn't ready for a partner, even though her attraction to him felt overpowering. It took all her strength not to follow him.

There was a tap on her should and she turned to find Janice standing there.

"What was that about?" she asked.

"Oh, you're here.

"Yes, and...?"

"Did you see the fight and the red card?" asked Lily.

"Yes, and...?

"He wanted me to go out with him."

"And you said yes, right?" asked Janice.

"Wrong."

"Should I kill you now or do you want to explain first?" Janice glared at her.

"I can't go out with him. I'm not ready for a partner. And I had that horrendous first date with him. He just told me what happened. Apparently everything the tabloids wrote was true."

"C'mon, you were on all those drugs, espresso and wine. And first dates are mostly hideous. When Tom and I first went out, I hated him. How can you pass up a guy like that? Aside from the fact that even soaking wet he's one of the most gorgeous men most of us have met in the flesh. He thanks you when he wins an Oscar, even after that date. He rescues you at the grocery store when you forget your wallet. He has groceries delivered to your house. Lily, you need to rethink this. I said it before, I know. But you dream and fantasize about him and when he shows up in real life, you reject him." Janice shook her head.

Janice's daughter had come off the field for a time out and was pulling at her sleeve. Tracy was in a huddle with a couple of friends, sharing a drink with one of them. They were all howling with laughter about something.

Lily didn't know what to say to Janice. She felt like a worm. Janice was right, but she didn't know the whole story. How to explain her little problem of accumulating children to Sean. It terrified even her when she really thought about it. She could barely cope now and had a peculiar feeling more kids were on their way. She didn't know how to make it stop or where it would end. She couldn't even go there.

Lily squished her feet around in her shoes more. Despite all the water, the sticky sports drink was still there. And how could it be so cold in April. It felt like February. It felt freezing. But if that were the case, her shoes would be filled with ice. Or maybe not. Did sugar water freeze?

How were Mom and Dad doing with all the other kids at the movies? She'd tried once again to tell them about everything. They couldn't see it happening. They just thought she was overworked and needed rest. Dad sent her money and they came to town more often to take the kids off her hands.

Which felt wonderful, but didn't come close to solving the problem.

If her parents didn't believe her then who would? Certainly not Sean.

No matter how much she wanted him.

She never really had worked through her ex's betrayal. If there had been no kids, she probably would have gone out with Sean again, even after that horrible date. Even though she didn't feel attractive, didn't really feel safe enough emotionally to go out with anyone. And she didn't want the kids to get attached to someone who might break their hearts when he left. She'd seen it with other single moms. She could handle her own heartbreak, if she needed to, but not handing the kids any more pain than they'd already had.

The game began again and she turned her attention back to it. She would not call Sean. Not under any circumstances.

But when he'd talked to her, even here in the cold and wet, she'd longed to cuddle up in his arms. Feel his warm breath on her neck, his hands beneath her raincoat and her sweater. Rubbing her back. Skin upon skin.

Lily sighed. She felt so torn. What should she do?

SEAN

SEAN PULLED UP OUTSIDE CASEY'S HOUSE JUST AS HIS CELL rang. The scent of her lilacs in full bloom wafted in through the open car window.

He pulled his phone out of a pocket. Nina Vicente.

"Hello," he said, his shoulders tightening.

"Sean?" Her sultry voice instantly recognizable.

"Hi Nina."

"How are you?"

"Good."

"My life is having its usual ups and downs."

It must be down for her to call him.

"So, why are you calling?" he asked, abruptly. He wished he'd worn shorts instead of jeans and a T-shirt. The sun was out and he felt too hot. He still hadn't figured out Seattle weather.

"Always to the point. Well, I haven't heard from you in so long and then you vanished into the rain forest way up north and I don't even get to see you at parties anymore. I wondered what you were up to."

"I'm on my way to a meeting and running late, so this call has to be short. Mostly I've been avoiding paparazzi."

"Now how do you accomplish that?"

"It involves using multiple modes of transportation and sometimes disguises. An out of step with the world hippie here, a street person there, that sort of thing. The more unexpected the better. Walking several blocks sometimes fools them, so they set off on foot, then I have a bicycle stashed somewhere or a hearse waiting or I'm the last person on the bus."

She laughed with delight. "And is there any reason you're evading them? A torrid love affair perhaps?"

So that was what she was after.

"No, It's just a little game we play. I like to mess with them. But there is that endless supply of naked baby photos and stories of childhood humiliations that my family could supply if pressured, so I try to keep the paparazzi away from them."

"Better be careful. The paparazzi will get you in the end. I don't want to keep you, but I'm shooting a film in Vancouver next month and wondered, if I popped down to Seattle for a day of shopping would you be free for dinner?"

Sean shifted in the car seat and took a deep breath. He didn't want to get involved with Nina again, that much felt clear. They'd dated and lived together for five years, although the last year of their relationship he discovered she had cheated on him, with several other men. Apparently, he bored her.

The evening before he won his first Oscar, for *The Way of the World*, Nina tore their lives apart. She'd gone to her stylist's to dress, do hair, makeup, etc. Apparently she'd done more than that. That evening Nina arrived at their house and looked ravishing as always. She was also totally strung out on cocaine, a new habit of hers. He tried to get her to stay home, but she wouldn't have any of it. They went to the ceremony. His tension level had been through the roof, he never felt comfortable at those huge events anyway. He hadn't minded the attention on the red carpet as Nina paraded around and stole the show. It took some of the pressure off him. But when she fidgeted during the entire ceremony and mumbled a continuous stream of catty remarks in his ear, it made him crazy. After the ceremony she whined through most of the interviews, until he sent her off to begin the rounds of parties, telling her he'd catch up.

"Sean? Wouldn't it be great to have a nice, quiet dinner to talk?"

When he didn't reply to her question again, Nina continued chattering about the great Bohemian shopping in Seattle. She would go on about this store or that one. His thoughts slipped back to the past to remember why he didn't want to get involved with her again.

He'd finished up the interviews and felt 'over the moon' as his grandfather Sean would have said. Then he walked into the studio party at the same moment a reporter tripped over a pair of feet protruding from under a banquet table. The tablecloth got ripped off and revealed Nina and one of his costars, James, having sex under the table. The press and other media had a feeding frenzy. Even with Nina's publicist there to quickly drag her off, the photographers got a lot of action.

Sean felt humiliated and bitter. That it happened on this most special of nights just made it worse. He went home and drank whatever he could find in the house until he passed out. The next day his shocked and heartbroken face showed up plastered over every magazine and tabloid that didn't have photos of Nina hugging Sam.

Nina gave interviews stating that Sean hadn't touched her for over a year, how desperate she felt for affection and several other lies. Over the next few months stories, which were mostly true, about sexual abuse by her father slowly leaked out.

Probably guided by her publicist. Nina very publicly went into drug rehab. Then she starred in a critically acclaimed movie about a woman recovering from an abusive relationship. She weathered the storm, was able to control the spin and sent her career skyrocketing.

He'd given no personal interviews, except one, in which he stated, "It would be wrong for me to give personal details about a relationship involving another person. I will tell you I don't believe her version of what happened between us and neither should anyone else." Then he packed up his belongings, sold the house and got on a plane to Kuala Lumpur for a year to film and hide. He didn't date again, for years. He just didn't trust anyone to let them get that close. And he didn't trust his own judgement about women.

Sean shook himself back to the present. A breeze blew through the open car windows.

He wouldn't get burned again. He was a different person now. Their relationship had been exciting and intense. Nina could be very seductive, but he trusted himself enough to know he could resist her.

The idea of a relationship with Lily felt much more intriguing, but he couldn't figure out how to make that happen. She didn't want a relationship. She didn't even want to see him. He felt like she'd slammed him to the ground. More than once.

But Nina apparently did want him. He still remembered the times when their relationship worked. They had been terrific. Well, he'd flip a coin about whether to see her. A desperate way to solve a dilemma.

He picked one out of the cup holder and tossed it. Heads.

"Sure. Come on down. It'd be fun to see you," he said, not sounding quite convincing to himself.

"Lovely," she said, relief purring in her voice. I'll call you once I'm in Vancouver and my schedule's confirmed."

"Great. Well, I'd better get into my meeting."

"See you soon, Sean."

He stared at the phone. Wasn't that intriguing? The woman he wanted turned him down flat and the one he didn't want seemed about to take up the chase again. Why was that? And had he just made a stupid mistake?

He got out of the car and walked up to Casey and James' blue bungalow. Clearly, she'd been out in the garden recently. Piles of pulled weeds and dried sticks lay around indicating she'd been interrupted by the kids.

He knocked on the door.

Someday. Someday, I'll have my own kids.

He sat at Casey's dark wood, kitchen table next to the window overlooking her back garden. She poured cups of steaming Earl Grey tea and then went to the fridge to get cream. He munched on a currant scone, still disconcerted from the phone call.

He tried to distract himself by looking at her perfectly tidy kitchen. She and James had decorated it. The walls were painted white with Wedgwood Blue accents, to match her china, and dark, antique beams and cabinets. It looked very English.

"So," she said, sitting down next to him, "I've drawn up a guest list. There's at least thirty adults on it and I'm afraid to count the kids." She pushed a pad of paper at him. The list of names took all the first page.

"Hmm. You sure you want to have the Anniversary Party here?" He loved all the kids, but there must be at least forty children from his siblings alone.

"Yes, I do. But we better think about renting one of those big outdoor tents, along with the chairs, in case it rains."

"That sounds good. These scones are great."

"Thank you. About time you noticed."

He stuck his tongue out at her.

"So, what do we tell Mom and Dad?" she asked.

"Why don't we just tell them that you and I want to take them out to dinner on their anniversary? I'll pick them up and then come here to get you. Of course they'll want to come in and see the kids. We'll have everybody hide and then we'll jump 'em," he said.

"That sounds plausible."

"Plausible, just plausible?" he asked. "Well, what's your plan?"

"I don't have one. You're the devious one. The evil twin."

"Well, my angelic twin sister," he said, putting a hand on her shoulder, "I've always found that when you're being devious, simplicity is best. Always follow the most logical actions and when lying stick as closely to the truth as possible."

She laughed and shook her head in disbelief. "So how's it working in your personal life?"

"I don't usually feel a need to be devious in my daily life. Except for the paparazzi. I try to save deviousness for my love life," he said, picking up the vase of lilacs from the table and inhaling deeply. The sweet scent filled with childhood memories of Casey and him playing spies in Mom's lilac hedge.

"So, how is your love life?"

"A couple of possibilities, none of them good," he said, leaning back in his chair and gazing out the window at the black/purple tulips. He felt strange talking about Lily. On one hand he felt like a complete failure with her. But he also needed to talk about their connection with someone who could understand.

"How can a gorgeous, brilliant, famous and rich man like you, sexiest man of the year, have a nonexistent love life?" she asked, raising an eyebrow.

He sipped some tea and said, "I don't know, but it sucks."

"How many kids are there?"

"Six at last count. With all the usual explanations: adoption, foster child, virgin birth and so on," he said, waving his hand dramatically. "But the coolest thing is, I was there when the last one appeared." He grinned at her.

"What are you going to do?" she asked, staring at him over the rim of her teacup.

"I don't know. My deviousness is failing me at the moment. I've tried several tactics, but since she flat out rejected my offer of paid childcare and dinner, I've felt like someone punched me in the gut."

"She's afraid, poor woman."

"Yeah, well this poor woman just drop kicked your brother. Again," he said, reaching for another scone.

"Serves you right. You've been getting to cocky."

"Gee thanks."

"But doesn't her family know? Parents, brothers, sister?"

"She was adopted by a childless couple who are now in their seventies. No signs of any siblings. Besides, did Mom and Dad notice with you? We had to tell them. You had to tell me. Even James didn't believe you."

"Oh, my god," Casey covered her mouth.

"What is she thinking? Tell me. You've been there."

Casey said, "She probably has no idea why this is happening to her and not a clue how to stop it."

"You said that before. What else?"

She grabbed his arm. "Sean, you have to tell her. She's probably feeling paranoid someone will find out or notice. That's why she won't let you get close. And I only had four kids, she has six. She must be completely terrified."

"Right. How am I supposed to tell her? I humiliated her, embarrassed her, stalked her. She hates me."

"You have to find a way or she'll end up with a million kids.

You know some of the stories that James found about the Gift were tragic. Women committing suicide before their soul mate manned up and consummated the relationship, that sort of thing. You must tell her. And soon!"

He remembered when children first appeared to Casey. She told him about it. At first he didn't believe her. It just sounded too bizarre, but there the kids were. She'd been so afraid someone would find out and take them away from her. Finally they had gone to her parents, who shed some light on the Gift and what they knew about it. The hard part had been getting James to understand.

"I'll keep trying, but I'm feeling rather hopeless about her." He sighed and said, "And ironically, Nina called today."

"Nina? That bitch? I thought she was long gone."

"So did I."

"You're not considering taking her back? Not after what she did to you?"

"No. No, I don't think so. I'm just meeting her for dinner."

"Sean, she's even more conniving than you and she *does* use it in her daily life. So watch out."

"Yeah, I know." He glanced at his watch and said, "Hey, we better wrap up this party planning. I've got a meeting in an hour and need to make it to Capital Hill."

"Okay," she said, staring at her clipboard. "So, I'll take care of the food, along with Janie. We'll put George in charge of the tent and chairs. Sam can deal with the music. Marcia can email and call everyone to get them here on time and let them know what their share of the cost is. You're in charge of getting Mom and Dad here and making sure they're surprised. Around five, I think. We'll put Jules in charge of beverages and Shelby and Ondrea can plan entertainment for the kids. Carlotta's such a great photographer, we'll have her do that. Is that everything?"

"Shiny. Why don't we just open our own catering and party business?"

"Don't tempt me. I'd love nothing better than to get us all to start a business together. Now get out of here, Mr. Movie Star," she said, shooing him out the door.

He grabbed another scone as he left, knowing it was expected. He'd save it for breakfast tomorrow.

"And tell her. Before I see you next," said Casey.

"I'll do my best," he said, waving.

He drove off heading for the bridge. He just couldn't figure out exactly how he was going to accomplish that. He hadn't realized Lily must be suffering so much. The side of her he always saw was calm and cool. Except for the clumsiness thing. But that had been there, even when they first met. She wouldn't let him close enough to see any fear or anxiety.

How was he going to get her to talk to him long enough to tell her?

LILY

LILY CRAMMED ALL THE KIDS INTO THE CAR AND DROPPED the four older ones at their different schools. She needed to get a van. Not everyone had seat belts or even seats now. Then she drove to Green Lake and loaded Emily and Katie into the new high tech stroller Mom and Dad had bought. She felt grateful to her parents. It wasn't something she could have afforded on her own.

She looked up at the overcast sky, but pulled off her sweatshirt anyway. It was still chilly, but she'd warm up as she ran. So, stripped down to a tank top and running shorts, she took off on the 2.8 mile path, jogging slowly and pushing the stroller. There were already lots of people out. Running, walking with and without dogs, cycling and skating. She'd never, ever been the only person on the trail around the lake.

Ducks paddled through the water, rooting around in the mud near the banks, and she admired the growth on newly leafed out trees. Spring was finally showing up. The temperatures slowly climbed, not enough to really feel warm, but enough to give her hope that summer might show up this year. The air smelled clean after this morning's deluge.

Emily alternately squealed and snorted at dogs as they passed, depending on whether she liked them or thought they should be run over. She especially liked Dalmatians. They rated a minute long squeal.

Babies and other kids were Katie's specialty. She always screamed with laughter when she came across them. Lily pegged Emily for a veterinarian or dog breeder and Katie to be a therapist or camp counselor.

Lily had been cranky all morning. She woke up to find all three boys having a water fight in the kitchen. There were broken dishes she couldn't replace. Only three weeks left of school until summer break. All the kids were antsy and slightly out of control. Some more than others.

It didn't help that a delivery person arrived a few minutes after she found the dishes. He carried an obscene amount of lilies and roses, along with a note from Sean. Even thinking about it now made her angry.

Lily picked up the pace, until it was as fast as she could run and still breathe. Why wouldn't he stop pursuing her? Hadn't she made herself clear? Apparently not. She'd have to do better next time she saw him. And she felt certain there'd be a next time. She had to get rid of him. Tension built up in her shoulders. She felt tense, about losing the kids, all the time now.

Still, she appreciated the overpowering scent of lilies and roses. It filled the entire house, almost washing away the smell of burnt eggs.

As she passed the halfway point, the sun began to peer out from between the dissipating clouds. She was finally getting used to this routine, having never exercised before Tracy came into her life. Her body was beginning to feel good, but she still needed more endurance to keep up with all the kids.

Emily was having a fabulous dog watching day. Lily slowed a little, passing a particularly ugly, shaggy dog. She was enjoying the sunshine and smelled a rather pleasant, wet woody smell when *he* showed up running alongside. Sean smiled and passed them.

Lily stopped in her tracks.

Katie said, "Oomph," as the stroller stopped as well.

He kept running.

"Hey, come back here," she yelled, her Mom voice taking over without her permission.

He turned, running sideways and pointed to himself as if to say, 'who me', when he saw her staring at him.

"Yeah, you."

He ran back and said, "Is something wrong?"

"Are you following me?" she asked, her grip nearly bending the metal alloy of the stroller. She couldn't be sure which irritated her more, his following her or the flowers.

"Why would you think such a thing?"

"Oh, it's just a coincidence you're here now?" She tried to ignore the slightly rumpled look which made her want to run her fingers through his hair, despite the fact she also wanted to kill him.

Lily slowed to a walk, breathing hard. She had made it three-quarters of the way around the lake at a really good pace. She smelled a fishy, froggy, muddy smell. Maybe this side of the lake was stagnant. She hadn't noticed it before.

"I didn't say it was just a coincidence," he said.

"Are you following me?"

"I thought you'd never notice," he said, with the charming look that got him on so many magazine covers. His big brown eyes smoldered at her, the cleft in his chin just sat there looking sexy. And the dimples, she could swear they winked at her when he smiled.

She shook her head.

"How long have you been following me?" she asked, her knuckles turning white from clenching the stroller handle. Katie giggled at him. Emily was silent, watching.

"Oh, at least a couple of days."

"Why?" she asked.

"Well, you're such a puzzling woman," he said, walking beside her.

"Oh, well just feel free to ask any questions. I sure wouldn't want to keep any of my life a secret from you," she said, starting to run again. God, he made her nervous. And angry. And she was working as hard to hold onto it. As hard as he was working to dissipate it. He kept succeeding. She found it difficult to be mad at him for pushing so hard, even though he smiled the same smile he used in *Razor Dreams*, where he played the psychiatrist who humored the twelve-year old, mass murderer until he confessed. Now, she knew why the kid killed him in the end.

"Well," asked Sean, "Exactly how many children do you have?"

"It varies."

"How many right now?"

She felt almost afraid to answer the question. "Six?"

"Oh well then, those guys who've been following you must not be yours," he said, pointing to two identically dressed boys, ages five and six, who she had vaguely noticed halfway around the lake. When he pointed to them, she knew immediately they were hers. Or going to be. Then he smiled his familiar cat who just ate the chickadee smile.

She shivered.

"Mom, are we almost done?" they asked together.

She stopped and looked at them.

The older one, Beau, had been running and had not one hair out of place. His jeans were clean and looked new, his white T-shirt was spotless. "Boo wants chocolate ice cream," he said, pointing to his brother.

Boo, with the mussed up blond hair, torn jeans and mud spattered red T-shirt, said, "Beau wants licorice flavor." He pointed at his older brother, then looked down at his shoes before looking back up into her eyes.

"Boo?" she asked.

He nodded seriously and said, "Look at the cool feather I found."

She glanced at Sean who stood looking at her like a cat with a feather hanging out of his mouth, arms crossed, waiting for her reaction.

She said to the boys, "We're almost done here. Race you to the parking lot, but stay on the trail."

The boys ran off. She loped after them, leaning slightly on the stroller and vaguely hoping to lose Sean. She felt like a large, awkward giraffe.

It didn't work. He ran alongside, easily, and she could feel him watching her.

"Eight. Eight kids. I occasionally have memory lapses, you see. My ex couldn't take it," she muttered, feeling cornered and afraid.

He smiled and raised an eyebrow. He didn't believe her, she could tell. No woman forgets she has eight kids. She only wants to.

"Big family," he said.

"Mmmmmm, and getting bigger all the time," she mumbled, feeling in shock. And somehow he had noticed. That realization filled her with fear.

They were back at the parking lot. She walked across it to

her car, making the boys hang on to the stroller. She unlocked the car and the boys scrambled in, Boo in the back and Beau into the front. She opened the other back door and began the process of strapping the girls into their car seats.

"Buckle up," she said, automatically to the boys, as she stashed the stroller in through the tailgate.

She felt pretty sure that having a child that young in the front seat, even in a newly appeared booster seat, was illegal and unsafe. There was no alternative in this car. She officially needed a van to carry everyone. How would that happen? Stress tightened her shoulder muscles even more than the fear had. She tried to breathe and relax them, but it didn't work.

"Can we just get together for coffee?" asked Sean.

"I'm too busy. The kids will be out of school for the summer soon," she paused. "The rest of the kids. I'll need to entertain them or at least make sure no one gets killed or maimed."

She just wanted to get away from him. He knew. He noticed the kids appearing. She didn't know what to do. Her stomach felt all knotted up.

What if he told someone? What if other people began to notice? What if the paparazzi, who stood over by his car, noticed? She might have to run away with the kids. And quit working. But how was she going to support all of them anyway with her income?

She closed her eyes and tried to breathe.

"We could go to the zoo? Please, Lily."

"I'll call you if I get some free time," she said, getting into the car and starting it.

"Lily, I need to talk to you...."

She drove away without fastening her own seat belt, he'd rattled her so much. Looking in the rear view mirror, she saw him standing there, looking dejected. She felt a stab of pain, felt sorry for him. It was soon replaced by fear. He noticed.

She swore under her breath all the way home. This was getting too spooky. She really didn't want another man in her life. One had been enough. Her mind was busy trying to figure out how her part time job could feed nine people as well as buy a van. Next she'd have to spring for a school bus.

She'd either have to get a second job or ask her parents for more money. Either one felt terrible. Working more would take time away from the kids and cost money for childcare unless one of the older kids was available. And her parents had earned all their money, they deserved to enjoy it themselves. Yet they never complained and they always came through for her. Joyfully.

Ignoring her budget, she stopped at the grocery store for cartons of ice cream and then home.

After the kids were done, she sat down with her own carton of Rippling raspberry and chocolate. And a spoon.

She was right. Beau and Boo belonged to her. They came out of nowhere, just like all the others. There were no missing children listings. They couldn't remember any other home and knew the other kids instantly, knew all the routines and rules of the house. Clothing and beds magically appeared, a neighbor cleaning out their basement asked if she wanted them. The boys fit in seamlessly. It felt bizarre to have eight kids and never been pregnant.

Lily still felt a need to explain them and told Janice they were her cousin's kids. That the cousin, who was single, had died in a plane crash and Lily had been named in the will as the guardian and would adopt them.

Janice accepted the story without question. Lily knew that by the time she got them registered for school in the fall, their records would be there and would tie in with her story and correspond with what the boys knew. She had no idea how it worked. That it worked was about the only thing keeping her sane. If she had to make all the details fit her mind would have been gone after the first child arrived. But the fear that one day things wouldn't work out lingered in the back of her mind. What would happen though if come fall, she had to register five more kids?

Somehow, she knew more kids would be coming. Finances were thin and she needed a van. The clothes dryer had broken down and she couldn't afford a new one of those either.

She strung up a clothesline, telling everyone it was better for the environment. Good thing summer was coming. Drying wet clothes in drizzling rain didn't work so well.

Luckily, her house was big enough for more kids. She might have to build more bedrooms downstairs. Or maybe a barracks. She got hung up on worrying about explaining more kids to her neighbors and other people. No one had ever questioned her, before Sean. But someday, people would and she kept trying to keep all the kids' stories straight. No one would believe her if she told the truth. They'd either sell her story to the tabloids or lock her up and take the kids away. Or both.

The kids had all given her such wonderful gifts. Each one enriched her life in ways she would never have thought possible. Jim taught her how to use her computer. Tracy, how to enjoy exercise, Teddy, about all the new music coming out. Max about vulnerability and asking for help as well as accepting it. Emily, about laughing uproariously. Katie about the beauty of small things. What would Beau and Boo teach her?

Lily found more compassion, humor and gifts within herself than she ever knew existed. She couldn't live without the kids and didn't want to.

Then there was Sean, who made it clear he'd seen the boys arrive. Why was that? Was he looking for something to hold over her? He must have been waiting for something strange to happen. Which made her pretty sure he'd seen Max arrive.

Everything about Sean seeing the kids made her feel truly paranoid. She needed to let that go. There was no controlling what he did, no matter how afraid she felt.

She could only control herself, sometimes. She needed to get him out of her life.

That night after the kids went to bed, she gathered up all her photos of Sean, all the magazine articles, the CD's, DVD's, everything except his signed book, which she couldn't find. She carried the whole bundle out into the back yard and piled what would fit, onto the charcoal grill. She went back inside and finally found matches on top of the refrigerator.

She set the paper on fire. As things burned through, the awful, black smoke spiraling upwards and burning her throat, she said, "God, Goddess, Allah, Ramtha, Buddha. She Who Watches, Kwan Yin, Isis, Venus, whoever's out there. I'll make a deal with you. I'll stop all this fantasizing. I don't want this man in my life. He's way too high profile. Someone will find out about me. Please stop sending me children. Just make it possible to keep the ones I have. Don't let anyone take them away from me or find out. Let me find the money to take care of us all. Please."

She felt a knot in her chest and wiped the tears streaming down her face away.

She'd keep her part of the bargain. Tomorrow she'd ask Jim how to delete the internet history from her computer and delete bookmarks. No more fantasizing. No more accepting groceries or flowers. She'd move to a different town if she needed to.

As she added more paper to the fire, the smoke turned a bluish color. She moved upwind and continued to burn things until it had all been consumed by the flames. She felt empty and drained. She hoped that it meant being cleansed of any desire and attraction to him.

SEAN

SEAN SAT ON A STACK OF PALLETS IN A BRICK WALLED AND paved downtown alley in Pioneer Square. He watched his friend, Eric, sparring with another actor. As they went through the choreography, the camera followed.

He pulled his black sweatshirt on. The alley was in complete shade, even though the day was sunny. It was maybe fifty outside. Seattle summer. At least he worn jeans, they were warm. He drank more from his water bottle.

This scene was supposed to be done an hour ago, but there were lighting problems. He'd been hoping Eric could get away for lunch, but that didn't look possible now. He hadn't seen Eric since leaving L.A.

Eric was in costume, which in this case meant stripped to the waist, wearing tight black leather pants and boots. All the better to see his perfect abs onscreen. His blond, curly hair was cropped short for the film and only made his startling blue eyes stand out more. He was younger than Sean, still in his thirties. Eric's hunkiness, combined with his considerable abilities as an actor, made him much sought after by directors. Both women and men wanted him as a lover and Eric was happy to oblige either. He'd been after Sean for years.

While Sean felt flattered, he really only was attracted to women and made that clear. They'd fallen into a little game. Eric offering and Sean refusing.

The sparring stopped when a production assistant said something to the two of them. Makeup toweled them both off and fussed with their hair and makeup. Eric grabbed a bottle of water from an ice chest and sat down by Sean.

"It looks like they're starting in ten minutes. Sorry it's taking so long."

"It's okay. I know how it goes."

"When are you gonna work again?"

"When the headaches are gone. I had a doozie the other day. Couldn't have worked if I'd wanted to."

"You still getting those?"

"Yeah, but we're closing in on why, so I'm hoping to have the whole thing dealt with soon. So what's new in L.A.?"

"When I left, it was fabulous as usual. Wish you hadn't moved. You've missed so many incredible parties. Dana had one last month, Winter Wonderland. Outside the temp was about a hundred, inside it was a frosty fifty degrees. We all wore fur, mostly fake, and the place overflowed with ice sculptures, live seals and penguins. Truly amazing, even for Dana. And Nina looked spectacular, she wore a fur thong with fuzzy high heels and the tiniest patches of fur to cover her nipples. Froze her butt off though. I asked if I could warm her up and she looked at me as if I was crazy. Maybe she's not into blondes. A woman of many charms, as I'm sure you're well aware of."

"Yes." Nina was always the exhibitionist. Glamor at any price. She and Eric would make a good pair. "She's in town today, you know?

"No, I didn't," Eric said, cocking an eyebrow. "I'd love to get to know her."

"I'm having dinner with her this evening. Want to come?" Eric would diffuse any tension between the two of them and who knew what might come of it?

"I can't. I'm in this evening's scenes. Damn."

"That's too bad. I think the two of you would really hit it off." It had been worth a try.

"Sooo, I take it your having dinner with Nina isn't an attempt to get back together with her again."

"Not on my part. Been there, done that. She called me, don't know what she wants," said Sean.

"I wish I could come up with some horrible twenty-four hour disease, so I could sneak out and join the two of you for dinner. Now she'd be worth becoming monogamous for."

"Like she could," snorted Sean. He still cared about Nina and felt compassionate about her and her problems, but he held no illusions about her limitations. Her dramas always made him rethink his compassion.

They talked until the makeup people needed Eric again.

Sean walked down the block towards his car, then drove to Ballard. He grabbed a quick lunch at a drive through and ended up at Bob's new house. Lily's car was gone. He felt disappointed. He'd hoped to catch a glimpse of her, maybe get a chance to talk. He really needed to find out what she knew about the Gift.

Bob didn't answer the door, but his white pickup was in the driveway. Sean tentatively opened the unlocked door and walked in.

"Bob, are you here?" he yelled.

"I'm downstairs, Sean."

Bob was replacing a couple of water damaged beams and put Sean to work helping him.

"Maggie and the kids are packing. I brought a load up with me. I'll be glad to get up here and get Sam away from his friends. He's been in counseling, but now he'll have a chance to choose better friends. Ones who aren't into drugs."

Sean asked, "Met any of your neighbors?" as he held one end of the tape measure.

"Most of them. The retired guy next door is still out of town."

"You met Lily?"

"The woman across the street?" asked Bob, marking a new beam and cutting it with a crosscut saw.

Sean marveled at the ease with which his brother did things. He was practiced and smooth, whereas Sean always felt and looked clumsy.

"Nice lady," said Bob. "I'm glad the kids will have other kids to play with."

"What do you think of her?" asked Sean, unsuccessfully trying to unscrew screws with the power screwdriver.

"Well, I only met her the once. Looks like she's got her hands full, but she keeps a pretty tight rein on her kids. Why do you ask?"

"Oh, no reason," said Sean.

"Don't give me that. You always have a reason for everything you do."

"Did she say anything about me?"

"Only that she ran into you when you looked at the house. Oh no, you're not...?"

"Yeah. I am."

"Hooo. You've got your work cut out for you," said Bob, looking up from his work and shaking his head.

"Think so?"

"Yeah. I'd guess working and raising nine kids alone leaves her no time to date."

"Nine. I thought there were only eight," said Sean, trying to cover his surprise. He shouldn't have been surprised, he realized. He'd send more groceries, whether she wanted them or not. He knew she needed them.

"No, nine. She introduced them all to me. I counted nine."

"Well, math never was my strong point," said Sean, covering his mistake. Things were really heating up. What if Casey was right, she had no clue about where the kids came from?

Bob said, "Good thing you have an accountant to keep track of all your money."

They continued working on the beams. So, there was another child. That meant six kids in the month and a half since he'd seen her again. He felt a knot in his gut. He just didn't know how to get through to her that he could help. That she needed to let him help. That she didn't need to do this alone.

He wanted to help.

His stomach was rumbling by the time they finished up with the beams. Bob packed his tools to head back to Oregon. He had a job for the next week.

Sean walked out into the driveway and saw *her* car pull up. Lily and some of the kids got out. She glanced at the two of them standing in Bob's driveway. They waved at her. She hesitated for a moment, then halfheartedly returned the wave.

Sean felt hungry as he stared at her, taking in the off white shorts and a peach colored tank top in which her nipples stood out. Lily's long hair tumbling down around her shoulders.

He yearned to spend time relaxing with her and for the two of them to have time playing with the kids. He wanted to talk to her about his dreams and find out her hopes for the future.

Watching her follow the older kids up her sidewalk, while she carried Katie and held hands with Emily, he noticed the new kid. A little girl, maybe five, cavorting in circles around Lily. Nancy's hair was short and sort of spiky.

"Yep, your work's cut out for you. If she was interested, she'd have come over," said Bob.

"I know. Well, do what you can for me. Tell her what a wonderful and lonely guy I am."

"You mean lie?" asked Bob.

Sean laughed and punched him in the shoulder. "Call me when you're back in town again."

"Will do. Hope we'll be moved in by next month. We'll see," said Bob.

Sean drove off, preoccupied with coming up with ideas to change Lily's mind. He'd never really wanted someone who wouldn't have him. He didn't handle rejection in his personal life very well. He had enough of it in his professional life.

He got home and ran through the shower, changed into a pair of slacks and a clean shirt. He needed to pick up Nina in forty-five minutes. And a good chunk of that time would be spent losing the paparazzi, which was getting more difficult. They expected it and they also knew Seattle better than they had a few months ago. Right now there were only three of them: Harry, Roderigo and Geoffrey. The rest had taken a break from his boring life to cover Eric's movie set and the hotel the actors were staying in.

Sean hoped she wasn't planning a seduction. They hadn't been lovers in over six years and wouldn't be ever again. He'd long since forgiven her, but that didn't mean he'd trust her with his heart again. As fascinating and sexy as she was, he wouldn't set himself up for that kind of hurt from her again. No matter what happened between him and Lily.

This dinner was just about making peace. Becoming more comfortable around her, since it was obvious they were going to run into each other. Directors kept calling with offers that involved the two of them working together again.

Sean knocked on Nina's hotel room door. She answered, wearing a stunning black dress with spaghetti straps. Her perfect body practically poured in the dress and her dark hair dyed a deep red for the current film. She looked much younger than forty-one.

Coming here was a mistake. He could almost smell her muskiness and his body responded, just like it always had. As if time hadn't passed and she hadn't betrayed him.

"Come in, come in," she said, wrapping her arms around him for a hug and kiss. Just a short one, but close enough for her to feel he was hard. "You *did* miss me!" She pulled away

"Not as much as you think," he said, feeling defensive. It was just a physical reaction. Nothing more. Like a sneeze.

She pulled on a thin, short sweater, maybe a sweaterlet.

"Did you have fun shopping today?"

"Shopping was glorious. I found a couple pair of shoes and a perfect dress. And lingerie."

Why she needed underwear confused him. She rarely wore it and he doubted she wore any tonight. He watched her slip heels on over bare feet.

"Did you know Eric Jorgenssen is in town filming?" he asked, as they walked to the elevator.

"No, I didn't. But I'm leaving in the morning. I have to get back to Vancouver and be rested up for the next day. I just came down to do interviews for a film opening next week. And shopping," she said, flipping her long, red hair out of her eyes.

What exactly was she shopping for? Or who?

They got into his car and made small talk as he drove to Ballard. She wanted Italian food and he knew a cute little cafe. She'd find it quaint, for a late dinner. The sun had finally come out and warmed everything up.

Bella Ristorante was a small cafe, seating perhaps twenty people. It was half full when they arrived. The teal walls, accented with swags of burgundy cloth, gold framed mirrors and paintings made the place seem cosy and inviting. They were seated at a small table with hard, wooden chairs, looking out onto the street.

Dinner flowed smoothly. He'd forgotten how fun and charming Nina could be. Always full of great stories, yet able to listen as well. She seemed genuinely interested in his family. She'd met all of them during the rare holiday visits he'd spent in Seattle.

There were only a few other people in the restaurant. People alternated staring at the two of them and being completely absorbed in their own meals and conversations.

"So Sean, how's your love life?"

"Ah, there it is." He felt justified in his suspicions that she came down here with an agenda for meeting him, but he wasn't about to discuss his love life with her.

"Yes," she said, bending over the table, exposing her lovely breasts as she rubbed her foot on his shin.

He knew that no matter how calculated it looked, she was actually not conscious about it. Her body simply followed her desires.

She sipped red wine and said, "I've thought about you a lot over the years. I know I hurt you badly and I've tried, again and again, to apologize."

"I recall that I accepted your apology," he said, quietly.

"But you haven't forgiven me," she said.

"Yes, I have forgiven you. I simply won't trust you on that level again."

Nina sighed and pushed back her hair. She seemed to be searching for the right words. Unusual for her. She nearly always said the right thing at the right time. He admired her for that ability.

"What can I do to regain your trust? I want you back in my life again. I've missed you so much."

That surprised him. That she wanted him enough to grovel. He also felt a little guilty. He didn't want to hurt her.

"Nina, this isn't going to happen." Then he blurted out, "I'm in love with someone else," instantly regretting it. Sean pushed the plate of half-eaten chicken away, his appetite gone. He drank some of his wine, tasting the bitter dregs from the bottom of the bottle.

She toyed with the remains of her pasta and asked, "Who is she?"

"You don't know her," he said, shifting on the now painfully hard chair.

"But who is she? How did you meet her?"

"She's a neighbor of my brother's," he said, knowing that Nina wasn't going to give up easily now.

"What's she like?"

"Tall, blond, athletic, funny. I don't know. I'm not good at descriptions."

"You don't know her well enough?" asked Nina, leaning back in her chair and looking vaguely like a cat who's got a mouse cornered.

"Perhaps not. Time will change that."

"I'm sorry. I had no idea. I wouldn't have come if I'd known," she said.

He didn't believe her. She'd simply changed her tactics. He wasn't exactly sure what game she was playing now.

"I probably should have told you over the phone. I didn't know you were interested in me," he said, looking down and rubbing his index finger along the leather folder which contained the receipt from dinner.

Nina looked too composed, a bad sign. It usually preceded a volcanic eruption. He slipped the receipt in his pocket and the credit card into his wallet. Ready to run. She made him feel nervous, tiptoeing around her. He'd forgotten how that felt.

"Well, let's go," she said. "I was going to ask you out for drinks and dancing, but I'd guess you'll say no."

"Sorry, I can't," he said, wanting to be gone before she exploded.

They walked towards the car and a teenage girl with a double ice cream cone nearly collided with them.

After he got over the surprise, Sean recognized Tracy. He and Nina rounded the corner and saw Lily and the rest of her kids coming out of an ice cream store.

She looked beautiful as always, having changed into a lilac tank top and cutoff jeans. Her hair casually piled on top of her head with wisps escaping to caress her neck and cheeks. Her fresh beauty made a sharp contrast to Nina's very calculated look. Sean wished he was walking with Lily. He had to force himself to look away from her.

He went to his car, which was parked in front of the ice cream store. Unlocking the passenger door, he opened it and turned to see Nina watching Lily and the kids walking their direction.

Sean realized Nina noticed him watching Lily. Lily hadn't actually seen them. She was busy balancing Katie and an ice cream cone.

For an instant he really thought he could get Nina out of there quickly without Lily noticing him.

Nina said, loudly, "Some people have no self control. Can you imagine having all those brats?"

His cheeks began to flame with embarrassment. He wanted to vanish.

Lily heard and looked up to see him and Nina.

He should cut and run. Avoid a scene. But he didn't want to be rude to Lily. There might be a shred of possibility with her. He still clung to that hope.

"Hi Lily."

"Hello," she said, a puzzled look on her face.

"Lily, this is Nina Vicente. Nina, Lily Toureau."

It wouldn't be too long before Nina made the connection. She might confront Lily and jealously tear into her. He needed to do something.

Teddy said, "Mom, we gotta go or we'll miss the game." He'd clearly wolfed down his ice cream and he took Katie from her arms.

The other kids started edging their way up the block.

"Nice to meet you Lily," said Nina, curling her arm around Sean's.

"Good to meet you," said Lily, "I like your work."

"Well, we'd better be going too," said Sean. "You have an early plane to catch," he said to Nina. To Lily, he said, "Nice to see you again."

He pointedly held the door open for Nina.

"Not so fast, darling," she purred. "This, I assume is the woman you referred to earlier?" She stepped in front of Lily and stood there, sizing her up.

Lily looked uncomfortable and stood on the sidewalk by his car, concentrating on eating her ice cream cone, which looked very soft and was dripping.

He couldn't decide whether Lily didn't know what to do or if she understood she was driving Nina crazy and just kept at it.

Most of the kids wandered off down the street towards home, only a couple blocks away. The older ones holding hands with the younger ones.

Sean continued to hold the door, disentangling himself from Nina who still stood in front of Lily.

At that moment he saw movement out of the corner of his eye. Two paparazzi leapt out of their car. He recognized Roderigo and Harry. He had a hard time losing them, but clearly they'd found him again. The third stayed in the car, ready to drive. Both cameras came at them, flashing.

Images swarmed through his mind. Lily and the kids exposed. His family exposed. The history of the Gift was filled with misunderstandings, murders and suicides. And fear. In this day and age he could imagine witch hunts for people with the Gift taking over the country's consciousness. Large families investigated and at best, ostracized. At worst, murdered and tortured. Damn. Lily would have been better off if he'd simply left her alone.

"Oh, don't say anything, dear," said Nina to him, clenching her fists. She either didn't notice the paparazzi or didn't care.

Sean knew the eruption was coming. He stepped back out of the way, trying to decide if he should just cram Nina in the car or run.

"You don't have to say anything. Yes, she is cute in a June Cleaver kind of way," she said to him, snidely. "All those babies. She's a rabbit. All she'll ever do is make babies. She'll be even older in just a few years. Looks haggard now. I can't believe you'd fall for her. How could you want a breeding bunny when you could have a playtime bunny, as if I would ever do such a thing?" She covered her mouth with her hand and gasped. "Is it because I can't have children? Is that it? I know you wanted a big family, but we could adopt," she said, tears streaming down her face.

"Get in the car Nina. You've said enough."

He turned to Lily, "I'm sorry. Actresses, they have to cause a scene wherever they go."

Nina, who'd been half in the car, flew out of it towards him.

"Don't you dare apologize for me. I haven't said enough. Now you've got me started."

By now Nina was screaming and jumping up and down, in full tantrum.

"Honey, did he tell you, he's lousy in bed? That's the real reason we didn't have kids. And as for monogamy, you can forget it...."

When she started swinging, Sean grabbed her. Nina's gestures and language got wilder as Sean worked hard to stuff her back in the car. She was playing it up for the paparazzi and the small crowd of onlookers.

Finally, he stopped pushing and said in a low growl, "Get in the car Nina, or I'll drive off and leave you. I'm sure you can get a cab or hitch a ride with the paparazzi, but I'm leaving now."

He knew she'd get in. She hadn't given up hope on him that easily.

"Bastard. That is what you're rejecting me for?" she asked, getting into the car and slamming the door.

"I apologize once more," he said to Lily.

He felt so badly for her, wanted to talk to her, make everything all right. He wanted to throw Nina off a cliff somewhere and watch her splat into the ocean. That would be satisfying.

"Charming company you keep," said Lily, cooly. She walked away ignoring Roderigo who was following her, snapping photos.

"Hey Roderigo, the real show is going to happen when I drop Nina off. If I were you, I'd follow along," said Sean.

Roderigo smiled, shook his head no and continued to follow Lily. Harry jumped into the waiting SUV.

Sean walked to the driver's side of his car and got in. Without a word, he started the car and drove Nina to her hotel, not bothering to lose the paparazzi. She sat in the seat next to him, clearly smoldering with fury.

In contrast he felt ice cold.

Lily really wouldn't want anything to do with him now. Not that she ever had. He'd messed things up royally in his pursuit of her. This would be the clincher. He drove, feeling numb, knowing a deep pool of rage lay beneath all his ice. Wrath that all his dreams of a family and Lily were crushed. His life felt ruined.

The ride back to Nina's hotel was silent. Absolutely silent. The sun shone its way to a blazing summer-like sunset, but Sean felt only gray and bleak winter. He saw only gray streets, silver and white cars and gray concrete buildings.

He could tell Nina was staring at him, finally aware that she'd pushed him too far. Once again. He refused to look at her, lost in his thoughts about what Lily might be doing or thinking right now. Had she even given him a second thought?

He pulled up to the hotel entrance.

Nina said, "Sean, I don't know what came over me."

He just sat and looked at her, frost filling his gaze.

"Please, talk to me," she said.

"We have nothing to talk about."

She sighed and looked at him with her big, dark eyes. "Well, goodbye then. You have my number if you change your mind. I'll be here until tomorrow morning and then back to Vancouver. You know what I can do for you. She can't give you what you need."

"Goodbye."

Nina got out of the car and walked slowly into the hotel. Harry was already out of the SUV, waiting for her, taking photos. She had one hell of a walk. But like nearly everything she did, it was calculated for maximum effect.

He drove off. The SUV driver, probably Geoffrey, followed

him. Sean drove aimlessly and parked. He got out and walked around. Then drove, parked and walked again. For hours in the dark and cold, feeling devastated.

Geoffrey and his camera, faithfully shadowed him like a dog, but kept his distance taking the occasional photo.

Sean sat in a park on a cold concrete bench, overlooking downtown and Puget Sound. He was trying to decide whether it would be useful to anyone if he drowned himself.

Geoffrey sat down and thrust a hot latte into Sean's half frozen hands.

Sean looked at him and said, "Thank you."

Geoffrey nodded and said, "Women...." Then he fell silent and sat, staring at his hands.

The coffee felt warm and wonderful in his chilled body. The smell went a long ways toward bringing him back to life.

He felt torn between going over all the mistakes he'd made with Lily from the first date to the disaster of tonight. And feeling hopeless, knowing she was his twin soul and that they were meant for each other.

If she wouldn't talk to him, he couldn't tell her about the kids and they would never stop coming. He didn't know what to do about it. Write a letter and give her Casey's number?

Lily would be hounded by the paparazzi and soon, someone would figure out she was the 'date from hell'. He didn't know if anyone would notice the kids arriving, probably not. But he knew she'd most likely feel terrified about that and all the media attention.

He should leave her alone, but then more kids would come. And her finances and time and energy had limits.

He could see no way out of this mess. The hopelessness won out. Finally, exhausted, he gave up trying to work it all out.

Sean stood up and shook Geoffrey's hand. "Thank you. I'll be okay now. I'm going home and to bed."

"You know I have to follow you," Geoffrey said.

"I know. Just letting you know where I'm going."

Geoffrey's eyebrows raised in surprise.

Half an hour later, as Sean crawled into bed, he realized exactly how discouraged and ravaged he felt. Almost exactly like he felt after that first Oscar and Nina's betrayal.

LILY

Lily stood in her kitchen, arguing with Mom and Dad. She was still in her bathrobe and holding a cup of coffee even though it was long past lunchtime. She'd been up a lot last night with Jim, who'd had stomach flu, but seemed miraculously recovered today, eating five pancakes and keeping it all down. Kids, how did they recover so fast?

"Nonsense, we'll have no problems," said Lily's mom.

"Listen honey," said Dad, "we've done this before. The kids will be just fine. The older kids always help take care of the younger ones."

"It's true," said Susan. "You don't think we're getting too old...," she put her hand over her mouth in mock horror.

"No, no. It's not that," said Lily, half falling for her trick.

"Good, because if you did, I'd tan your hide," said Nick, pushing his baseball cap back over thick, gray hair.

Lily laughed. Her parents had never raised a hand to her even after her worst adventures as a child. "It's just that nine kids are a lot to handle."

"We're just going to a baseball game. And nine is a lot easier than twenty-five," he said, bending over and arching an eyebrow at her.

"Dad, you taught high school, not younger kids."

"Even worse. You have no idea of the machinations in the minds of sixteen year old boys."

"Now, there's no more arguing," said Susan. "I want you to take the night off. No housework. Either stay home and take a nice, long bath or go out for dinner and a movie. Or call up that nice young man who sent you groceries the other day. But relax and have some fun. We'll be home sometime after the game ends."

Lily felt heat creeping up into her cheeks at the reference to Sean. She'd asked him not to send groceries again, then backpedaled. But why would he keep doing it if he was seeing Nina again?

Mom was thrilled that a man was interested enough to take care of Lily. She didn't tell her about the video store gift certificate he'd sent. Mom and Dad quietly hoped she'd marry again she knew.

"I hope the game has extra innings, then we'll get our money's worth," said Nick, punching Teddy playfully in the arm. Teddy retaliated and they began a mock boxing match in the kitchen.

"Okay now, everybody has a sweater or jacket," Susan said, going down the line of kids for an inspection, as she'd taught them. She'd been a first grade teacher years ago. "And everyone has shoes?"

"And fingers, don't forget the fingers," said Nick, mocking her. The kids laughed, Emily the loudest.

"Oh you, I'll deal with you later," said Susan to Nick. "Okay, we're set. Money, blankets, tickets...." She looked at Nick.

"Money, blankets, tickets," he said, checking under Jim's jacket and winking at Lily.

"Okay then, we're off," said Susan. "Bye dear." She hugged and kissed Lily.

"We'll be just fine," said Nick, hugging her as well.

Lily watched them all pile into the van her parents had rented when they came to town. Lately they'd been threatening to buy one and leave it with her to drive. She sighed. She needed one. She couldn't even fit all the car seats in the station wagon at once. Let alone all the bodies. Which meant someone always had to stay home.

She closed the front door and locked it. Of course, they'd all be just fine. Her parents were amazing. They always rose to any occasion.

She shook loose the tension in her shoulders and rubbed her forehead, breathing deeply. She blamed the headache on the reporters. One of them followed her home the other night after the onslaught by Nina. Two nights later they began to stalk her. She and the kids went for ice cream again and the reporters tried to get information about any relationship she might have with Sean. Nina had alluded to it in her jealous tirade. Rabbit indeed.

Lily's shoulder tensed again as her anger at Nina surfaced. She really wanted to deck the bitch. Or Sean for that matter. The reporters tried to get the kids to talk about him.

Beau had been happy to and said, "He's my daddy," before Lily could get them to be quiet.

Lily tried to point out the improbability of Sean keeping a child a secret for that long to the press. She whispered to them that Beau always made things up and had perhaps seen a few too many of Sean's movies.

She thought they believed her in the end. Maybe. Her dad was keeping busy trying to think of practical jokes to play on them, while her mom pointed out they were simply doing their jobs and providing entertainment for people who paid money for that sort of gossip.

Attention from the reporters left her feeling exposed. She didn't want to jeopardize the kids. Reporters sat outside her house until one in the morning. Maybe they hoped Sean would show up. But why would he, when he could have Nina? Lily never understood why he'd want her anyway, tall, gawky and clumsy? She'd never really believed it.

She sighed again. She knew exactly what do, at least for right now. It was such a hot, muggy day and she felt sticky. A nice cool bath sounded wonderful. By then it would be around five. She'd go have dinner some place, inexpensive with outside dining.

She called Janice to ask her along, but no one answered. She left a message.

It had been a hell of a week. First, it became more and more clear that Sean knew she had more kids. Even worse it was possible that he'd even seen Max or Beau and Boo appear out of thin air. He'd increased the amount of groceries delivered. And sent her a huge gift certificate to their favorite video store. Which meant he'd followed her there, or hired someone else to do it. Did he also know they went to the ice cream shop every couple of weeks? Had he planned that encounter between her and Nina? It scared her that he knew about the kids. Made her feel powerless and at his mercy.

And this week Teddy had been caught shoplifting CD's at a local department store. He claimed it was his first time. He'd been banned from the store and fined, with a warning that if he were caught again, he'd be arrested. She'd been racking her brain trying to figure out what to do about him. She spent last night talking to her parents about it. They gave her several ideas and she was still mulling them over.

Then there was Nina. Lily wasn't used to being insulted like that. She wasn't sure which bothered her more, the insults or that Sean was seeing her again. Of course it was all over the tabloids and some of the better magazines too.

Nina had made comments like, "I've never gotten over Sean."

Interestingly enough, there were no comments from Sean in the magazines.

She felt so divided about how she felt about him.

She lit the dusty candles in the bathroom, turned some soft music on the living room stereo and ran bath water. She poured in the only bubble bath she could find. Bubble gum. It was Tracy's. Lily usually could only find time for a quick shower, these days.

She slid into the delicious cool water. It felt wonderful, despite the overwhelming fragrance of bubblegum. The tub was a little short for her, but she stretched out as much as she could. The water felt silky on her skin. Bubble bath was a great invention. It made one feel playful and sexy all at once. All those little bubbles forming, disintegrating, reforming. She shaped gloves onto her hands and made space creatures with them.

Her parents had given her such a wonderful gift with this time alone. They were so thoughtful. She never told them how sometimes she wanted to escape her life. Even though she loved her children and didn't really want a life without them. When the burden of caring for the kids became too much, she fantasized about dropping everything and leaving to live somewhere else. Alone. Sometimes, she just wished a friend would take the kids away on a vacation. For about three months. One child was exhausting. Nine felt completely overwhelming,

Nina's comments came back to her again. That she looked old. She was beginning to *feel* old. Worrying too much. And she wasn't a rabbit, damn it. She was an intelligent, talented woman who simply couldn't figure out what she was talented at, other than making children appear out of the ozone. Well, maybe she was a rabbit, after all.

She sometimes missed being free and having no commitments. No one else to take care of. No missing socks to hunt for, no grades to worry about, no tooth fair and no disciplinary action for a failure to eat vegetables and most of all, stealing CD's. What would it be like to put something where it belonged and to go back days later, finding it in the same place? Maybe she'd live in a fancy condo downtown with a view of the sound.

That was all fantasy. She had nine kids and at this rate, she'd have another twelve by the end of the year. She *was* a rabbit. Just not in the normal way.

She made a rabbit out of bubbles.

It was stupid to spend her precious, leisure time worrying about things. She could worry anytime.

She bent her knees and sank up to her neck in the tub. Closing her eyes, she envisioned herself in a beautiful, secluded lake. Floating naked in the sunshine. Feeling the coolness of the water invigorate her body as she lay there drifting.

Suddenly, into her fantasy swam Sean. He glided closer, gathering her up in his arms as he stood on the sandy bottom near the edge of the lake. Their legs entwined, he cupped the back of her head and pulled her closer for a kiss. She closed her eyes and felt the softness of his mouth. He nibbled on her lips, teasing her. Kissing them then pulling away. Coming forward again and brushing her lips, then retreating. As she embraced his shoulder, he kissed her ears, sucking on her earlobes, his tongue flicking behind her ears and sending her tingling. He pulled her closer again, their bodies rubbing together and his hands stroked the length of her back and buttocks. She felt heat building in her body despite the chill of the water. He kissed her again. His tongue rimming her lips, then meeting hers.

As he moved his lips along her neck, she arched up onto a smooth, warm boulder. His mouth found her breasts and sucked on her nipples until she writhed with excitement. He gently lifted her further out of the water, his mouth caressing her belly, her hips and down the outside of her right leg, then up the inside, pausing to pay special attention to that spot behind her knees that made her squirm even more. Then he did the same thing to her other leg.

She wanted him so badly, she shook with eagerness. He opened her legs and brushed his lips against the wet hair covering her vulva. Slowly, he spread apart those lips and took his time exploring the folds with his tongue, sucking on her as she moaned and he brought her excitement even higher.

Lily felt the warm sun adding to the heat of her body. He moved on top of her, his hard cock sliding inside her, his hand rubbing her sex, his mouth on one of her nipples. She arched as her breath came in short gasps, the rhythm of his fingers increasing with her excitement. She moaned with pleasure.

"Surrender," he said. "Surrender yourself to me."

She cried out in an explosion of ecstasy. After too short a time she went limp, lying on the smooth rock and feeling part of the earth again. She opened her eyes and kissed him, hard this time, inserting her tongue in his mouth. He responded by shifting his weight and thrusting deeper inside her. She wrapped her legs around his hips and he slipped in and out, moaning. The tempo increased until he came. Shouting, then collapsing in her arms, surrendering in his own way. They lay in each other's arms, basking in the sunshine.

Then her cell rang. She was back in her bathtub, into real life. And alone. Her body had been cooled off by the bath water and she felt cold. She reached towards the counter for her phone.

"Hello."

"Hey kid, you called me?" asked Janice.

It took her a minute to realize who it was. She shook her head, reluctantly, to clear away the fantasy. "Yeah, I have a free night. No kids. My parents took them to a baseball game. I wondered if you were free and wanted to go out to dinner?"

"Oh." Janice sounded disappointed. "I can't. Tom and I are going to his company thing. I wish I could. It'd be much, much, much more fun."

"Oh."

"But you go off and have fun anyway."

"Yeah, I will. Talk to you later."

"Bye."

She put the phone down and sank back underwater up to her chin, her knees sticking out above the foam. She felt disappointed. It would've been fun to go out with Janice.

Well, it was time to get out. If she stayed in longer her skin would turn into a wrinkled prune. An old wrinkled prune.

She washed and rinsed her hair and pulled herself out of the water. After drying off and putting lotion on, she slipped into a blue sun dress. The thought occurred to her that she could call Sean. Ask him out to dinner. Maybe a few months ago, that would have worked. Now, his gorgeous ex, Nina was back in the picture. How could he go back to her after the way she humiliated him years ago?

Well, it didn't matter. She couldn't ask him out, couldn't get involved with him, or anyone for that matter.

She decided to go to an Italian cafe in Fremont. Janice raved about it. Reasonable prices and if she got there before five, she might score an outside table.

As she drove, her mind wandered back toward Sean. He did

seem like a nice guy, considerate, sensitive and funny. She wished the situation could be different. Wished she was normal and could get involved with him. He would make a good father, but what would he do if kids just kept appearing?

Where would it end? fifteen, fifty, a hundred? She could just open up a huge orphanage. Did he really notice the kids showing up? Or was that just her paranoia? Was he like everyone else and didn't see it. No. That was wishful thinking.

She found parking around the corner from the cafe. There were a couple of tables still available outside. She ordered a glass of red wine and sat back to peruse the menu and watch the line for a table begin to form.

Then it occurred to her. What would happen if she told him? She'd told her parents. His reaction would certainly be more extreme than Mom and Dad's thinking she was simply overworked. Would he run? There were all the paparazzi and he was so high profile. If she had fifty kids then the whole world would find out anyway.

It would be interesting to find out how he responded.

Maybe she'd call him and do just that.

SEAN

Sean looked over the railing and down the stairs of his condo. It was a warm, sunny June day. That the sun shone in June was apparently unusual. From the balcony by the stairs he could see across the street. Three SUV's worth of paparazzi were camped out now. One black, one green and one white. Most of them stood under the horse chestnut trees, talking, but a driver sat in each car. Ready to take off at a moment's notice. And he knew someone waited on the sidewalk just outside his parking garage. There wasn't any parking allowed on that street. But the paparazzi had a lookout.

He still felt furious about Nina. Her little scene had been splashed all over the tabloids. He knew she enjoyed it immensely, despite all the apologetic messages she left. She had a movie opening next week and the extra attention would only help the numbers. But it made his life more difficult.

He ran his fingers through his wet hair. It used to be fairly easy to avoid being followed when there was only one car of paparazzi. Even though Harry, Roderigo and Geoffrey caught on to his tricks. They began to carry a bicycle on the back of their SUV. He hadn't tried skates, but anywhere he could go on skates they could go almost as quickly on a bike. Almost. A Vespa, or something like, now that had possibilities.

He didn't have much confidence he could lose all three cars though. And they didn't get bored. That was the problem.

Time to try a disguise, he thought, walking back inside the condo. He felt pissed off enough at Nina and the world in general, just to mess with them for the hell of it. All he wanted was to go out for dinner, even though it would take at least an hour for this little maneuver. Maybe two if traffic was bad. It wasn't like he had a hot date or anything. Just wanted to be miserable in peace. He called a cab and gathered up a baseball cap and jacket, shoving them into a backpack.

The paparazzi stood poised for action.

They ran for him when he came out of the building.

He said, "Not tonight boys, I've got a flight to catch." He waved off their questions and got into the cab.

"Hi Sam," he said, recognizing the driver. They'd done this before. "The airport I think this time."

"More games again? I don't envy you, Mr. O'Neill."

"It's the price I pay for people giving up their hard earned cash to let me play around on the screen."

Sam asked, "What if you talked to them? Scheduled interviews."

"I do tons of interviews. But the paparazzi, they want candid photos. And there's too many of them. It's not just the American tabloids, but the British, French, Italian and so on. They go on forever. Always looking for something more personal and twisting it to find more drama. Then selling the photos to the highest bidder."

"There isn't much dirt for them to find on you, is there?"

"I only wish there was, but the most exciting thing I do these days is play games with the paparazzi."

They drove to the airport followed by all three SUVs. Sam dropped him off at ticketing. He leapt out of the car and slung the backpack over one arm. Several paparazzi followed. He walked to the automatic ticket machine and pretended to punch numbers in to get a boarding pass. He checked his watch and did a sleight of hand with a slip of paper, making it look like the machine just printed out a boarding pass.

Making his way into one of the more crowded restaurants, he wove his way through and went out the opposite door, slipping into a nearby restroom. In one of the stalls, he put on the jacket and baseball cap, then tossed the backpack into a garbage can and left through another door.

He spotted the paparazzi standing outside of the restaurant. Sean followed a crowd of people to baggage claim, taking an escalator to the lower level. So far, so good.

Two airlines down, he caught another cab and took it back to Fremont. To the cafe up the hill from his condo.

He paid the cab and got out, walking around the corner to the entrance. Despite his success at evading the paparazzi, he felt down.

His parents' anniversary party had been last night. Everyone had a wonderful time, except him. He spent the evening watching everyone. He felt alone with no partner and no children. Normally, being alone with his family felt wonderful, but his longing to create his own family overpowered everything else in his life. She was his family, but he'd run out of ideas to convince her of that. Now, he'd run out of motivation as well. He'd tried to bulldoze his way into her life with absolutely no success.

Perhaps she wasn't connected to him at all. Maybe he'd made a mistake. Someone else was the trigger for all the children in her life.

He entered the courtyard of the cafe and waited to speak to

the host and put his name on the waiting list. He really wanted to eat outside, but there didn't seem to be much chance of that. Then he saw Lily sitting alone at the table next to the herb bed. He'd walked right by her and hadn't even noticed. She was looking at him and must have seen the surprise on his face. She looked radiant.

Damn. Now she'd think he was following her. He turned to leave.

"Sean," Lily called as he walked past her on the way out.

He turned and said, "I didn't follow you. I'm sorry. I didn't know you'd be here."

"You're welcome to join me," she said, then looked uncomfortable.

"I don't want to intrude."

"No, please. Besides, there aren't any other tables. I'd like some company," she said. She wore an indecipherable look on her face.

She's only trying to be polite. He sat down and took off the jacket and baseball cap, putting them on an empty chair.

"Do you come here often?" she asked.

"A couple times a week. I live just down the hill."

The waitress brought another menu and said, "Hi Sean," as she set a glass of red wine, his usual, in front of him.

"Oh, thanks June," he said.

She read off the specials and left.

"So, you've stopped following me?" she asked, an amused smile on her face.

"You gave me the distinct impression that even if I was the last man in the universe you wouldn't be interested. I don't have a high tolerance for rejection. I use it all up in my professional life."

She looked almost hurt. He didn't mean to hurt her. An

awkward silence followed. He filled it by pretending to read the menu, which he could have recited from memory.

"Would you like to split a pizza or did you come for something else?" he asked after a while. He just wanted to sit and stare at her. Run his fingers through that blond, silky hair.

"I'm sort of overwhelmed by all the choices," she said. "I usually eat fast food when we go out. That's what everyone will eat."

"Well, the barbecued chicken pizza is truly amazing, if you'd like to split one. If you don't I'll get it anyway and take the leftovers home for tomorrow," he said.

"That sounds terrific," she said, looking more relaxed.

After the waitress took their order and left, he said, "About the other night, I...."

"You already apologized twice. You weren't even the one who insulted me."

"I know. I guess I felt that I shouldn't have brought her to Ballard for dinner. I shouldn't have even gone out with her. It was a mistake. My relationship with her is dead and I won't be used again."

The waitress brought their salads and Sean began to eat, only now realizing how hungry he was. The fresh strawberries and creamy dressing whirled around on his tongue, contrasting with the slightly bitter spinach and arugula.

After he polished off the small salad, he asked, "What brings you out here alone?"

"My parents took the kids to a ballgame and demanded I take the night off. I decided to go out to eat someplace I'd never bring the kids."

"A lot of people bring their kids here."

"A lot of people don't have nine kids. Mostly well-behaved kids, but nine kids to one adult is a ratio that's tough to handle in a restaurant."

"True," he said. "You make a lot of compromises for your kids, don't you?"

"I think all parents make compromises for their kids." She seemed defensive.

"But being a single mom with several kids you probably make more than most," he said, sipping his wine and savoring the deep, rich taste.

"They do sort of rule my life, although I think they give me more than they take away. What's your point?"

"Don't know. I think about you a lot. I've often wondered, if you didn't have kids, if you'd have gone out with me again. Or if it's just me that you don't like or trust."

She squirmed in her chair, looking uncomfortable.

"I'm sorry. I shouldn't have brought it up," he said.

"No. It's okay." She played with her salad. "I probably should be honest with you. Tell you why I can't go out with you again."

"I'm eager to hear it," he said.

She shifted in her chair again and had a sip of wine. "Because I'm afraid once you find out who I really am, what's happening to me, then you'll vanish or think I'm crazy. And I'm afraid anything between us wouldn't last and I can't put the kids at risk."

"Like past relationships?" he asked.

"Yeah. My marriage. Except it's worse than just fear of being abandoned. I didn't have kids then or any of this craziness."

"So Casey's right. My twin sister said this was about the kids."

"Well, it's not what you might think."

"I'm pretty sure it is," he said. He felt like a kid about to tell the biggest secret in the world.

"What then?" she asked, challenging him.

"Well, I'm guessing the ever-increasing number of kids who

keep materializing in your life is pretty frightening." He sat back and let the comment sink in.

Lily's mouth dropped open in shock and she gasped.

The waitress arrived with their pizza. Sean cut the pieces, sawing through the stringy cheese and put slices on their plates.

Lily continued to stare at him, looking a little wild eyed. She was clenching the edge of the table.

He was right. No one else had ever noticed.

He began to eat his pizza, trying to calm himself. He wanted to handle this just right.

Finally, she asked, "What do you mean ever-increasing number of kids?"

"Well, when I saw you at Food King I know you had four. Teddy, Tracy, Jim and Emily. Then in April, Katie and Max arrived. I was there when Max just warped into existence on your front porch. I saw and felt him and immediately knew his name. I was also there in May when Beau and Boo showed up. Now, you have nine, the little dark haired pixie, Nancy. And I'm pretty sure there'll be more kids."

"You're not shocked?" Lily asked, shaking her head.

"Nope," he said, thoroughly enjoying himself. He'd caught her off guard. Maybe he still had a chance.

She ate some of her pizza, clearly disturbed.

"No one and I mean no one, not my parents, the kids, my neighbors, no one beside you has ever noticed before. I don't understand. And you sit there looking like the Cheshire Cat."

"I've had some time to adjust, after all I've been watching you and trying to get your attention for months. Besides the Gift runs in my family as well." He sipped his wine again, breathing in the fumes.

"What?"

"I can't give you details, they're not my stories to tell. But this accumulating of children is genetic. Our family calls it the

Gift, although it can cause a lot of problems. Since you're adopted, I'm assuming no one has explained it to you."

"You even know I'm adopted?" she asked.

"It's on public record. Like divorces."

"What don't you know about me?" Lily asked, looking worried and her brows furrowing. Was she irritated by him?

"What I don't know about you would fill up the world. Which doesn't mean I don't want to know."

"I still don't understand why you're interested in me. I could end up with twenty kids," she said, knocking over her water glass.

He righted her glass and mopped it up with his napkin. "I love big families," he said.

She shook her head and continued to eat a slice of pizza, staring at him.

She seemed so shocked that he didn't think she could absorb any more right now. The rest of the information about the Gift would have to wait. They talked about trivialities for the rest of the meal.

June brought the check. He pulled out his wallet and tried to pay for the meal, but Lily insisted they split the check.

He walked her to her car. "Do you really need to go home this early?" he asked, as she got inside.

"I don't know when the game will end, but I'd better be there when they get home. My parents will be exhausted."

"When can I see you again?" he asked.

"I'll have to think about it. I'll call you."

He felt helpless, she was slipping away again.

She tried to start the car. Nothing. No sound. The engine wouldn't turn over or even make that sad little clicking sound. She put her head down on the steering wheel.

"Should I call you a tow truck?" The only thing he knew

about cars was how to drive them and where his mechanic worked.

"I don't know." She paused, then said, "Yes, I guess so."

"Do you have a mechanic?"

"Yes."

"Well, let's get your car towed there. I'll give you a ride home."

"I don't want to inconvenience you."

"No trouble whatsoever." He pulled the phone out of his pocket and called.

Twenty minutes later the car was hooked up and ready to go. While she was getting her things out of the car, he slipped the driver his credit card.

As the tow truck left, she said, "Oh my god. I forgot to pay him."

"It's taken care of," he said.

"No. I don't want you to do that."

"Please, let me take care of this. You'll have enough with the repair bill."

"No."

"You're a stubborn woman."

"Yes, I am. So how much was it?"

"Thirty dollars," he lied.

"So, I owe you thirty. I'll send you a check," she said.

"My car's in the garage at my condo. It's just down the hill," he said, hoping the stakeout at his condo was over for the evening. They walked the two blocks to his place, making more small talk. He could feel her looking at him intently. He hoped it meant she was rethinking her opinion of him, in a positive way.

He didn't see any paparazzi and assumed they were still searching for him. He knew that sometimes they just randomly drove around in neighborhoods that he frequented hoping to come upon one of his cars.

"Would you like to come up?" he asked.

"No, I really need to get home."

It took fifteen minutes to drive to her house. No one had followed them. He got out of the car and walked her up to the front door.

"They're not home yet. Good," she said.

"Well, I should be going. I'm sure you need some time alone." He turned to walk away and said, "Oh bloody hell." He turned around, walked back to Lily, pulled her close to him and kissed her.

Just one slow, luscious kiss.

He'd taken her by surprise. Kissed her before she could protest or deck him.

She surprised him by returning the kiss. Passionately.

Holding her in his arms made him hard. He both wanted and didn't want her to notice.

"You smell wonderful," he murmured, inhaling her perfume.

"It's probably the bubble bath. Bubble gum," she said, screwing up her face.

"You wear it well," he laughed. Reluctantly, he pulled away slightly. "Will you call me?"

"Yes, I'll call you."

"We could make this work. And I have so much more to tell you about the Gift. We could all be very happy together. Please give me a chance," he said, gently brushing the hair out of her face.

"I'll think about it," she said, quietly, as she unlocked the door and went inside.

He turned to walk to his car and saw the familiar three carloads of paparazzi stalkers, surrounding his car. Unconsciously, he'd heard the click, click, click of cameras, but it hadn't registered. They whooped with victory and dove into their SUVs, still shooting.

He felt so buoyed by that kiss, he was beyond caring what damage they did.

The next thing he was conscious of was driving into the parking garage at his condo. He couldn't even remember the drive home. He was still lost in that kiss and the feeling of her in his arms.

LILY

Lily lay in bed, stretching. The sun streaming in her window warmed her. She could hear dishes rattling around in the kitchen. At least some of the kids were up. She should get up. Maybe her parents had come in from their RV, which was parked in her driveway. Then she remembered her car at the mechanics. She should call them.

She wanted to stay in bed and relive that kiss.

Instead she dragged herself out of bed, sliding her feet into slippers. Her hair was tangled and she tried to detangle some of it with her fingers. She opened her bedroom door and walked into the kitchen, yanking her XXL t-shirt down.

Nick and Susan sat at the table, drinking coffee and conspiring quietly about something. Then Susan picked her cell off the table and dialed.

Tracy, Teddy and Max were in the kitchen. Max was pouring juice into glasses. Teddy was pulling plates out of the cupboard and Tracy was cooking pancakes. With chocolate chips in them.

"Good morning," said Lily. "Can I help?"

"Nope, we're making breakfast," said Max.

"I didn't get Emily or Katie up," said Tracy. "They were both asleep."

"Well, they'll let us know when they're ready."

She walked into the living room. The younger kids were quietly watching a movie. Lily opened the front door, the sun blasted in making her cover her eyes.

Then flashes went off and twenty people seemed to be crowded on her front porch.

"Lily, is it true you and Sean O'Neill are having an affair?" asked a dark-haired man she didn't recognize.

The warm summer morning was filled with voices asking questions.

She just stood there and when the din died down a little, she said, "First, where's my newspaper?"

Eventually she was handed her slightly used paper.

"Why would you think Sean and I are having an affair?" she asked.

Someone pushed a tabloid at her. On the cover was a photo of Sean kissing her at her front door. The headline ran 'Sean O'Neill at Secret Love Nest'. She started reading the article and when she got to the part which said, 'Nina Vicente said that Sean and Lily have been lovers for years and Sean is the father of all Lily's children,' she began howling with laughter.

Nick appeared behind her in the doorway. She pointed out the passage to him. He read it and began laughing as well.

"Thanks everybody. You've made my day. Now, I need some coffee," she said, lying. She turned and walked back into the house with the tabloid.

She heard Dad say, "Show's over folks, nothing else to see. Now run along." She heard the front door close and lock, including the tall chain lock that the younger kids couldn't reach.

Lily poured herself some coffee and sat at the table across from Susan. Nick sat down as well, looking at her.

"I didn't think you'd go outside or I would have warned you," he said.

"They were there when you came in this morning?" Lily asked.

"They began arriving in the middle of the night," said Susan.

Lily drank some coffee and put her head down on the table. She felt hung over, but she didn't have that much wine last night.

"Mom," said Teddy.

She lifted her head.

He set a plate of pancakes in front of her.

She stared at them, feeling numb. She was awake though. Wide awake.

So now was what she'd been dreading. That she'd be under scrutiny. That people might notice the kids. But the only mention of the kids had been about Sean being the father. As if.

"I've got a plan," said Susan.

Lily looked at her.

"Eat your breakfast dear," Susan said. "After we all eat and pack up some clothes, we'll pile into the rental van and go shopping for a van for you. I found several choices online and we'll go look at them. Now, I just called Janice and told her you've got a plague of paparazzi camped out on your doorstep. She suggested a camping trip. I agree. So after we buy a van, we'll park at her house. She's going to buy a tent or two for you, sleeping bags and air mattresses. Then she'll pick up food. So you can load up over there and get out of town for a week. Nick and I will come back here, close up the house and pick up the RV and turn the rental van in and drive north to go to a friend's daughter's wedding."

Lily considered the possibilities of Susan's plan. Mom was thorough. She had that to say for her.

"By the time you get back, all the paparazzi will have moved on to other things," said Dad.

"Maybe," she said.

"Probably," said Susan.

"Definitely," said Nick.

"What about my car. At the mechanics?"

"We'll have it towed to where ever we buy the van. Make it part of the van deal. Or something," he said. "It'll all work out."

It took a couple hours for everyone to eat and pack clothes and entertainment. Jim was completely panicked to leave technology behind for an entire week.

"No dear," said Susan. "Nothing electronic. Think of it as an experiment. This is how people used to live all the time. They read books, sang songs, played cards."

Teddy was stressed about leaving his music behind, until Nick went out the RV and brought in a guitar and said, "Time to start making your own music."

Teddy's eyes lit up as if the idea had never occurred to him. Nick showed him a few chords and basics.

When they went out to load stuff into the rental van, Lily found the paparazzi population was cut in half. They snapped photos and when they tried to talk to her, Nick started in telling stories which distracted the reporters long enough so she could get everyone settled in and buckled up. Susan took the wheel and Nick popped in at the last minute.

Four cars of them followed her, but they quickly got bored with car shopping, especially after one of the managers of a dealership threatened to call the police.

Lily found a used van which would fit everyone with room to spare. A little room at least. Her parents helped with the down payment and along with trading in her battered Subaru the mechanic had gotten started, the monthly payments were doable.

By four in the afternoon, Janice and Lily had packed up the new/used van and they were all on their way out of town. Lily felt wonderful driving a vehicle where everyone could now be safe. Not to mention it was fifteen years newer than her old station wagon.

They chose the Nick and Susan method of traveling. Max closed his eyes and pointed at the map and they drove, deciding the first night would be staying at a hotel since they had started out so late. Pizza was on the menu for dinner. She silently thanked her parents again for the cash they'd pressed into the hand before leaving.

"I can't wait for my turn to point," said Nancy, bouncing up and down as much as her car seat would let her.

At some point during the week, Lily went to call Sean and realized her phone was dead. She'd forgotten to bring the charger in the haste of packing. She felt guilty. This time she'd actually meant to call him and blown it. What must he think of her?

The camping trip was fun with only a couple of complications. Jim broke his arm walking across slippery river rocks and Nancy got an ear infection. But even they had a blast. Before she knew it they were all back home, parked in their driveway with no one around. Lily was glad there were no paparazzi in sight.

It was after midnight when they drove in, so Lily left the van to unpack tomorrow and got everybody settled in their beds.

"I'll come over tomorrow and help unpack," Janice said.

"I have to be at work by ten," Lily said.

"Oh, that's right. Why don't you take my car and I'll get the kids to help unpack? I'll get them started on laundry and stuff."

"You're a lifesaver. I have to leave at 9:30," said Lily.

The next morning, Lily ran through the shower and got breakfast for everyone. She pulled on a pair of shorts and a tank top.

There was a knock at the front door. She opened the living room curtains and saw five paparazzi out in the front yard and Janice and her daughter coming up the front steps.

She opened the front door and the cameras started snapping shots. At least she'd brushed her hair.

Janice carried a huge box of doughnuts and her daughter held two cups of coffee. Lily let them through. One of the paparazzi, the one who'd followed her home the night she met Nina, handed her the daily paper.

"Thanks," she said, and closed the door.

"I didn't know they were still here," said Janice.

"Neither did I. They must be cruising by every day, just in case," said Lily. "But I thought this would have blown over by now."

Lily grabbed a Bavarian cream doughnut with chocolate frosting and slipped into a pair of sandals as she chewed. Then she put her now charged phone in her purse, resolving to call Sean. Today.

She looked towards the front door and said, "I don't have time for this nonsense. What if they follow me to work?"

Janice said, "Go out the back door and through my yard. Car's in the driveway," she said, dangling the keys from her hand. "We'll get the van unloaded and things aired out. After that, it's time for your kids to learn how to garden. If the paparazzi give us any trouble, we'll toss slugs at them."

Beau and Boo whooped. Apparently, throwing slugs at anyone counted as major fun.

"Okay, thanks. I better run before I get fired." Lily hugged the kids and dashed out the back door. She went through the new gate Janice's husband had made between the two back yards. She got tangled in the overgrown blackberries coming from her own yard. After getting free, she went out Janice's other gate to her driveway, which was around the corner from the paparazzi. Lily got into Janice's Honda and drove to work at the hotel.

She finished the coffee Janice brought in the car. She picked up another one from the hotel bar and flew into the dressing room. The other models were already there, made up and nearly dressed. Lily did what she could with her face and hair. Jeannie came in, saw her and glared. Then she left.

What the hell was that about? Lily didn't participate in the chatter. She got dressed in a copper high waisted nightgown, slit up the right thigh. After work, she'd either call Sean or maybe go to his condo and find out why the paparazzi were still haunting her. And go by a cash machine and get thirty dollars to pay him back. But she couldn't live with the paparazzi shadowing her every move. It made her crazy, wondering when they'd discover the increasing kids. Did Sean really know something about the Gift, as he called it? Maybe he knew how to stop it.

She followed the other models out into the lounge and walked across the stage and among the tables as Jeannie described their clothes for the audience.

One older gentleman asked her the price and Lily stopped to tell him and give him a spiel about the wonderful flow of the fabric. She could tell he simply wanted to talk, not buy anything and she needed to move on. She felt sorry for him. Probably just a guy who was lonely, but she sure wasn't who he needed. Not with her little problem.

The next trip through she wore an indigo lace, merry widow with a thong and black stockings. She didn't talk much to people about what she did for a living. She had always felt self conscious when people asked, but after years of modeling swim suits, this felt like being fully clothed. And it was her most stable and best paying job these days. She really needed it with all her expenses from the kids.

She walked onstage, annoyed at the gold charm bracelet, it didn't fit with the merry widow, way too cutesy, but worse it kept getting caught on the lace. Jeannie had just gotten a contract from a jeweler, so they'd begun modeling a lot of jewelry as well as lingerie.

She stood in the middle of the stage, looking out over the audience, while Jeannie described her outfit. She continued walking, then saw Sean sitting at a table in front. She shook her head. Tried to clear it. Maybe she was just imagining things. Looked again as she pivoted. Damn. He was still there.

She took a deep breath and began walking. The heel snapped off one of her shoes. She stumbled, running into Jeannie at the podium. Lily's gold bracelet got tangled up with own her garters and Jeannie's ruffled dress.

Lily tried to free the bracelet. It only made things worse. Finally, she gave a yank. Something would give.

The bracelet flew into separate parts. Some of it stayed stuck to her garters. Some to Jeannie's dress. The rest went up in the air.

She slipped on one of the charms. And landed flat on her ass. In the middle of the spotlight. Jeannie, only five foot tall and a hundred pounds ended up in Lily's lap. There were gasps from the audience.

Lily looked at the audience. Sean fished part of the bracelet out of his drink. It was a heart. He winked at her. Then stuck it into his mouth to clean it. Then tucked it into his shirt pocket, patting it. And smiled a very predatory smile.

Jeannie struggled to her feet, one of her sharp heels coming down on Lily's calf. Hard. Besides tearing her stocking, it hurt like hell. Lily wondered if it was intentional.

Jeannie put the podium upright again. A few snickers came from the audience.

She spoke into the microphone, nervously patting her hairspray encrusted hair. "I guess that just proves the lingerie we sell is stronger than gold. Durable, yet feminine enough for your little lady."

Rising, Lily surveyed the ruins of her stockings and tried to smile as nonchalantly as possible, despite the pain in her calf. She slipped out of the shoes and kicked them backstage. She walked through the audience trying to work out the pain. The remains of the bracelet still stuck to her garter, jingling every time she moved her leg.

Lily knew she looked calm, but this job was history. She'd get sacked. Jeannie had fired models for less.

Panic streamed through her. What would she do for money? What would happen to her and the kids? How was she going to deal with the party on her front lawn? What if they figured out about the kids?

She went into the dressing room bathroom, locked the door and stood there for a few minutes in the darkness, hyperventilating. She felt nauseous. The restroom smelled like newly cut grass. Must be some strange air freshener.

After the show, Jeannie fired her, in front of everyone. Complaining about her lateness, being clumsy and for the clincher, Jeannie pulled out the 'Sean O'Neill at Secret Love Nest' tabloid.

She said, "Now, some people would see your association with this as money in the bank. I think it's trashy and tawdry and I will not have one of my girls involved in something that makes the cover of a tabloid." Then Jeannie left the room, head held high and smiling with self-righteousness.

Lily felt humiliated and furious. The other models commiserated with her, told her they'd keep in touch, especially about other jobs.

She packed up and went to the childcare center out of habit. Sean waited there for her. She glared at him, unsure why, and walked past him to the counter before realizing she hadn't left Emily or Katie there.

She hadn't meant to glare at him. It wasn't fair. He didn't get her fired. He couldn't help it if she lost it every time she saw him.

"Hi Lily," said Theresa, as she got a Pokemon lunch box down. "Sorry to hear about your job."

New travels fast, Lily thought. "Yeah, well that's life, I guess."

"Jeremy was a little rowdy today."

"Jeremy?" she asked, trying to play along.

"Yeah. He smeared paint all over Andrew. But Andrew probably deserved it. His mom lets him get away with murder. Then Jeremy tried to flush the bean plants down the toilet."

"Troublemaker," said Lily. Another child and she'd just lost her steady job. She felt any hope of financial survival sink into oblivion.

When Theresa brought him out, the boy had the universal 'I'm being rescued by Mom' expression on his face. It was the same one Katie and Emily had whenever they got picked up at childcare.

Lily turned to go out the door with Jeremy holding her hand. Sean looked at her and raised an eyebrow. He smiled at her.

She stuck her tongue out at him and said, "This is all your fault."

Lily wasn't sure what that meant, but something had to be

his fault. He was just too cool, too calm, too perfect, too patient.

He followed her to the parking lot. "Yes, it is. You didn't return any of my calls. I stopped by your house, but no one was home. I couldn't think of anything else to do. I needed to see you. I guess I shouldn't have sat in the front row of tables though. I should have chosen one of the dark corners in back, like last time."

"Last time?" she raised her voice, while fastening Jeremy into the car seat that had magically appeared in the back seat of Janice's car. She closed the door and walked around to the other side, opening the back door and dumping all her stuff inside and opening the front door as well, to let more heat out.

"Yeah. I've been here several times. It's where I first saw you when I came back to Seattle. I still had a beard and long hair from the last film. You didn't notice me and I didn't want to say anything to you. I didn't want you to think I was just another lonely guy looking to get laid."

"But you are! What is it you want? To ruin my entire life? I just lot my job and I have nine children to care for. I'm having a meltdown. And I really don't know what to do, but I don't want to do this in public."

He pulled her into his arms. She held her own arms rigidly crossed against her chest.

Sean said, "I want to find out who you are, I want to take you out dancing or swimming or for a walk in a park with the kids. I want to sit with you and explain the Gift to you. I can't get you out of my mind and I don't want to."

"That's what my ex said and that didn't last long."

"I'm not your ex husband."

"No, you're not, are you, but I don't know who you are," she said.

"Well, stop running away from me and you might find out."

That made her really mad. She knew he was right. And the childish part of her wanted to be right. To throw a tantrum and cry and scream. She felt so afraid and angry.

She took several deep breaths and relaxed in his arms, embracing him.

After a few minutes, she said, "Okay. If you want to come over on Friday for dinner, consider this an invitation. We're grilling fish. But beware, I'm probably going to have to invite all the reporters who're camped out on my front lawn. And it's the fourth of July, so who know's what will happen?"

He winced. "Have you seen '*The Universe*' yet?"

"How could I help it? One of them shoved a copy in my face the morning after the photo was shot. I was still in my pajamas. Apparently, your friend Nina hasn't helped matters."

He looked her in the eyes and asked, "What do you want me to do?"

"Is there anything you *can* do?"

"I'll try. Nina's as stubborn as a boulder, but I'll find something to make her recant, for whatever good it'll do. Were you serious about dinner?" he asked, stroking her back.

Her skin tingled at his touch. She wanted him to keep touching her.

"Yes," she said, feeling confused and guilty about laying into him. She still felt angry about the paparazzi and losing her job.

"Would it be possible for me to bring my twin sister, Casey? I think you two should talk."

"Sure. The more the merrier. You're welcome to bring your whole family. Like I said, we will be inviting anyone and everyone. My parents will be back in town. The neighbors are coming over."

"What can I bring in the way of food?"

"Dessert, I guess. Ice cream bars or something."

"Chocolate," yelled Jeremy through the open door.

"You just buckle yourself in young man," she said. "What color paint was it?"

"Red," he said, hunting for the seat belt.

"Chocolate, it is," said Sean.

"You know where we live," she said. "I'll see you and your entourage around six."

She hoped this wasn't one huge mistake.

SEAN

Sean stood in Casey's well-ordered living room. His niece, Dana, sat on the couch. She was trying to tearfully explain the toddler on her lap.

He shifted weight to the other foot and picked lint from his blue T-shirt, feeling uncomfortable.

Dana's twin brother, Daniel, stood behind her. He looked worried, but supportive, his hands rubbing her shoulders.

They were only eighteen, just graduated from high school. The scene seemed reminiscent of the one both he and Casey played out nearly twenty years ago with their parents. So much angst could be avoided if only parents warned their kids what would happen. But they didn't, maybe hoping the Gift would run its course and disappear. It never did. He would have thought Casey and James had told the twins, especially after all James' genealogy research.

Sean glared at Casey, pacing back and forth and jumping at the sound of a string of firecrackers shooting off days before the fourth of July.

"Damn fireworks," she said.

Clearly not the real problem.

"Why?" asked Sean. "Why didn't you tell her?"

She turned on him and snapped, "Because I thought eighteen was too young. She's just a baby."

James remained calm and asked, "Dana, who's the father."

"I told you, how do I know? Believe it or not, I'm still a virgin. Even though I'm sooo old. Jamie was sitting in the car. Strapped into a car seat, toys and all, when I came out of the store. I don't understand it. He keeps calling me Mama and I knew his name was Jamie and all about him.

"Did you lock the car?" asked James.

Casey shot him a dirty look and James put his hands in the air and said, "Well, I just want to make sure nobody's missing their child and we don't need to call 911 to let them know we found him."

"Daaaddd. I always lock the car. I learned my lesson since the stereo got stolen a year ago. Besides, the car seat was in our car, so were his toys and diaper bag," she said, defensively. "You don't actually think he crawled in there with all that."

She held on to Jamie as if her life depended on it and he clutched her long brown hair in his tiny hands. She wasn't about to let anyone take him from her. Sean had never thought of her as maternal.

He hid his smile from Casey, who was clearly not amused by the irony.

His thoughts drifted to Lily and her ignorance about the Gift. He was worried about her; even Lily knew she was melting down. And he hadn't thought of a way Nina could help. Tomorrow was the party at her house. He'd find a way to make things right. Somehow.

He realized the room was silent and everyone stared at him.

"Earth to Sean," Casey said.

"Sorry, I was wool gathering."

"She doesn't know who it is. What do we do now?" asked Casey.

"Well, first it would probably be a good idea to explain the whole thing to her," he said.

Casey and James looked sheepishly at each other, trying to figure out where to start. When he and Lily had twins, they'd do better. He hoped.

The doorbell ran and Casey answered it. Bob came in, pushing a wooden crib.

"What's that?" asked James.

"Well, Sadie had wanted to keep this, so we moved it up here with us. Then she changed her mind and I was going to take it to donate, but this morning I just had this unshakeable feeling that you needed it," said Bob.

Casey just stood there, mouth open, then looked at James, who shook his head no at her. No one had called Bob.

Sean rubbed his eyes in disbelief. Sometimes, life was just too strange.

James snatched his glasses off the coffee table, just before Jamie did. He handed the toddler a coaster which Jamie accepted as a suitable substitute. He wandered off with it in his mouth.

"What's going on?" asked Dana.

Sean said, "Oh, for Pete's sake." He sat on the coffee table across from Dana. "Daniel, sit down. You're going to go through this too, so you better listen and remember. I don't know how or when this started, but it was ages and ages ago and has been passed down for generations. It's probably some sort of genetic mutation or maybe it's magic. No one knows. But our family has it."

"What is *it*?" asked Dana.

"It is what Gram and Gramps call the Gift. It happens to twins. So, there's a set of twins, a boy and a girl. They grow up and the girl starts finding children come into her life. Like Jamie and you. She knows the child is hers, that she's its mom. As time passes perhaps more children appear. In the best case scenario, the twin knows what's happening and knows who her soul mate is. He also, is always a twin and is somehow the catalyst for the kids appearing. Once they figure it out and get together and consummate the relationship, the kids stop appearing and a set of twins is born, setting the cycle in motion again."

"Consummate?" asked Dana. "What does that mean."

"Have sex, get pregnant."

Her face turned beet red.

Daniel said, "Are you all crazy?" He looked at Casey and James.

"Nope. Well, we are actually, but not about this. And like I said, it'll happen to you. Maybe sooner, maybe later. It happened to your mother and I didn't notice anything strange at the time. Just saw kids showing up in her life for all sorts of reasons."

Now, if only he could tell all this to Lily just as clearly.

Sean asked, "What do you remember Bob?"

"I didn't notice anything strange about Casey. She was at the University and I was in Portland having kids of my own, the normal way. And with Mom and Dad, well I never remembered much before I was six. Mom and Dad told us we were adopted, so I never thought much about it. Didn't wonder who my real parents might be, because I had a great home and the best family ever. I know all of it sounds nuts, but it fits somehow. Seems natural for our family." He shrugged his shoulders and leaned against the crib.

"So, if it happens to twins, why hasn't it happened to you?" asked Daniel, staring at Sean, his arms crossed in total denial.

"It has happened to me. Is happening to me."

"So where is she?" he asked.

"In Seattle, but I'm having a tough time getting through to her," he said, feeling frustrated and a little embarrassed.

Daniel looked crestfallen.

Casey began laughing hysterically. "You've just blown your image, big brother. Daniel always thought you were infallible.

Sean laughed, snorting. That was rich.

He turned to Dana and asked, "Is there someone you know who's irresistible, that you've got a huge crush on or you seem to have great chemistry with?"

Dana looked thoughtful and said, "No one," as she rose, vaulted over the coffee table and grabbed Jamie before he pulled the tablecloth off the dining room table. "Mom, I think it's time to baby proof the house."

Daniel said, quietly, "Peter."

Dana said quickly, "It can't be him," and gave Daniel a warning look.

"Why?" asked Daniel, ignoring the look.

"He's five years older than I am."

"Who's Peter," asked Casey.

"You know, Coach Swanson," said Daniel.

"Your soccer coach?" screeched Casey, her hands gripping the back of the couch, nearly ripping holes in it.

"He's not interested in me," said Dana, looking at her feet.

"Yes, he is. I've seen the way he looks at you, but of course he can't say anything to you," said Daniel. "That would be so wrong. He's your coach. Some guys wouldn't respect that boundary, but he does. He's a nice guy."

Casey relaxed her grip on the couch. Sean smiled. His sister had nearly strangled her future son-in-law, in absentia.

"Let's have Peter over for dessert, tonight. Now," said Casey.

Sean could tell she was working hard to wrap her mind

around the fact that her baby, not only wasn't a baby anymore, but now had a baby.

"No," said Dana. "I'd just die."

"You'll do nothing of the kind," said Casey. "We'll just have him over for dessert and to meet Jamie. See if he has a twin sister and whatever else we can dig up."

His sister seemed to have learned the gift of scheming from him. He smiled.

Sean left shortly afterwards. He wondered how many children Dana would have before things worked out.

He pulled over in a parking lot and decided to give Nina's number a try. He had an idea.

There was no answer, so he left a quick message, "Nina, I need to talk to you, pronto. It's Sean."

He'd already left a message with his publicist's receptionist. But James was on a trip to Australia, so wouldn't get the message until he landed.

Sean wanted everything solved immediately.

He was about to put his phone away, when it rang in his hand. He didn't recognize the number, but answered it anyway.

"Hello."

"Sean, this is Lily."

"Hi."

"I need to cancel the party on Friday. Tomorrow." Her voice shook.

"What's wrong?"

"Teddy's been hurt. I'm at the hospital."

"Which one?"

"Sisters of Mercy."

"Emergency room?"

"Yeah."

"What happened?" he asked, putting on the bluetooth and pulling out of the parking lot, heading towards the freeway.

"I'm not sure." Her voice quavered. "He was out with some other kids. There was drinking, a stolen car. I don't know how he's involved yet."

"Have they told you how he is?"

"No, I'm in the waiting room. Waiting. Listen, I've got to go."

"I'll be there as soon as traffic allows."

"No, please don't come, I'm a mess."

"I'll be right there, fifteen minutes. You shouldn't be alone. No arguing."

"Thank you," she said.

He liked to think she sounded relieved because she really wanted him there.

LILY

Lily paced restlessly around the mostly crowded waiting room. It was painted a cream color with beige chairs and beige carpet. Was it supposed to be soothing? It wasn't working for her. It was just ugly and lifeless and boring. One would think in an ER that they'd have a decor that would be distracting. Something to entertain people while they sat around in pain or waiting with their loved ones who were hurting. She pulled the long sweater tighter over her T-shirt and capris, but didn't button it.

Why had she called Sean? She'd called Janice, who came over to take care of the rest of the kids. When she got to the hospital, she called her parents. They hadn't wanted to talk long so they could get on the road and come back to Seattle.

Sean was always asking to be let into her life. She needed someone to talk to, to be there. Maybe it was time to see if he was the man he claimed to be.

She watched people come and go, then finally sat in a chair in the corner and flipped through a newspaper someone had left. A few minutes later she put it down without having read a word.

She sighed, rearranging herself in the chair and wrapping her arms around herself. If only she'd been there. If only she'd watched Teddy more closely. If only she'd asked for more help when he first started acting out, gone to see a therapist or something.

The reality was that she couldn't handle all the kids alone. Maybe she was a good mom like everyone said. Maybe not. But it wasn't enough. All the stress of wondering where the kids came from, whether they'd be discovered and taken away from her, when they'd stop coming, keeping Sean at bay, worrying about money and getting fired, had taken its toll. She was snapping. Had snapped. She couldn't do any more or any better. That was the crux of the problem.

She buried her face in her hands.

"Lily," said Sean, putting his hand gently on her shoulder, as he slid into an adjoining chair.

She looked up, wiping the tears from her face with the sweater sleeve. Her eyes and nose were all red, but she really didn't care.

He put an arm around her and pulled her as close as the two chairs would allow. His other hand brushed the hair out of her face. "Have you heard anything?"

"No, he's in surgery right now. Maybe a punctured lung. I should have taken better care of him."

"This isn't your fault. Sometimes kids have to make their own choices and fail in order to learn." He squeezed her and said, "I'll see if I can find anything out."

She watched him walk up to the admitting desk. Her face tingled where he'd touched her skin. She felt warm and just wanted to glue herself to him. How could it be that she felt safe near him? A man she barely knew. She found a tissue in her purse and pulled it out, hoping it was clean.

The nurse, a tall thin man, looked preoccupied by paperwork and spoke without looking up from his piles. Sean replied to him. The nurse finally looked up and did a double take. Sean had clearly been recognized and was very gracious.

She watched their conversation for a few minutes, before realizing the nurse was flirting with him. Sean flashed his charming smile at the nurse as the man picked up the phone and dialed. There was a back and forth conversation and then the nurse hung up. They had a conversation and the nurse shuffled through some papers and handed Sean a paper. Sean signed it. Lily was puzzled. Was he signing an autograph? She watched Sean hand it back to the man and they chatted a little more, then he came back and sat beside her.

"The doctor is coming out to talk to you. Teddy's out of surgery."

"Thank you."

"Who's taking care of the kids?"

"Janice, my next door neighbor. She drove me here and dropped me off. I was too upset and crazy to drive. She went back to my house and was going to stay until Mom and Dad got there."

"What else can I do to help?"

"I don't know. I'm not feeling clear about anything at the moment."

"Then I'll just stay here with you."

Lily wished she could think of something to say, but nothing came to her. The waiting room was nearly deserted now. An older couple sat and waited. The woman, clearly in pain, held her arm. In a distant corner a young woman nervously leafed through magazines, her entire body tense.

Lily watched the admitting desk fill up with staff trying to look busy. They kept sneaking peeks at Sean over their clipboards. He looked like it was normal and just smiled at them. She stared out the window, trying not to start crying again.

A petite woman with short, dark hair walked over to them. Still dressed in green scrubs, she said, "I'm Dr. Shelby." She shook Lily's hand first, then Sean's. "Teddy's out of surgery and doing well. He's in the recovery room and will need to stay a few days, but he's out of immediate danger."

She paused, perhaps waiting for questions or to make sure she'd been understood.

Lily nodded.

The doctor continued, "Teddy has a collapsed lung and three fractured ribs. We've re-inflated the lung and repaired the damage. He should be just fine. He'll be sore for quite a while. And he'll be sleeping for the rest of the night, but he's a teenage boy and they bounce back quickly."

Lily felt some of her tension drain away.

"He could have died, couldn't he?" she asked.

"Yes, he could have if the ambulance hadn't arrived soon enough."

"Can we see him?" asked Sean.

"Certainly. They're taking him up to room 620. Like I said, he will be drowsy until sometime tomorrow. And he's stable."

"Thank you so much for your help," said Sean, standing.

Lily stood and said, "Thank you."

"You're very welcome." Dr. Shelby turned and left.

Sean took her arm and they walked towards the main part of the hospital.

She felt shaken to the core. Relief flooded through her, but along with it came anger and frustration. Clenching her jaw, she tried to distract herself with her surroundings. Trying to hold back the flood of emotion and tears which threatened to overflow and drown her.

They waited outside the room, while the nurses bustled about and got Teddy settled in. Sean seemed to know she didn't want to talk and just stood with his arm around her.

Once inside, she felt shocked at how pale Teddy looked. She stroked his hair and began to cry.

After a few minutes, she pulled an iPod out of her purse, turned it on and listened to check the volume, then put the headphones in Teddy's ears. She tucked the iPod under his covers.

"At least he'll have music he likes to listen to," she said.

Sean nodded at her.

"I have a favor to ask you," she said, wiping her face.

"Anything."

"I need to run home, pick up a few things, send Janice home and check on everything, stay till Mom and Dad get in and then I'll drive myself back here. Could you give me a ride home?"

"It would be my pleasure."

She turned back to Teddy, leaned over him and whispered, "I love you sweetheart. I'll be back as soon as I can."

Sean took her arm and they walked to the elevator. Once inside, he held her in his arms. She leaned into him, inhaling his smell. Tried to concentrate on him and ignore her life, for just a while.

She got into his car and he closed the door behind her.

He got in and asked, "Do you need to get some food?"

"No, I'm fine. And my parents could be there any time. It'll be chaos at my house, what with the paparazzi and all. They're probably back. They seem to show up most evenings."

"I'm so sorry about that. I put in a few calls and I'll make a few more. See what can be done."

The ride to her house was quiet. As they crossed town, they

drove into the rain. She stared out the window at the wet streets. She felt cold. He must have as well, because he turned the heater on. She remembered watching him at the nurses' station at the ER.

"What were you signing at the ER?"

"What do you mean?" he asked.

"The nurse handed you a paper and you wrote on it."

He sighed deeply. "I asked them to send Teddy's bill to me."

"What?"

"I can't let you pay for this, even if you had the money, which I'm guessing you don't. I know you don't understand all of what's going on with the children. I need some time to explain it to you, but I'm thinking now is *not* it." He looked at her.

"You're right. Now is not it. I'm on overload already," she said.

"So, let me just say, that I bear some of the responsibility here. If you disagree after we have time to talk, I'll give you the bill when I get it."

She nodded at him. He was so damned mysterious. Part of the reason she felt attracted to him, she supposed.

He pulled up in front of her house. Mom and Dad's RV was parked on the street since her van was in the driveway. Two paparazzi stood under umbrellas. As Sean parked behind her van the rest came out of their SUVs.

"Can I walk you to the door?" he asked.

"Not with all these witnesses."

She kissed him and said, "Thanks for coming to help. I'll call you tomorrow."

"Goodnight. You sure you don't want me to drive you back to the hospital."

"I'm sure. I feel better, knowing he'll be okay."

She kissed him again, harder. As he returned the kiss shivers ran down the back of her neck and continued along her spine. She reluctantly pulled away and went out into the rain, ignoring the paparazzi who swarmed around her.

She heard a whistle and saw Sean standing beside the car.

He said, "C'mon gentlemen, oh hello Alice, ladies as well. Let's go for a ride. Any of you who meet me at the Scarlet Door within twenty minutes will get to hear stories about Nina Vicente that will curl your hair." He slid back into his car, slammed the door, backed down the driveway and drove off.

The paparazzi paused and looked at each other, for about half a second, then fled, leaving only two staked out on her lawn. She slipped through the front door just as they turned their attention back to her.

Would he really go to the tavern? And would he talk about Nina? Probably not, since finding a parking place at the tavern would take at least half an hour.

The house was quiet. All the kids must be in bed. How did Janice manage that?

There was a light on in the kitchen and she found Janice, Nick and Susan drinking cups of mint tea.

Then it occurred to her that if Sean would kiss and tell about Nina, he would do the same about her. How many years down the road?

After all neither of them had a great track record for relationships.

SEAN

Sean made another cup of coffee and sat at his dining room table, wearing a pair of jeans. They were new and way too stiff and uncomfortable, but he felt too lazy to change. He looked at the debris of the morning newspaper. Lily called very early this morning and said Teddy was doing much better. She thanked him again and said the fourth of July party was still on for this evening. She felt bad for Teddy missing it, but all the other kids had been so looking forward to it, she didn't want to punish them.

He felt relieved. Somehow, he needed to get her alone tonight and talk to her.

So, today he'd get all those pesky phone calls out of the way, read a script this afternoon and check his business messages. It had been a week and he knew the messages were backed up for miles. He had endless hours to fill until it was time to leave.

He pushed the button, listened and deleted. Only one tempting offer, an indie film with an up and coming director. But he didn't think it would be more tempting than spending time with Lily and the kids.

Sean got up, stretched and looked in the mirror. He needed to shower and shave. And call Casey to tell her he would meet her at Food King this afternoon. He couldn't shake the paparazzi now. Too many of them. They hadn't found where she lived yet and he wanted to keep it that way.

He sighed. Time to call Nina again. She hadn't returned his call from yesterday. He knew she was back in Vancouver shooting.

He sat down and picked up his cell.

He was surprised when she answered.

"Hello dahling, have you forgiven me?" she asked.

"Not yet sweetheart. Not after what you told the paparazzi."

"What? I haven't told anyone anything."

"Can it, Nina...," he said, warningly.

"Oh!"

He could almost see her stamping her feet in frustration.

She said, "You were so beastly, wouldn't even talk to me."

"I'm talking to you now." He gripped the chair arm, forcing himself to plunge ahead and not fall for her attempts to direct his attention where she wanted it.

"It's time for you to create a wonderfully, juicy scandal about someone else. Maybe even you. Somewhere else in the world. I want you to take the paparazzi off Lily's doorstep today."

"Even if I could do that, why would I want to?"

Sean took a deep breath to keep from yelling at her. She knew so well how to push his buttons.

He said, softly, "I know you can. And you will do it because I've always been very quiet about what happened with our breakup. I've always refused to talk to the press about certain facets of your past and your personality, even while you painted me a blaggard. I've also had standing offers for an interview with every single news show in existence, with interviewers on your dream list. So, if you don't move the paparazzi's attention off of Lily, and myself for that matter, then I'll schedule a media blitz, including an autobiography, that will sear your eyelashes off."

He sat back, waiting for her to squirm.

There was a lot he could reveal about her, but he'd always felt it was no one's business. She'd always put a spin on what leaked out into the press to make herself look like a victim overcoming bad circumstances, or a martyr. This time, he wouldn't let that happen. He was now more than willing to show the other side of her. He wouldn't lose Lily over this.

"Sean, that's not fair. And it wouldn't look good to kiss and tell."

"Normally, I wouldn't. But I love this woman and you've made her life hell. She's lost her job and she doesn't have a security team to take care of her. Now, are you going to do this or shall I call my agent?"

She sighed, dramatically.

"I'm not bluffing. You know I don't play games."

"I know. What do you suggest? I don't have any ideas."

"You're devious enough to figure it out."

"I can't think of anything I could do that would upstage you and a new woman."

"You have a movie opening soon. Eric Jorgessen's just finishing up filming here in Seattle. He thinks you're amazing. Why don't you two start a very torrid, very public love affair? I think you'd get on wonderfully and the publicity for your film would be great.

"Eric. I always thought he was a little wild."

Sean smiled with amusement.

"Wouldn't you like to be the one who tames him? Just a thought. I'm sure you'll come up with something. Fly down from Vancouver and see him. Today. And take all these reporters away with you. I know you just wrapped. So do it."

"You sure know a lot."

"I keep my ear to the ground."

Sean realized he was probably right about the two of them. Eric needed someone spontaneous and dramatic, but someone who needed to be taken care of, like Nina. And she needed someone who would worship her, but boss her around every now and then.

"How do I know you won't change your mind and spill all my secrets later?"

"Nina."

"Okay, okay. I'll see what I can do. But I can't promise they'll leave," she said.

"Just promise me you'll do something wildly dramatic."

"You really love this woman, don't you?" she asked.

"Yes, I do."

"She's very lucky."

"You will be too, if you call Eric," he said.

"Okay."

"Do it now. I want them gone today," he said.

"Okay."

He gave her Eric's number, then hung up. He texted Eric 'expect phone call from Nina soon, if she doesn't call, you need to call her.' Sean had spoken to Eric late last night and given him her cell number, along with the possible scenario. Eric had been ecstatic. So, hopefully that would clear off some of the paparazzi.

Around four-thirty he took a shower and smoothed gel on his chin. What words could he come up with so Lily would believe him? And want him? He wanted there to be some magic words.

He'd tell her about his parents and Casey and James. Maybe meeting Casey would help.

Sean rinsed the razor and began shaving. His hair needed a trim again.

The script he'd read this afternoon was intriguing. His agent was right. The film would most likely be incredible. Great director and production team. But this was his chance to have Lily. He wouldn't pass her up. At some point he needed to choose a film to do or else he'd lose his chances of getting good films. Had he already passed that point?

Finished with the shower, he dried off and put on sunscreen. Brushed his hair. He pulled on some khaki shorts, a sky blue T-shirt and sandals.

He checked messages, but there were none. He hoped Nina was getting off an airplane. Otherwise he'd be making a few late night calls.

It was 5:00. He just had time to try to lose the paparazzi, make it to the store to get ice cream bars and meet Casey.

He wanted to be at Lily's at six. Not early. It was never okay to show up early for a function held at someone's house. And it was even more dangerous if the people had kids. His siblings had taught him that.

He'd been wracking his brain for an idea of how to get rid of the paparazzi if Nina didn't come through, but still didn't have a back-up plan.

Lily needed at least one problem off her back.

LILY

LILY PERCHED ON THE EDGE OF THE LAWN CHAIR, THE WARM breeze blowing her hair in her face before she finally pulled the strands into one bundle and tied it into a knot. The airflow felt nice even though she was dressed for warm weather: tank top, cutoffs and bare feet.

She was trying to get the coals lit. It took three tries before they caught. Everyone else was in the house, getting food ready or giving tours of the house and their toy collection to guests. Janice and her family hadn't arrived yet.

Sean had come with Casey, her twins and a small boy, who belonged to Casey's daughter.

He said, "I didn't know how many people would come." Then he handed over a couple grocery bags with ten dozen chocolate ice cream bars and a dozen vanilla. His sister brought two enormous salads.

She was secretly amused that a man was interested enough to try and bribe the kids. Sean was promptly waylaid by Jim, who wanted to show Sean his model airplane collection. Jim had already shown them to the twelve paparazzi who'd been on the front lawn when she declared the party open. She hadn't been joking with Sean about inviting them. She was tired of strangers hanging about and decided the paparazzi needed to not be strangers anymore. So they were now scattered throughout the house being entertained by Lily's kids or her parents or perhaps Sean. She felt sure Dad was making up incredible lies about something or other. He loved telling stories and playing games.

She blew on the coals just to be sure and stood up. The yard was beginning to look like a real home. Janice and the kids had planted shrubs and flowers and had helped the younger kids start a vegetable garden. The lettuce and zucchini thrived. Teddy had planted a couple of rose bushes.

Lily sighed. What was she going to do with him? He was going to be okay, physically. But he'd nearly gotten killed. There was going to be a lot more rules for him once he got out of the hospital. And counseling. And he certainly wasn't going to see those friends again. She was considering locking him in the room he shared with Jim and Max, for all eternity.

Twenty firecrackers in a row blew up. Maybe a block away. They were illegal, but on the fourth there wouldn't be any enforcement happening.

Casey, Dana, Tracy and Susan began bringing food out to put on the table. Nick came out with a sheet pan holding slabs of salmon that he and Mom brought. Max brought out hot dogs.

Janice, her husband and daughter came through the gate with corn on the cob and marshmallows.

"Hey, glad you guys could make it," said Lily.

"I'm so happy we changed plans. I really didn't want to drive around today. So much nicer to walk next door," said Janice.

Dad came over and asked, "How're those coals coming?"

"Almost ready, Mr. Chef."

"Great, I'll run in and get my equipment."

Dad loved to grill things.

More food came out of the house. Lily felt glad she'd borrowed a couple of Janice's extra tables, and a lot of chairs. With all the food taking up a whole table, there still might be room to eat.

Lily should probably buy a couple of those tables, so all of her family could eat together.

Sean was still being given the tour. He waved from Nancy's window. Did he need rescuing? No. This would give him a taste of what her life was like. He needed to know the reality. What did an actor know about real life?

She went into the kitchen searching for the paper plates and napkins she'd tucked away. But where?

Part of her felt overwhelmed. Too many responsibilities. Too many paparazzi still hanging around, just waiting for a story. She still felt paranoid that they might notice the kids, she felt sure more kids were coming.

She muttered to herself, "I'll just sell my story to the tabloids and the whole family will become freaks. '*Woman attracts kids like metal to magnets. Estimates of eight per year, all virgin births.*' Okay, the last part is a lie, I'm far from a virgin. And I didn't given birth to them. But the rest is accurate. At this rate I'll have to start giving them away. Or start my own school, but there won't be room for anyone else's kids."

Finally, all the food was cooked and set out, along with plates. Beverages were in a couple of ice chests. Everyone dished up and sat at the tables.

Most of the kids sat at one giant square table. And they knew they had to behave or suffer the consequences. No TV for half a century.

Sean ate slowly, it must have felt more like an interview for him. Dad, Max and Jim asked him a lot of questions. The paparazzi had set their cameras aside, and weren't taking notes, although they could have been recording, but they were being subtle about it if they were.

Lily was eating salmon with a fork in her right hand, but every time she went to drink some wine Jim was playing with her left hand. Wrapping a bread tie around her fingers, then his fingers, then hers again.

"Honey, I need to use this hand to eat."

"Sorry," he said, taking the bread tie off, playing with it and putting it in his pocket.

Was he trying to get attention from her? She needed to give the kids more attention. She was pretty sure that Teddy needed more. But how to make everything work?

After dinner the kids decided to have a water fight. First they helped clean up the food and take it inside. Then they folded up Janice's tables and carted them next door. All the chairs and the picnic table got moved into the safe zone on the side of the yard. Along with the ice chests and snacks.

The kids gathered up squirt guns, balloons and other water toys and began to fill them. Those not participating retreated to the safe zone. Roderigo and Frances, two of the paparazzi joined in the water fight.

Lily leaned back in a chair and savored her glass of merlot. She really wanted to talk to Sean. Alone. To find out what he had to tell her. But he was being polite and mingling with everyone at the party. She'd have to figure out how to get him alone.

Nick and Susan sat down beside her.

Lily turned to them and said, "Mom and Dad, I'm sorry for calling you all the way back to Seattle. But I'm really relieved Teddy's going to be okay."

Susan said, "Well, it was starting to rain on the coast anyway."

"Not rain," said Nick. "It was a hurricane. We planned on

coming back to civilization anyway and hoped the weather would be better. Then when it hits here, we'll go back to the coast. Outwit mother nature."

The two of them looked at each other and laughed. Then they took off running to the other side of the yard to start off the battle. Susan grabbed the hose. No puny squirt gun for her. Lily watched as Susan adjusted the sprayer attachment, calculating which slot would give her the hardest jet possible. Then she turned the hose on and blasted Jim, who clearly hadn't expected it. His gaping mouth filled with water.

Nick laughed and said, "Never, ever fight with your grandmother, my boy. She always wins!"

He grabbed a water bazooka, shot vaguely at Susan, missed and ran around the side of the house to hide. The paparazzi and kids joined in and the battle was on.

Sean was having a serious conversation with one of Casey's twins, Dana. Casey and Janice were involved in a long talk about cooking. It seemed they loved to cook the same kind of food. The other twin, Daniel was playing with Dana's son and Katie and Emily. He looked like he was having a great time.

Lily felt somehow alone. But she didn't want to join in the water fight, she just wanted to talk to Sean.

The far gate to the front yard opened and Nina Vicente walked in, followed by a man with short, short blond hair and startling blue eyes. Lily recognized him as Eric Jorgenssen, an actor who'd been in a couple of movies with Sean. Nina wore a slinky, leopard print dress with spaghetti straps and gold sandals. Even with flats she was almost taller than Eric. They were followed by at least ten more paparazzi.

She watched Nina take in the chaos of the water fight and try to decide how to pass through it. Lily couldn't decide whether to welcome her or not. After being insulted by Nina, she sure didn't feel like it. Still, it was her house.

Susan saved her the trouble.

"Truce!" she yelled at the top of her formidable lungs. "We have diplomats who need safe passage."

Everyone froze. Nina made an elaborate thank-you bow to Susan, who returned it. Then Nina, Eric and the paparazzi walked through the war zone to the safe zone.

"Commence fire," yelled Susan, walloping Tracy with a jet of water. Tracy responded with a water balloon to Susan's head. Susan howled with laughter and got her again.

Nina pulled up a chair and sat next to Lily.

"Hi. Sorry to crash your shindig, but I owe you an apology." She extended her hand to Lily. Eric sat next to Nina, smiling.

Lily shook her hand, waiting to be bitten.

Some of the paparazzi edged closer, on the pretext of picking up their drinks or snacking.

Nina said, "I had far too much to drink the other evening when I insulted you. And far too little self control. My jealousy came out. I was angry that you obviously had Sean's attention, but more than that, you had so many children, when I can't have any. I hope you'll forgive my rudeness."

Should she believe Nina meant the apology? "You know all these children are adopted, or foster kids?"

Nina sat back, her eyebrows raised in surprise. "Are they really? You mean they allow single women to adopt? I mean, I'm not young anymore, but I heard adoption agencies were prejudiced against older, single women."

"You would have no problem financially supporting a child. Their rules change." She shrugged.

"That's something to look into."

Sean spoke from behind Lily, rubbing her shoulders. "Nina, if you really wanted kids, you'd need to make a few life changes. Kids take up and enormous amount of time and energy. Every single day."

Nina looked at Eric, then to Sean. "Oh, I've got quite a few life changes planned."

"That's what we came here to talk about," said Eric, grinning.

"We're on our way to the airport. This evening we'll fly to London, then take a train to Gretna Green and get married. Eric is so romantic." Nina put her arms around his neck and kissed him.

"You two don't even know each other," said Sean.

Nina laughed, "Sean, we've known each other for years. We simply never dated. He never asked me out and I always thought he was too short. Little did I know there's nothing short about him."

Eric smiled and said, "I told her she needs to wear flats more often anyway, better for her feet. Besides, she's not tall, just long legged."

All the paparazzi had now abandoned the water fight. Several of them dripped with water. They were grabbing towels from the huge piles left on a couple chairs.

Nina stood and said to the paparazzi, "So, are you all going to escort us to the airport and London? I'll tell you how Eric and I met." She watched them hesitate and added, "I'll tell you all about our wedding night plans. And if you come, we'll even invite you to the wedding. We're eloping and not inviting friends or family."

At that moment a massive red water balloon sailed over the paparazzi and hit Nina in the back of the head.

Nina's eyes flew wide open, then narrowed. She was absolutely silent.

"Oh crap," said Nick. "Sorry, I was aiming for someone else."

Nina turned around and looked at him, as Eric grabbed a towel for her.

Nick looked sheepish. Had he done it on purpose?

Susan said, "I'll get him back for you" and turned the hose on him again. At that point all the water balloon, squirt guns and bazookas went off at Nick. He danced around howling with laughter.

Most of the paparazzi were too busy with their phones to pay much attention. They were probably booking flights to London.

Nina carefully patted her face dry and wrung out her hair.

She smiled and said, "A little water can't ruin my day, but it's time to get going, so we can make our flight."

Another cease fire was called. Nina and Eric walked toward the gate, waving to everyone. The paparazzi waved goodbye. Many of them shook hands with Lily and thanked her for inviting them to the party.

Roderigo said, "Thank you Lily, this was a wonderful barbecue."

Edward agreed, "Your hospitality is greatly appreciated."

She felt surprised and realized that with their work, they rarely got treated as equals, but usually like a pack of hounds. Treating them nicely had returned some humanity to them.

"Well, I think it's time to break out the ice cream. Mom, Dad, do you want dessert yet?" she asked.

"Not yet, we need more exercise," said Susan.

"She Who Must Be Obeyed has spoken," said Nick.

The water fight resumed as she walked into the kitchen, followed by Sean. Her eyes adjusted to the dimmer light inside.

"Honestly, I think my parents are more childlike than the kids."

A strong smell of honeysuckle filled the kitchen. Maybe Janice had brought her a bouquet, but she didn't see one anywhere.

"They're old enough to appreciate being childlike. They're

not hung up on what their friends think or all that other angst about growing up that kids have," said Sean. "Speaking of children," he nodded his head for her to look behind her.

Lily turned to see a plump, thirteen year old girl, twisting her shirttail in her hands. Sheryl.

"What honey?" Lily asked.

"Mom, can I please have some ice cream?"

"You can have some after you run and play in the water fight for twenty minutes."

"Okay," she said, running out the door.

"Sheryl's on my side," screamed Max.

Sean took her hand and asked, "Want to talk about it?"

She felt defensive. "I can't understand why you understand about the kids. No one else does," she snapped.

"I understand because my mother was in the same situation, as was my twin, Casey.

"What?"

"Casey's daughter, Dana, is in the middle of it right now. Jeremy is her first, but there will surely be more."

"But she's still just a child herself."

"That's what Casey thought and so didn't tell her about the Gift."

She didn't know what to say.

"Have you ever wondered why I come from such a large family?"

"The question did come to me once or twice."

"My mother met my father, they married and that same day he shipped out on a boat to go to war. No honeymoon, no consummation of the marriage. When he returned from the war a couple years later, she had six kids. No one noticed anything strange, except him. Dad felt furious, wouldn't talk to her, thought she'd been unfaithful, but he still loved her. After many more children appearing in a month, and a little math on his part, he realized it didn't matter if the other kids were adopted, appeared out of nowhere or if she'd been messing around. He couldn't live without her. They reconciled, finally had their honeymoon and nine months later, Casey and I were born."

"Twins."

"Yeah. It's always twins."

"Wait, you said born."

"Yes, born. She gave birth to us. After us, there were no more children. Do you understand?"

"No," she said.

"When their relationship was consummated, something changed. She got pregnant. No more children appeared. The same thing happened to Casey. She met her husband, James, in college. He came from a large family and James also had a twin, his sister died in a boating accident when they were seven. His parents died during his first year of college and didn't pass along any information about the Gift. So Casey, who also didn't know a thing about it, and James fell in love. Children began appearing."

Sean continued, "Casey lived in Seattle and Mom and Dad were in California, so they didn't know about the kids. Casey wouldn't tell them. Casey panicked and dropped out of college. She had four kids and was working in a bookstore when James found her again. He found it all pretty unbelievable, but she'd only been gone a few months. They married, had twins and then no more children. Since then James has done a massive amount of research on the Gift. Does any of this say anything to you?"

"That you're damn lucky to be a man,' she said, pulling four boxes of ice cream bars from the freezer and setting them on the counter. "Does it ever happen to the man?"

"Not that I've heard of," said Sean. "We just get headaches

or other chronic problems. Maybe nature decided we were hopeless as single parents." He poured himself a glass of water and drank it. "Do you know about your twin?"

"No. My birth mother left me in a picnic basket at Meriwether Lewis Memorial Park, among the lilies. Nick and Susan were traveling through and found me. After no one claimed me, they adopted me," she said, feeling her chest tighten and throat knot up.

Sean pulled her into his arms and held her while she tried to let all the fear go.

He said, "Everything's going to be okay. We can stop this," he said, stroking her hair. Her entire body tingled. "Have you ever been pregnant?"

"No, I found out after we got married, that Buddy didn't want kids."

"When did the first one show up?"

"Teddy showed up the day after your signing at the bookstore. The day of our date. Tracy came the next morning. Jim a month later. In March, Emily arrived. The others you know, I think."

"So you've gotten ten, no twelve, or however many children in the last eight months?"

"Yes, I think. I lose count all the time," she said, sighing deeply. Being responsible for that many people felt like a heavy load at the moment.

"I've known for some time that I'm the father. It's why I never stopped pursuing you, never let you push me away. I bet if we sat down and compared calendars, we'd find the kids' arrivals dovetailed perfectly with my debilitating headaches. I know we're meant to be together, unless you've got another candidate?"

She laughed, "No. There's no one else possible. When would I even have had time to look at another man?"

"Good," said Sean, "I've waited a long time for this, thought it would never happen to me. Besides, I've had a headache since I arrived, so you really need to marry me and make these nasty headaches go away."

"Aaah, but the kids won't go away," she said, smelling a strong citrusy scent that she hoped was dishwashing detergent.

"Nor would I want them to. I love kids," he said, holding her even tighter.

The sound of the screen door slamming broke them apart. "Mom, Jim hit me with a water balloon," said a dripping, seven year old girl with red hair and pale skin. Sally. Her name was Sally and she loved blueberries.

"Well, take the ice cream out to the picnic table for me please, then go get a water balloon and hit him right back," Lily said. "You're growing up and you need to make him respect you."

"Okay," Sally giggled, grabbing the boxes of ice cream bars and running back out the door, leaving a pool of water in the middle of the kitchen.

"Another one," he said, smiling.

"Another one." She drooped a little.

"So, when are you going to marry me?" he asked, pulling her into his arms again. "I am in love with you, you know."

"You don't even know me. And besides, all we really have to do is just have sex, right?"

"Probably. But James has a theory that all this is genetic and that what nature is really trying to do with the Gift is form family units. Not just the normal guy sows his seed and moves on. We might have to have sex more than once. Or maybe there's something inherently relaxing about being in the cocoon of a relationship that allows the woman to get pregnant. Nobody knows for sure."

She didn't understand why she wanted to run. Everything was so clear, but part of her still felt afraid.

"And I know a great deal about you. I know you can't raise this many kids alone. I know you're completely overwhelmed right now. How well did you know your first husband when you married him?"

"Really well. We'd know each other since Middle School."

"But you didn't know he didn't want kids."

"No." Lily felt like she was being outmaneuvered.

"I can wait as long as you can. I love big families. And I can find a way to support as many kids as come along. I have a feeling that there might be some things you want to do with your life other than raise children. Of course we could hire a nanny, or two. And probably add another story to this house," he said, smiling the sarcastic smile he used as the schizophrenic football coach in *Purple Dawn*.

"Nannies?" she asked, feeling stunned. "Remodel?" She could feel herself begin to hyperventilate.

"At least agree to another date with me. Let me pay for childcare and make you dinner. Come to my place. Please give yourself a chance to get to know me. Give me a chance."

She still wanted to run, but managed to say, "When?"

"Tomorrow," he said.

She nodded.

"Good," he said, "seven o'clock work for you?"

She was still breathing fast when he embraced her again He stroked her cheek and kissed her. She nearly melted, felt soft and hard all at the same time. Voices became louder and the back door opened. Still, she stayed in his arms. Even though she wasn't comfortable with the whole marriage thing.

Susan said, "Don't mind us."

"We're on an expedition for ice cream bars," said Nick.

"Chocolate ice cream bars," said Susan.

"Picnic table," said Lily.

"All gone," said Susan, opening the freezer. They took a couple more boxes and left the kitchen, giggling.

"Shall we go steal the hose while we can?" asked Sean.

"Might as well. We can't be the only two dry people around. They'll get us sooner or later."

SEAN

Sean lit candles throughout his apartment, enjoying the scent of sandalwood as it drifted from room to room. He turned on exotic and sensual music, loud enough to hear on his balcony, but low enough to not intrude on the conversation.

The food was prepped, so he set the small table on his tiny balcony. Just enough room for a cafe table and two chairs. The sky was mostly clear with a few clouds on this balmy evening. It should make for a spectacular sunset.

He looked in the mirror. The slacks looked okay, but his T-shirt had spatters on it from sautéing vegetables. He quickly tossed it in the laundry basket and grabbed a purple one out of the drawer; pulling it on. Then rearranged his hair again. Purple was not his color, but it would have to do.

His intercom buzzed and he pushed the button, "Hi Lily."

"Hi."

"I'll open the gate," he said, pushing another button.

While he waited, he did a couple of yoga poses, feeling the tension in his muscles. God, he was nervous.

He opened the door and looked down the stairs. Couldn't see her yet.

"Everything will turn out just fine. She'll fall madly in love with me, marry me and we'll live happily ever after. At least until she gets tired of the paparazzi, the fans, the hours and me in general," he said to himself.

When he saw her, he said, "Hello."

"Hi. I haven't been getting my workouts in, since school ended. Too busy. I think I need to start running the stairs at the amphitheater at Green Lake."

He took in her pale green dress that buttoned up the front and was held up by skinny straps. She wore tan sandals and her long hair was pinned up, although a few wisps had escaped. He wanted to unpin her hair and take her dress off. He could feel himself growing hard.

Instead, he said, "Come in. You look lovely."

"Thank you. So do you."

"I'll get dinner going. Feel free to poke around while I cook. Would you like a glass of wine?"

"I'd love one," she said, putting her purse down on the dining room table and coming into the kitchen area.

He poured a glass of red wine and watched her walk around, while he cooked the pasta and added prawns and fresh basil to the sautéed vegetables. He tasted it, the richness of the prawns rounded out the intensity of the basil.

He carried salads and parmesan out to the table.

"I thought we could eat outside, watch the sunset," he said, going back for the pasta and wine.

"That would be wonderful."

He felt relieved the pasta turned out perfect. As they sat enjoying the last of the wine, the sky began to color. She seemed more relaxed. Perhaps it was the wine. He took her hand and kissed it. She smiled at him.

"Are you ready for dessert?"

"There's dessert as well?"

"Of course. What kind of cook do you think I am? Letting people off without dessert."

"What was I thinking? Of course I'll have dessert."

Sean cleared the table and pulled the mousse and dessert wine from the fridge, putting them on the tray, along with two new wine glasses. He pulled a small box from the cupboard. In it lay an engagement ring and a wedding band. He rinsed the engagement ring under the faucet, slipped it into one of the glasses and poured dessert wine into both. As he carried the tray outside the glasses clinked together, echoing his nerves.

What if she said no?

He set Lily's wine and mousse in front of her and unloaded the rest of the tray.

"More wine. Are you trying to get me drunk?"

"The thought did occur to me," he said, smiling. "But, I'll be happy to drive you safely home. Unless of course you'd care to spend the night."

She ignored the comment and sipped her wine. "This is divine. I've never tasted anything like it."

"Late Harvest Gewurtztraminer. From a local winery." He tasted it, feeling the cool, honey-like sweetness roll across his tongue, followed by the favor of spicy fruit.

Lily put the glass down and noticed the ring. She looked at him as if in shock.

He took her hand in his, caressing it. "Lily, I don't seem to have any of the right words. If you marry me, I'll love and cherish you, as well as our children, to the end of my days. And I'm planning on living a very long life. I'll always be there for you. Please marry me."

She closed her eyes and sighed.

He stood and pushed his chair out of the way, kneeling in

front of her so his face was level with hers. He put his hands on her cool, bare shoulders.

"Lily, talk to me."

She sighed again and looked at him. "I'm afraid."

"I can feel that. What are you afraid of?"

"I haven't been in a relationship for so long. I never was very good at it. I don't know how to do this without screwing it up."

"We'll both need to learn. And we'll make mistakes, but it won't be the end of the world, because we'll be together. Marry me."

"Yes," she whispered.

He pulled her forward and held her. Then pressed her with a long, languorous kiss, full of promises.

"Will you wear this ring? If you don't like it, we can choose another."

She fished it out of the bottom of her wine glass, stuck in it her mouth to clean it, then dried it on her napkin.

"It's beautiful," she said, as he slipped it on her finger. "How did you get the right size?"

"Jim, last night. The thing with the bread tie.

"You scheming devil," she laughed.

"You have no idea," he said, sucking leftover wine off her fingers. Lily looked as if she would melt.

He got up and pulled his chair back in place, sat down and pulled her on to his lap. Then he fed her chocolate mousse, alternating with sips of wine, while he ate his own dessert.

Finally, she asked, "Are you trying to seduce me?"

"Yes, how am I doing?"

"Oh, I'd say you're doing just fine," she said, slipping her sandals off.

After dessert and the sunset, they sat on the balcony, kissing. Their tongues explored each other. His hands caressed the soft skin of her shoulders and the silky dress down her back and along her thighs.

He slowly kissed her face and sucked on her neck, inhaling the fresh clean scent of her skin. She trembled and her breath came unevenly and his fingers touched the neckline of her dress and began unbuttoning the front.

Cupping her breast, he put his mouth to her nipple feeling it harden and kissing it. When she arched her back, he sucked.

She moaned with pleasure and he unbuttoned all the buttons to her waist.

He moved to the other breast and repeated his actions.

She grabbed the bottom of his T-shirt and pulled it off and began caressing his chest, weaving her fingers through his chest hair, making him want to tear her clothes off.

He pushed her dress up her thighs and hips, caressing the skin as he went. When it was around her waist he stated the obvious, "You're not wearing any underwear." He smiled.

"It's too hot for underwear."

"After we're married, we're moving to the equator." He ran his fingers up and down her thighs and over her belly, until she opened her legs, allowing him to delve into the folds. She writhed on his lap, making him even harder.

He groaned and plunged his finger inside her while caressing her sex. She continued to writhe and gasped for breath until she cried out and shuddered in his arms. Then she was still, her eyes wide as she looked at him.

"That felt incredible. Thank you," she said.

"You're very welcome, we can repeat it any time you want."

She gathered herself together, stood and undid his pants, pulling them to his knees as he raised up, allowing them to slide down. He kicked them off, feeling a little uneasy being stark naked on the balcony.

Lily straddled him, taking his mostly hard cock in her hands and making it completely hard.

"So who's wearing no underwear," she said.

"Never do."

"Never?"

"Not in my private life."

He groaned as she continued, stroking him.

"I can't take much more of that," he said.

"Good, because neither can I," she said. She sat on him, enveloping him with her softness as he thrust into her, sliding his hands beneath her and grabbing her cheeks. The pleasure almost overwhelming. The sensation of her skin and his slip-sliding inside her. It felt like no time passed before love, passion and desire spilled out of him like a flood. He felt like his heart would burst, then lost himself in a sensation of floating.

He came back to himself and her, his face between her breasts, smelling their two scents mingling together.

"You are so amazing," he said.

"Why?" she asked, wrinkles forming between her brows.

"A few months ago you would hardly talk to me and now you're going to marry me."

"A few months and lots of kids," she said.

"Is it only the kids?"

"No. I figured I was never going to get rid of you, so I might as well enjoy you instead, cabana boy."

"I'm at your command," he said.

"Good, that's just how I like it." She stood up, grabbed the wine bottle and pointed to the glasses. "Glasses."

Then she walked inside. He picked up the wine glasses and followed her. In the dining room she slipped completely out of her dress. He moaned, his cock coming to life again.

She continued on to his bedroom, putting the bottle down on his night stand and pulling the covers off the bed.

Clearly she didn't have any plans for sleeping.

He poured two glasses of wine and handed her one.

"By the way," she said, "I will require breakfast in the morning."

She's spending the night. He couldn't decide which part of him felt more excited about that.

"My world famous scrambled eggs with smoked cheddar and roasted red peppers?"

"That will be fine."

"Just how did you get out of morning duty at the orphanage?"

She laughed and said, "As I was leaving, Dad pulled me aside and said, 'Young lady, your mother and I expect you *not* to come home tonight. We'll see you tomorrow afternoon.'"

"Your dad said that?"

"Yep. He delights in being outrageous," she said, sipping her wine.

He dipped two fingers into his wine and brushed it on one of her nipples.

She put her glass down and moaned as he licked the wine off.

She pulled him closer and they fell onto the bed.

LILY

The next day they got a marriage license and set the date for the wedding. Three days, the legal waiting period in the county. Getting the license set the world abuzz again.

They invited family and a few friends to a wedding and reception at Casey's house; she'd insisted they use her house. The entire back yard was tented to discourage helicopters. Several paparazzi were invited to the reception. Things were very informal with entertainment provided by her parents and a gazillion children.

She and Sean managed to elude the press with a series of clever disguises and much switching of cars, enabled by her parents who thought the whole thing was great fun, to slip away for a two day honeymoon in a tent, on the Olympic Peninsula.

When they got back to Seattle, Sean sold his condo and moved into Lily's house. With his brother's help they added on two more floors. Sean began redecorating and reading movie scripts. Her parents got their own room to stay in as often as they wanted, keeping everyone in stitches.

Nine months later the twins, Darla and Don, were born.

That brought the grand total up to way too many kids. Sean promptly got a vasectomy. That was fine with her. She was only going through childbirth once.

She decided to study channeling. Once everyone was sleeping through the night. She felt called to find out where the kids came from and what happened to her twin. She'd spent most of her life in the lower chakras, dealing with sex, food and her body. Survival issues. Now it was time to move up. At least when she wasn't running into coffee tables, spilling wine or dropping vases of flowers after catching sight of Sean and before it sank in that she was married to that gorgeous man.

She couldn't really claim to live happily ever after. You can't be happy all the time, especially when you wake to find one child has shaved another bald and another broke their leg jumping out of a tree house. But they all loved each other. All of them. Love and laughter solved a multitude of problems.

That was the most important lesson of all.

If you enjoyed this book, please leave a review at the online store where you purchased it, or Goodreads. Reviews help readers find books they love. A review can be as short as a few words about what stuck with you about the book. Thank you so much!

LINDA JORDAN
Author of Bibi's Bargain Boutique
Living
in
the
Lower
Chakras
A Romantic Comedy about Obsession,
Magic & Destiny

ABOUT THE AUTHOR

LINDA JORDAN writes fascinating characters, visionary worlds, and imaginative fiction. She creates both long and short fiction, serious and silly. She believes in the power of healing and transformation, and many of her stories follow those themes.

In a previous lifetime, Linda coordinated the Clarion West Writers' Workshop as well as the Reading Series. She spent four years as Chair of the Board of Directors during Clarion West's formative period. She's also worked as a travel agent, a baker, and a pond plant/fish sales person, you know, the sort of things one does as a writer.

Currently, she's the Programming Director for the Writers Cooperative of the Pacific Northwest.

Linda now lives in the rainy wilds of Washington state with her husband, daughter, four cats, a cluster of Koi and an infinite number of slugs and snails.

Her other work includes:
-*Notes on the Moon People*
-*Continental Divide*
-*Horticultural Homicide*
-*Bibi's Bargain Boutique*
All her work can be found at your favorite online bookseller.

Get a FREE ebook!
Sign up for Linda's Serendipitous Newsletter at her website:
www.LindaJordan.net

Visit her at: www.LindaJordan.net
She can be found on Facebook at:
www.facebook.com/LindaJordanWriter
Metamorphosis Press website is at: www.
MetamorphosisPress.com
Goodreads: https://www.goodreads.com/author/show/
2021274.Linda_Jordan

Writers love reviews, even short, simple ones and honest
reviews help other readers find the book. Please go to where
you bought this book, or Goodreads, and leave a review. It
would be much appreciated.

www.ingramcontent.com/pod-product-compliance
Lightning Source LLC
Chambersburg PA
CBHW031230120726
47905CB00002B/540